TALK TO ME

TALK TO ME

THE SWITCHBOARD DUET
BOOK ONE

HEATHER LONG

If they shenan once, they'll shenanigans.

This is for them.

FOREWORD

Dear Reader,

Thank you so much for picking up Talk To Me. I can't wait for you to dive in and meet the characters that utterly consumed me. The Switchboard Duet was nowhere on my writing schedule this year until one day, it was just there, whispering in my ear. I could hear the characters coming to life.

Not only were they "talking" to me, they wouldn't *shut up*. I had to start writing as soon as possible so I could also work on other things. What the muse wants, sometimes, you have to let the muse get. This book *demanded* to be written. The next book in the duet is waiting patiently—so far. I imagine I'll be elbows deep by the time you are reading this.

What I loved most about these characters was how their dialogue told me so much about them. How tied to each other they are. How involved. Also—just how many secrets they each have. I want to peel them apart, layer by layer, and get to know every aspect of them.

But like any good mystery, they aren't telling me everything upfront. As much as I want to know, I'm really looking forward to the journey and finding out.

For a little housekeeping. The Switchboard Duet is a dark romantic suspense why choose. This means all the romantic heroes are matches for the heroine and she will not have to choose. It's also worth noting that romance is not the key focus of the first book in the duet. This is a harrowing journey of discovery for all our characters.

TWs: Mentions of SA. Kidnapping. Intimidation. Torture. Interrogation. Car accidents. Threats of violence. Scenes of combat. Violence. Be kind to yourself, this is a dark romantic suspense duet.

Thanks for checking out Talk to Me, I can't wait to hear who your favorite is.

Happy reading.

xoxo

Heather

P.S. Human voices only. All the work involved in this and all my novels from the stories themselves to the covers, to editing, to the audio are human-produced materials and voices only.

PROLOGUE

If you knew this was your last day on Earth, how would you wanna spend it?

That question came up in philosophy class. It was tossed around at a girl's night while we were drinking. It was asked during a damn episode of *Grey's Anatomy*.

The thing was, every single time I heard that question, my answer changed. Today, I couldn't seem to shake the question or come up with a good answer. I used my keycard to access the elevator lobby, then again to send the elevator up twenty-two floors. Once there, I would need to pass through the business front to get inside one of the country's most secure watchdog hubs.

Though watchdog was kind of a misnomer. We were an operational center. More for off the books, black ops, designed to protect the security of our country from all threats foreign *and* domestic.

I'd taken an oath the day I received my security clearance. Everything about my employment was classified, from the offices we worked in to the people we reported to. Most were simply names in emails or an avatar on the screen.

"Morning, Fallon," Ralph Taylor greeted me from where he sat behind the semi-circle reception desk. He had video screens everywhere beneath the lip of the desk, as well as weapons. A retired former detective from the NYPD, he confessed to enjoying his babysitting job for the nerd squad.

I didn't mind being lumped in with the rest.

"Morning, Ralph," I said before I set the brown paper bag on the desk.

"You remembered!" He gave me a wide smile.

"I did. The pirozhkis were fresh too." The smell would have made my stomach grumble if I hadn't picked up two for myself to eat in the car.

"You're the best," he called as I carded my way through the last security door. It opened to an antechamber then closed and locked me in the room where I needed a retina scan and a code before it allowed me final access to the tank.

The light flashed from red to green, then a buzzer sounded as the door opened to let me inside.

"There's my girl," Marty Cartwright greeted me as I slipped inside. Cartwright was the senior supervisor here in the tank.

"Good morning," I said as I released my card back to thump against my chest. It was secured by a retractable cord that clipped to my jacket. His presence set off alarm bells. Hadn't he left to go on vacation two days earlier?

Not that we had nine to five, five day a week jobs. We came in when the work required it. He moved like a shadow, following me to my cubicle. In addition to Marty, there were five others already in and at their desks.

Headsets on, they had various assignments up on their monitors. I recognized some at a distance, but not others. I didn't focus, just headed to my own control center. Marty continued to move in my wake, his unsettling presence leaving me on edge.

I set my bag down on the desk, opened the drawer where I always locked it in and then closed it before I pulled out the chair. Not sitting, I looked at Marty. "What's up?"

"I've been thinking..."

Waiting, I tilted my head as I met his gaze.

"You've been handling most of the watch over Turkey and the Baltics."

I nodded.

"We need to bring in someone to train. Currently, you're the only one who speaks the language of that area."

I knew this. So why was he bringing it up?

"For the next couple of days, I need you to log off of those servers."

My stomach dropped. Did he know that I'd found out?

"Okay," I said slowly, as though I needed to rework my schedule. "I think today's tapes and calls are all Poland and the new canal."

"Excellent. If you get tagged into the Baltics,

just forward it to me." Then he winked. "Maybe we can get a drink later."

Never going to happen. I smiled. "If I have brain cells left at the end of the day, I'll think about it."

That earned me a laugh. Then he motioned me to my chair. "I'll leave you to it." But his humor faded before he'd even turned away. Then he was striding across the office.

Cartwright was supposed to be on vacation.

He wanted me to log out of the servers where I'd been running a dozen shadow operations for U.S. intelligence.

He also wanted me to forward him the intelligence and the open cases.

He knew.

My heart triple-timed against my ribs, but five years of cold calls and hot operations kept my hands steady as I settled at my desk, put my headset on and logged into my machine.

A brief flash told me the camera had been activated remotely, but I pretended to not notice. More, the keystroke logger was activated. I had two keyboards, however, and I slid the secondary one out as I brought the other machines up.

Normally, all the units would be slaved to the center console. But I'd partitioned them gradually over the last two months. Right around the time I realized what Cartwright was up to.

Not that I'd known it was him before. No, today confirmed that. I opened another drawer, slid out a piece of gum, folded it in half and tucked it under my tongue before I started logging myself out of the various servers. I made a point of boxing the files, then forwarding them to him as requested.

They were encrypted. It would take him a while to realize I'd just sent him the logs from three weeks of battle gaming on God of War. The files were huge and contained enough data to work as a decoy.

Flipping the screens, I switched to the Poland tapes and started playing them. The language filled my headset and I looked for all the world like I was translating. The AI program wasn't the best, but it worked to keep the keylogger entertained while I used my backdoor into the systems to clean out the treasure trove of information.

I hadn't broken it all down yet, but it was hard to ignore the data once I'd lined it up. Someone was shadowing the shadow ops. They were profiting off operations. Twice, men had been deployed to eliminate targets that were not enemies of the state but actual competitors.

The last time, they'd used a drone strike. The data from the satellite had been corrupted, but I'd managed to piece enough together to see the family that had also been murdered.

Collateral. They didn't care who was hurt. The fact money was being moved in considerable sums as well as exchanging arms and drugs—it was all there. You just had to know how to parse the data.

I was never supposed to find this. But now that I had—I wasn't sure who to trust with it. So I did the only thing I could think of.

I emptied the bank accounts, swept the money through a dozen different dark web channels to clean it and deposited it in encrypted accounts. The program would keep the money on the move until it vanished. The rest I backed up onto two separate drives.

One I would take with me. The other would upload to the cloud when the data dump at the end of the day was done. It would use the normal dump to cover the amount of information.

I would also be long gone before that one initiated. Once that was complete, I monitored the AI translator until lunch time. I wasn't the first one up nor the last. I waited for the tape to be done then filed it before I shut everything down and logged out.

Bag in hand, I stretched. I waved to Veronica as I passed her cubicle. She lifted her chin but her fingers never stopped moving. This had been my life for the past few years. A life where I'd been making a difference.

Or so I thought.

As I slid into the elevator and pressed the button for the garage below, I hummed a song. I didn't even know which one. It let me fidget and not seem suspicious. Once I was in the garage, I bypassed my car as I headed for the ramp exit.

I turned my jacket inside out and pulled my hair up into a ponytail. There were cameras everywhere, but I'd long since mapped the blind spots and found a route to get out of the garage without being recorded. By the time I reached the top of the ramp, I had pulled my backpack out of the bag, then stuffed the bag and purse into it. Sliding it on changed my profile entirely.

Not slowing my pace, I went to the light and crossed the street. The bus was just pulling up to the stop. I climbed on board and swiped a bus fare card I'd picked up the week before.

After, I headed to the back of the bus.

I didn't look behind me. There was nothing there for me anymore. I couldn't afford to look back. I tugged up the hood on my hoodie and tucked my hair under it.

I wouldn't be getting off until the last stop.

Then I would disappear.

This life was over.

CHAPTER
ONE
PATCH

FIVE YEARS LATER...

The alarm went off at four. I was already up and moving before I hit the button to turn it off. In the bathroom, I started the shower before I turned on the lights. While I waited for the water to heat, I brushed my teeth.

The shower took me seven minutes. I debated blow-drying my hair but I'd rather get coffee going. I checked my watch as I pulled on sweatpants and an oversized slouchy shirt. Fuzzy socks completed the work ensemble. I pulled the covers up in a show of making the bed then headed for the kitchen.

A pot of coffee was already hissing and spitting away. My espresso machine waited for me and I grabbed a protein shake out of the fridge to drink while I made myself a latte. When the coffee was ready, I poured it into a thermos, then carried everything downstairs to the basement.

The door unlocked with a single code and then I was sliding inside to my office. What had originally been a fallout shelter had required a facelift and a series of installations.

I put together the best set up I could by using a wide variety of contractors. A relative few had been given access to the house, but that was *before* I moved in. Privacy was important. I set the thermos on the desk to the right as I woke my systems up.

An array of fourteen monitors rippled to life as I settled in my chair. A pop-up appeared on the center screen as I settled the headset on over my damp hair. I entered the code for the VOIP and verified all firewalls were active before I hit answer.

"Talk to me," I said, then took a long drink of my latte.

"Hello, Patch. It's always good to hear your sexy voice. Did you roll out of bed just for me?" Justus Locke's name appeared on a screen as the log noted his location. He was coming into the switchboard from somewhere in the southern hemisphere. Ah, Sydney.

"Didn't want to miss my favorite guy," I teased. It took a few keystrokes to work my way into the street CCTV in Sydney. At least he was in one of the most surveilled cities in the world. They had some sixty thousand odd cameras. Triangulating his location took a couple of minutes.

Ah, there he was. He was dressed in a t-shirt, khakis and what looked like loafers. It was summer down under at the moment. He had a cell phone to his ear and a bag slung over his shoulder. His position on the bridge in Darling Harbor afforded him a nice view.

"You never let me down," he said with a sigh. I switched cameras, going for a close-up. It took me a moment to find one.

"You sound tired," I said, downing more of the coffee. Now that I was in my chair, the adrenaline joined the caffeine. He looked tired too.

"I am tired." That admission wasn't like him. "But I would never miss our date."

I chuckled. An alarm showed on the left-hand screen, and a second camera view opened. "That's one of the things I love about you," I murmured as I did my scan. The target was a bank building less than a half-klick from his current location.

"That I'm tired?" The retort just made me roll my eyes.

"That you never leave me hanging."

"I do like it when you talk dirty to me."

That earned him a snort. "So, are we doing this or just hanging out for a bit?"

"All business and no play, girl, makes Patch—"

"A busy woman. I can play while we work, remember?"

"You know what that does to me," he complained, but he was already in motion. He tucked his phone into his pocket but our call didn't drop. He had an earbud in.

"It makes you move your ass."

"Yeah yeah, you keep your eyes on my ass."

It was my turn to chuckle. "Then put a little sway in that step."

His snort required no explanation.

"At the next alley," I said. "Follow it to the back of the building." I was already into their security system. Their internal cameras were coming up on a third screen. "The upgrades we were worried about don't appear to be installed."

"Tell me more," he said, even as he detoured down the alley I indicated.

"Hold position," I told him and he stopped, vanishing in the shadow between two lights. The door to the alley opened and one of the security guards stepped out, pressing a brick into place to keep the door open. "On a count of five, move. Leave the brick in place."

The security guard repeated a routine he'd demonstrated over the past few weeks. In his attempts to vary that routine, he'd just alternated by hour and door. This was just the night he used the door in this alley. He moved to the opposite end, lighting a cigarette and planting himself where he could people watch.

Like most cities, there was a night life, and the guard enjoyed watching it. The fact he kept the door open for a five-minute window just worked to our benefit.

"I'm in," Justus said. "Stick with me?"

"I'll be right here," I promised. "You have this."

"Do you have a plan?"

"I'm working on one."

My stomach clenched and I swore I could taste acid on the back of my throat. He was winging it. Justus Locke was one of the best at what he did for a reason. He was so good, law enforcement hadn't even figured out he was one person and not a crew. Periodically, his lack of a code name annoyed him.

Not enough to tip his hat and leave them a clue, but he wouldn't mind the ego stroking.

"Locke," I said when two minutes passed and he hadn't moved or said anything.

"Easy, sweetheart," he murmured. "I got you. I know just what we're going to do to make this work."

Sweat trickled down my back as icy apprehension began to slither up my spine. I didn't like this. Making changes on the fly could cause all kinds of problems.

"You ever see *The Italian Job*?" Locke asked, as he left the safe and began a methodical search of the offices nearby. "Not the original, the remake."

"We're not blowing out thirty floors to drop that safe into the parking garage or the shopping galleries."

He snorted. "Not what I meant, but I appreciate the enthusiasm. Oh, there we go. You'll do nicely."

I bit my tongue to keep from asking what would do nicely. The point of me being here was to watch his back, and clear his exits if he needed them. Still, my hands were trembling when I reached for my latte cup again. It was empty, but I filled it with the black coffee from the thermos.

"If I can get this open in under two minutes, will you let me take you out to dinner?"

"What does that have to do with *The Italian Job*?" Deflecting instead of answering was a habit.

"Cause Charlize Theron's character never wants to see what's inside the safes. You never ask me when I don't bring it up."

He was back in the room with the safe, but the low-lighting made it hard to see what he was doing.

"I only ask you what I need to know." A clock popped up in the right-hand corner of the screen. We'd been inside for forty-minutes. "Our window is closing. You need to open that in the next sixty seconds, or abandon ship."

"I told you," he murmured. "I never pull out before the job is done." The safe gave a distinctive click and then he turned the big wheel and pulled the main handle to open the door. "Tell me the truth," he whispered. "You're impressed right now."

"Gobsmacked," I admitted. "Good thing I didn't take that bet."

"Killing me, Patch," he retorted, but the smile underscored his words. He was pulling items out of the safe and filling his bag.

"Clock starts in thirty seconds," I reminded him.

"Relax," he said in a soothing tone. "We're good to go." He closed the safe, resetting it presumably before he pulled the bag's strap crosswise over his chest. He was out the main doors and had them secured as the clock began running.

The programs I installed were already erasing him from the footage. They would replicate everything in the areas where he had been with footage from the night prior at the exact same times.

I'd scrubbed through it the morning before to make sure we didn't have any surprises waiting for us. Once he was in the stairwell, he would descend below the ground level to the shopping galleries, then down further to the parking garages.

"Level Two," he said after fifteen minutes and I sent the power surge to reboot the cameras on that level. It happened. Fifteen minutes after that, he was strolling down the sidewalk leaving the CBD and heading toward Darling Harbor once again.

"All clear," I told him. "I'll monitor for the next twenty-four hours, but you should be good."

"You're the best, Patch. I'd be lost without you."

I chuckled. "Goodnight, Locke. Get some rest."

"Hmm, probably sleep better if you were there, you know?"

"Uh huh." I didn't indulge him any further, just ended the call and leaned back in the chair. My heart was still racing and the cold sweat on my skin was a reminder that even one misstep and it wasn't my ass on the line but the ones relying on me.

I kept an eye on everything and had just poured a fresh cup of coffee when the next call came in. Something was wrong—McQuade was early.

"Talk to me…"

CHAPTER

TWO

PATCH

The alarm jerked me out of sleep and sent my adrenaline pumping. I reached for the phone before I'd fully sat up. Remington's name was on the screen.

"Talk to me," I answered, shaking off the cobwebs as I pushed back the blankets and slid out of bed. The rat-a-tat-tat and pop of gunfire echoed behind him.

"Job went sideways, luv, and now everyone wants a piece of me. Not feeling the welcome."

"Or the lube from the sounds of it," I murmured, but I was already on the move. "Target still in play?"

"Target down. I need an exodus." The low, dreamy quality of his voice was something I'd always enjoyed. Every word he spoke was always enunciated with care and perfectly precise. Even when he was in a hurry, he didn't sound like it. The lack of regional or colloquial touches didn't betray where in England Remington hailed from,

19

but he did sound elegant and smart no matter the circumstance.

"I'm on it. Standby."

Downstairs, I brought my machines up. I was already tracking his call and I transferred the connection to my main box and slid my head-phones on.

"You still with me, luv?"

"Nowhere else I'd rather be," I told him. My fingers flew over the keyboard. Every second counted. He was somewhere in Poland.

I was zeroing in to his signal and looking for street cameras even as I pulled up a map.

Fresh gunfire filled the line. "Bloody hell," he muttered. "Hold on." Then the phone sounded muffled like he'd pressed it against something. The gunfire was much closer this time. He re-turned fire and the report was a lot louder.

"Someone has a bigger gun," I said and got a throaty chuckle in response. I had him on screen. He cut a good-looking silhouette from black cap hiding his bald head to his smooth leather coat. He blended with the shadows, but he wasn't ex-actly one of them. "Let's go big boy, head east—half a kilometer down the alley on the other side of that ancient Ford."

"Moving."

"Three o'clock!" I warned. He pivoted, sighted, and fired before the other man got his gun up. I focused on the fallen assailant for a split second. Guilt added another thread to the noose around my neck.

That man was dead. I was complicit. I compartmentalized it and locked it away. I'd feel worse about it later. Right now, I had to get Remington out of there.

Tracking ahead and behind him, I mapped a dozen different ways. But he had a whole squad after him. Whoever the target had been, he pissed off a lot of people.

"Ten more steps then go left again."

He didn't hesitate, cutting down the side passage that couldn't be more than a couple of feet across. He had to angle himself to keep going but he vanished before some of the pursuers reached the mouth of the alley.

"Next right. You need to move faster. They are splitting up."

Two had gone down the narrow passageway I'd directed him to.

"I thought you liked it when I was slow and deliberate." The faintness of his panting breaths belied the tease.

"I like it hard and fast too," I said. "Left again. Then another sharp right. Zig zag."

"Fuck," he swore. But he didn't stop moving. "Are you sending me to the crypts?"

"Close." There were catacombs in Krakow and other cities. "This one isn't a tourist hot spot though and it's been closed for a while. Be careful when you get to the entrance."

"I knew you cared," he said with a chuckle.

"Stop. Silent running."

He froze on my screen. Two of the pursuers passed so close to the opening he was tucked into they could have probably touched him if they'd reached inside. But the slant of the brick wall gave it an illusion like the buildings were actually touching more than they were.

"Ten count, then move. Directly across the street. Down the stairs."

He didn't respond verbally but at the ten mark, he slipped across the street. The assailants were moving away from him. Their search was a grid pattern. He'd lost his passageway pursuers. It was a virtual maze through those old buildings.

I did another sweep as he descended the steps.

"At the bottom, travel directly ahead. There's an old gate over the door. You'll need to open both to get inside."

The shadows around the entrance hid him from view. Police dispatches had them closing in on the area and in pursuit of suspects. I offered a quick tip into their system where some of them were.

The more attention they took off Remy, the better. A faint tapping got my attention. Morse code.

Oh...

"Yes, it's clear to talk, just keep it low. No one should be close enough to hear you."

"This is a church, luv. You sending me to hell?"

"Is that a complaint?" The corners of my mouth lifted. "Cause you can go back to hang out with all your new suitors."

"Green is not your color," he said and I

snorted. Remy was always fishing for what I looked like.

"Every color is my color," I informed him. "I'm a goddess."

"Yes, you are." There was a rattle as the gate rolled upward, then the door opened. The crack of wood being forced made me grimace, but we both went still.

"You're clear," I said after another couple of heartbeats. He closed the gate behind him, then the door.

"Am I good to use a flashlight?"

"Yes, you're also off the cameras."

"Damn, and here I wanted to blow you a kiss."

"Save it for next time. The access to the catacombs is located among the crypts behind the altar. My notes say Mother Mary marks it."

"Good to know I get to blaspheme while I'm at it. You take me to all the interesting places."

It was my turn to chuckle. "You were the one who picked the city."

"How do you feel about Venice?"

"Like I don't swim. Once you descend into the catacombs, follow them steadily west for about ten kilometers. They will narrow when you get to the next church, it's a little one off an old dairy road."

"You mean near farms?"

"They were probably farms back in the day, it's a lot more industrial from the looks of it now. The church there also appears abandoned. Once you come up, you should be in the clear."

He blew out a breath. "This is the part where you say goodbye, isn't it?"

"For a little while. Communications are spotty down there. You need to focus on where you're going. I'll keep an eye on the exit to make sure you're clear."

"Patch?"

"Hmm?"

"Favorite flower?"

"Never really thought about it."

"Everyone has a favorite flower," he said and I switched screens to make sure his pursuers were nowhere near the church he was currently standing in.

"Do they?" I mused. "What's yours?"

"Honeysuckle."

The speed of his answer amused me. "That was fast."

"It's beautiful, smells fantastic, provides a food source for bees, butterflies, and humming-birds. Practically perfect. Just like you."

Now I did snort. "I haven't sniffed honey-suckle in a while. I'll have to check that out. Now get moving, Remy. I've got your back."

"Think about the flowers. I want to know." Then he disconnected before I could answer or evade the question. I did my best to not get personal with my clients, but sometimes it was hard.

Times like now, when he relied on me to get him out of a dangerous situation. He never hesitated or slowed down to argue with me. When I gave him directions, he went. Just like when I told him about the guy he killed earlier.

I tabbed through the screens. Law enforcement had found the body on the street. A couple of the assailants were being arrested. More calls were coming in. A politician had been found dead in his office.

Well, that told me who the target had likely been. Still, nothing in the dispatches indicated Remy had been spotted or was being tracked. I checked the church where he would be exiting and kept one eye on it as I documented any close-ups of his pursuers I could.

Snaps of them were added to the files and I lifted information from the police band for names and affiliations.

These men were not security forces only. Not from the looks of it. As tired as I should be, impatience crept through me as I glanced at the clock repeatedly. I was keeping a mental countdown for when Remy should resurface.

Until he was out of the catacombs and into a safe house, I would not relax.

He took longer than I cared for, but the buzz of an incoming call had me sagging a little in the seat. "Talk to me," I said when I answered.

"It would be my genuine pleasure," Remy said, the smile in his voice seemed to echo on my face as I grinned. "All clear out there?"

"Yes, it is. Do you need transport?" I probably should have asked that earlier, but we were a little busy. There he was, leaving the church. Limping.

I frowned. The problem with the cameras

here, I couldn't really zoom in. Even if I did, they pixelated like mad.

"I'm good, I figure I'll just lift a car here. They have a lot of older models. I can find something to hot wire."

I snorted, but I was already checking the vehicles and registrations that I could read for a square mile around him.

"Two blocks west," I said. "It looks like the car used to be a rental. I can start it remotely."

"Luv, have I told you how sexy your magic fingers are?"

"A few times," I told him, keeping an eye on him as he limped. Had he been shot? Pulled a muscle? Or wrenched his ankle? What? "The gray one," I informed him when he got there.

It was taking me a minute to find the service codes to get the car open. Master codes existed for mechanics and repossession agents. You just had to know what list they were on.

There we go. The car unlocked and the engine rumbled to life as I disengaged the alarm. They should have had this one changed *after* they bought it. The codes for the rental company still worked.

Not that they were supposed to without the key being nearby...

"Check the right rear tire well, near the top," I told him and he circled the vehicle. A moment later, he held up a magnetic box.

"It's like you left it here as a gift for me."

The stupidity of some people never failed to amaze me.

"We'll need to ditch it in a couple of hours, but it should buy you the time to get out of the city. Do you need accommodations or trip planning?"

"You have no idea how much I want to say yes, just to keep you on the phone. I'm aware it's rather late there." It was the early hours of the morning there, still too early for sunrise.

"Hmm," I said. "And I'm doing all of this without coffee."

"My goddess is the best goddess," he said. "Thank you for not smiting me."

I snorted. "Be safe." On the screen, he was already pulling away and heading east. "Remy...?" I couldn't help myself.

"Still here, luv."

"Do you need medical care?" I grimaced at myself for asking, but he had been limping.

"I knew you cared," he said with a soft laugh. "Go back to sleep goddess, and dream of me. I'll be fine."

Then he hung up and I dropped back into the seat, stress and adrenaline drained out of me like someone had pulled the plug on the drain.

Remy was safe. Or as safe as I could make him. He'd also driven away from where I could safely view him. I could track the stolen car, but probably not the best idea.

Checking the clock, I rubbed a hand over my face. Despite the hour, there would be no going back to sleep. I checked the reports from the police for the name of the body they'd found on the street.

The man I'd helped to kill.

It wasn't there yet.

"Later," I promised myself, then closed down the screens one at a time before I peeled off my headset. I had a treadmill upstairs. While I couldn't outrun the nightmares, I could at least delay them.

A run, then coffee.

I took my phone with me in case Remy ran into more trouble. I wish he'd taken me up on the medical offer.

Giving myself a shake, I locked up the office and headed up the stairs. I knew better than to get involved.

But sometimes... sometimes it was more challenging to keep my distance than I liked to admit.

THREE

PATCH

Wednesday.

Hump day.

Well, it used to be. Now it was *delivery* day.

A message pinged my civilian phone with the drop off details. The driver was here. I checked the external camera, zoomed in on the truck.

It was correct. Then the driver. The number was familiar, but there were only three drivers that brought my deliveries. The one time they sent the wrong driver, I refused to let them in. The service had been far more particular since then.

When the ring sounded on my phone, I hit answer. "Hello Jimmy, you're early today."

"First drop-off for a change," he said. "I have everything except the ice cream. They said they were out. But they will have it for next week's delivery."

"I'll live." At least they didn't try to replace it with frozen yogurt.

I opened the exterior garage so he could bring the groceries in. He always lined them up neatly on the table along the side of the garage with the cold stuffs closest to the door.

When he was done, he grabbed the trash can and the recycle bins and wheeled them up. One of the neighbors always grabbed them for me and put them at the curb. My drivers always brought them in.

"You all good, Ms. Kensington?"

"I'm great, thank you so much, Jimmy. Have a good rest of your week."

"You got it—oh, hey, your laundry service is here. Want me to stay and make sure they put it where it goes?"

"You don't have to do that," I told him.

"I know, but my wife would smack me if I told her I left while they were here."

A laugh escaped me. "Well, we wouldn't want that."

"No, ma'am," he said. "We wouldn't." So Jimmy hung around as the driver carried the fresh laundry up, then collected the bag from the porch. I'd put it out first thing. They collected laundry every week when they dropped off the fresh.

Locked inside my office, with a gun on the desk next to me, I watched as Jimmy supervised it all. Once they were done, he waved the driver off then waved to my camera.

I pressed the button to close the garage then added more to Jimmy's tip. Only after the external door was closed and secure did I let myself out of the office. I secured the gun to the holster at the base of my spine, then hurried through the process of ferrying everything inside the house.

Mail always came in through the slot. A package door had been installed before I moved in. The beauty of the Internet, everything was available online and could be delivered. Made maintaining a low profile easy.

Kettle on to make tea, I studied the fresh contents of my fridge. Fully stocked and I had no idea what I wanted to eat. Grilled cheese was probably where I'd end up. My secondary phone beeped and I checked my watch to see who it was before I tapped the button on my headset.

"Talk to me," I said as I answered.

"Hey, gorgeous," Boxer said and I closed the fridge.

"No," was my answer.

"You don't even know what I was going to ask," Boxer argued. Despite the playfulness, there was an undercurrent of sobriety in his words.

"I don't have to know, you only open the call with compliments when you want a favor." The kettle was boiling. "You only want favors when you want me to take on new clients *after* I told you I was taking a break from newbies."

"Goddamn, Patch." He *almost* managed to sound offended. "You don't think much of me, do you?"

"I don't have to think much, I *know* you. Now, if you want to invite me to game or if you want to shoot the shit or something else fun—"

He sighed. "I just—need a second set of eyes on this guy."

Uh huh. "What's wrong with him?" I poured the water into the pot and set the tea ball into it so it would steep. Probably good, because my soothing tea was going downstairs with me.

Boxer didn't answer immediately. While he wrestled with the balance between needing assistance and how much to disclose, I threw together a sandwich and carried all of it downstairs to the office.

Once I was in, I engaged the locks and brought my system up.

"I don't know," he finally said. "Just—something hinky. You have good instincts. Even when you can't put your finger on what's wrong, you can tell when something is."

Lips pursed, I considered his comment then shook my head. "Boxer, if you're feeling uneasy decline. One thing I've learned about this business—our clients have to trust us implicitly, but that means we have to trust them."

"I hate turning it down—it's good money."

"Money isn't everything."

"Says the operator with steady clients."

I shrugged, I wouldn't defend my work ethic or my clients. I'd whittled the list down this year. Normally, I only ran five to seven operatives. But currently? I had three regulars and two intermittent. Three more were on my list, but two of those were on an extended vacation. The third one had dropped completely off the map.

They could be dead, I supposed. Hopefully not.

A beep signaled another call coming through and it was McQuade. He was right on time.

"Boxer, if your gut says no—then say no. A job is not worth the stress if you can't be certain of the client."

The other operator let out a forlorn sigh. "Yeah, I guess." He didn't say anything for another long moment. "Thanks, Patch." Then he was gone.

Shaking my head, I clicked over to McQuade's call. "Talk to me, big boy." I put a little drawl on the endearment.

"No one else I'd rather talk to, sugar bear," he fired back, snappy and sassy.

A snort of laughter escaped me. "You win."

He chuckled. "Damn, you gave in almost too fast. There's no fun if you don't make me work for it."

"Next time," I promised, my cheeks aching from my smile. Thankfully, I hadn't choked on my tea. "But that was a good one."

"Well, since I won and you seem to like it so much, Sugar Bear, we'll go with it."

I rolled my eyes, but didn't argue. After all, he had won. "So, what are we doing?" I managed a sip of my tea without inhaling it or spitting it over my keyboard. "Your request didn't go into a lot of details—just, you needed to talk to me."

"Can't a guy want to talk to his sugar bear?"

"Keep it up, *big boy*," I teased. "Sure, you can,

but if we're just gonna log in to play a game somewhere, I need to switch headphones."

"Hmm... there's something sexy about imagining you plowing through the bad guys in Fortnight."

"I prefer Halo, though the new Fallout was pretty damn sexy too."

"Sugar Bear, keep talking to me all gamer-like, it's turning me on."

"Hmm-hmm. Spill, what did you need the special appointment for?" John McQuade was a lot of things, but he wasn't frivolous and he didn't waste time. When he asked for specific appointments, he usually had work to do.

"Promise to not get mad at me?" He sounded so hopeful, like a child who'd done something wrong and knew it.

"No," I informed him. "You tell me what you did and why it's now my problem and we'll go from there."

"Damn," he said. "Here I was hoping to avoid the doghouse."

"What did you do, John?"

He grunted something that sounded vaguely like German. Maybe Dutch. I took another sip of the tea and waited.

"Got a job," he finally admitted. "Feels off. Did the research, still feels off. Want to take a look at it for me?"

"You did the research?" I raised my eyebrows. "You cheating on me, John?"

"I would never, Sugar Bear—most of the

time." That nickname was going to stick, wasn't it?

"Uh huh." I clucked my tongue at him. "Why didn't you just ask me to look at it in the first place?"

A file popped into my dropbox and I was already opening them.

"I don't want to take all your time with business. Sometimes, I like talking to you for fun."

"Big Boy, I am more than capable of handling you and more besides, who did you go to for this?"

I was already separating out the different file components. The job description. The company. The targets. Incorporation papers were there, founding, board of directors—

It was strange because it was way too clean. Everything was—perfect. Humans were innately flawed. Everyone had secrets, and no one who succeeded at that level in business was quite that squeaky clean.

Not when they handled equipment, pharmaceutical, and weapons sales of both the legal and illegal variety. They were very good at burying their various deals and holding companies beneath a complicated and intricate series of shells.

"Marcus," he finally admitted. "He's good."

"I'm better." It wasn't bragging. "Marcus is a surface skimmer. He won't dig too deep unless you tell him to."

"I did tell him to go deep," McQuade complained. "Problem is, he said the deeper he went, the more nothing he found."

"But you don't believe that." It wasn't a question. I didn't believe it either. The deeper I dug, the more shells I found. Back tracing them was creating an intricate puzzle. What secret were they trying to hide behind this web of deceit?

"No," he admitted, and there was a growl punctuating that word. "Learned a long time ago to trust my gut. Doesn't matter how clean it is or how much they doctor the logo, if it feels like a cheap knockoff—"

"It probably is. Now this is interesting..."

"What?" I had his full attention.

"Each series of shells is covered by three more. It's almost like a shell game within a shell game, within a shell game. Each time I track to the next, it splits off again."

"Someone doesn't want us to know where everything ties back to."

"No, they don't," I said as I worked on a program to break through that algorithm a little faster. "It's also set up to create phantom shells. One in three of these are legit, but they are cloning them, then using a replicating pattern to keep the real ones hidden. It's a really sexy little game of dress-up."

"You sound like you're enjoying it," he murmured and it was like having some big cat rumbling a purr in my ear.

"I like it when someone, who is almost as smart as me, provides me with a puzzle that's a challenge."

His soft laughter encouraged me. "Damn,

Sugar Bear, you sound hot when you're in pursuit."

The algorithm did its job, and helped me crack through the clones and false fronts until I was able to track the whole thing back to a company in...

"You can't take this job," I told him. It didn't matter what they were calling the business. They'd changed the incorporation papers, but I recognized the man behind it.

"Why not?"

"Yuri Androvich."

"It's a trap," McQuade sounded almost delighted. "Really?"

"Yes, really. Why are you so happy about it?"

"Androvich is almost like the guy who got away. And the son of a bitch never paid me for the two jobs I did before he tried to kill me."

"John," I said, refusing to be charmed by his engaged tone. "He didn't plan to pay you because he wanted to kill you. Then you screwed that last job for him—it not only cost him a few hundred million, but it put a price on his head."

"Couldn't happen to a nicer dickbag. So he set a trap for me." He clapped his hands.

"You're going to spring the trap."

"Yes, Sugar Bear, I am. Guess I'm off to Morocco. Want me to bring you back something nice?"

"Well, you coming back alive would be good," I said.

"If you insist," he teased. "I'll call you when I'm ready to move."

"I'll be here."

Then he was gone and I stared at the information on the screen. Where was Androvich right now?

CHAPTER

FOUR

PATCH

"You're bored," I told Remy as I pulled up his current location. Thanks to Google maps, I had access to street level as well as three-dimensional maps. It wasn't like I could just repurpose a satellite to scan his location.

If push came to shove I could, I supposed, but that would bring heat in the form of hellfire down on us. Not a benefit really.

"I am bored," he admitted. "*But*, I do need details on those guys. Soft background, habits, regular destinations—the usual."

"We looking for a good spot to ambush them or a reason to?"

Remington didn't say anything immediately. His quiet could be because he was actually considering his answer. Or it could be he was in danger of being overheard. It was far more likely the former than the latter. He could and had, found perches and nests where he'd spent days waiting out a target.

I would prefer we didn't discuss how he handled his bodily functions, particularly after he told me the longest he'd ever made it in a nest was 89 hours. My imagination provided enough detail. I was sufficiently grossed out enough to *not* ask more questions.

"Maybe a little of column A and a little of column B," he answered finally. "You ever wonder if there was something else you could be doing right now?"

"Well, I was binging the *90 Day Fiancé* when you called."

He snorted. "Luv, I meant a different line of work."

I shrugged, despite the fact he couldn't see me. "I know, I think my answer still stands." It took me a minute to figure out where the best location for his sniper's nest would be. Then I studied the local traffic cams.

He was invisible on all of them.

Remy was good.

"Uh huh, okay, so if you weren't on the phone with me, you'd be binging Netflix."

"More or less," I answered, flipping screens to the research. The names were just that. Names. They might be targets. They might be associates.

They could be his partners in a bowling league.

"What if you had a different job entirely?" He seemed fixed on this particular topic. "Like how do you even go to school for tech goddess of the universe?"

I snorted. "Who said I went to school?"

"Me," he retaliated. "You're too damn intelligent to not have like fourteen different degrees. I bet you've even got a PhD floating around. I'd play doctor with you anytime."

My face heated at the less than subtle innuendo, but I kept my laughter light. "You'd lose that bet, I'm afraid. I never even finished my Master's."

"Damn. MIT, though right? You seem like you'd be running MIT."

"Remy..."

"Yes, Patch my dear?"

"Focus."

"I am focused," he said. "We have time. You're doing research, and I'm curious."

"I don't have to stay on the line while I do the research. I can always just finish up the files and drop them in your box for you so you can review them when you're done."

It was how we normally did this.

"Ouch," he said with a huff of faint laughter. "C'mon, Patch. Indulge me. It's been forty-eight hours since one of these pricks stuck their head out to check the weather. I could be here for days and die of dehydration or boredom. Maybe both."

"And questioning me about my life is something to do?"

"Well, you practically know everything about me. Where I grew up..."

"Idaho?" I mused aloud.

"Stoke-on-Trent." The snap in his voice had me biting back a smile. "You've got jokes now."

"I've always had jokes," I told him. "You just have to pay attention." I was putting together a profile on the first name. They were—very clean. Almost too clean. Work history. School history.

Even their credit history.

All very normal. Middle of the road. No huge investments. No huge losses. One bad item of bad credit that rolled off after seven years. Small, insignificant loans. Car loan.

House refinance.

House sale.

House sale? I pulled up the papers on the property and the tax records for the property. Though it showed payments for ten years, and in his name before—no wait there it was. He *assumed* the mortgage.

Yeah, it was a really good job of an identity build but this was a cover ID. I flagged the file with a warning for Remy. If he'd been given someone in WitSec as a target, he needed to think about that hard.

So did I.

Sure there were some shitty ass people in WitSec, but not all of them. There were also marshals just doing their jobs.

"Play with me, Patch," Remy cajoled. "Twenty questions, truth or dare—just—tell me something about you that I don't know."

"I hate cell phones," I told him after I zipped up the file on the first name and sent it off. I started building one for the second. After how much had been done to cover the first, I wanted to make sure I didn't set off any alarms by digging too deep.

"Why?" He sounded legitimately surprised.

"You know anything about horses, Remy?"

"Some," he said. "Probably enough to be dangerous. Like I know how to ride, for fun. Why?"

"Well, you know how they tell you that when you control the head on a horse, you control where it goes. But to do that, you need a halter and a lead rope."

"Yes," he said slowly.

"The thing is, sure, you have a grip on a thousand pound animal, but they have one on you."

"Cell phone offers convenience, but it's also a leash."

"Exactly," I said. "I don't like that part of them. I think about when I was a kid and I didn't have a phone—and how badly I wanted one. My dad told me I was too young, etc etc." I shook my head. "I had no idea how good I had it and once you get one—it's like you're now permanently leashed."

All someone had to do was reach out and pull on that electronic lead to yank you back in. I'd worked hard to cut those cords. It was why I had three different phones now. One for each aspect of life. Not counting the burners in my go bag.

If I ever had to abandon this life, it would suck, but I had everything in place to do it.

"Were you a girly girl or a tomboy?" Remy asked. "When you were a kid."

"Oh, I thought you were asking about now." I deadpanned the delivery as I stared at the facts populating about the second name. Just as clean as the first, but also a co-worker.

That could be a problem. They wouldn't usually put two witnesses in close proximity. Possibly just a friend developed in the new life? Or family member?

They might bring a family member—

Oh, I backtracked the name then looked at the locations and the history. It was different. Almost too different from the primary.

"If you want to tell me about now, I won't object," Remy said. "But I'm trying to picture blonde, blue-eyed you with pigtails…"

"Who said I had blonde hair and blue eyes?" Amusement curved my lips. As skimming attempts went, it wasn't a bad one at all.

"Damn, you're a hard nut to crack." The protest on Remy's part carried a lot of humor.

"I thought it was a game, not an interrogation," I reminded him.

"Who says it can't be both?"

I zipped up the second file and sent it off. "Me."

There was a beat of silence, then he blew out a long breath. "Understood, luv. Understood. Backing off."

"Thank you," I told him. "I have one more name here to finish building a profile for. Did you really need these or was it an excuse to talk to me?"

"Both," he admitted. "You ever feel like something is too good to be true?"

"Every day." The fact I'd survived this long? Definitely too good to be true. "What's your gut telling you?"

"Walk away," he said and the issue he was

struggling with crystallized. Remy took a lot of black bag jobs, wetwork, and assassinations. I didn't ask too much detail about his targets and he didn't defend them.

It was all a job. A transaction. Once he accepted a contract, he fulfilled it. He just didn't accept all contracts. If he was on this...

"You're scouting a potential contract," I said abruptly and then winced at my big mouth.

"Yeah," he admitted. "Got this offer before, turned it down. They came back with almost double the fee. So I wanted a good look at the target. Want to know why they want them scratched off."

"You don't know why." It wasn't a question. I was tempted to dig deeper into the location. Strip mine the area for data and see who he was tracking.

"No," he said. "That part bugs me. Bugs me that they are offering twice as much for something that seems a pretty straightforward job."

"Then why not go to someone else? Someone with less discerning taste?" Because as much as I admired Remy and enjoyed his acerbic wit. He'd been my client the longest of all my regulars. Also, my first in this new life and job.

We went back...

Something tickled in the back of my mind. McQuade had a similar issue. My clients didn't generally cross paths. Though McQuade and Remy had been in the same place during the same conflict once. Thankfully, their different jobs never brought them to blows.

"You never ask me about my targets," he murmured and I kind of wish I could find him on one of the street cams. As it was, I had a good idea of where he was.

"You tell me what I need to know. You ask me the questions you need answered."

"That's it? No looking deeper?"

"Do you want me to look deeper?"

"Do you know that answering a question with a question is annoying?"

I smiled at the drop of humor in his voice. "Is it?"

He chuckled. "Never change, Patch. Never change."

"I don't intend to. This works because you tell me what you need and I find it." I zipped up the last file and sent it off. "The reason that job bugs you is they want *you* to do it. They aren't being dissuaded by your no. The fact they are offering you more money is bait."

"If I turn it down, what do you think they do next?"

"Depends on how badly they want you to do the job."

"That's what I'm worried about."

"Do you want me to look into this target?"

He went quiet. The silence elongated, until I wondered if we'd been cut off. "Not yet," he said, finally. "If this is a trap for me, I don't want you triggering it."

So he did see it, and that let me breathe a little deeper.

"I'm here," I reminded him.

"That's what I adore about you," he said. "Tell you what, next time we talk—tell me what your favorite kind of music is and if you know how to dance."

"Next time?" I verified.

"Yep. Next time. Go watch your crazy show. What season are you on?"

"Why?"

"Cause I plan to watch it. The fact you like it means it might be important and I always do my research."

A little shiver went through me. "Am I the target, Remy?"

"Never," he whispered. "Always."

"Thanks for clearing that up."

His soft chuckle echoed in my ears as he ended the call and I leaned back in the chair. He didn't want me to dig into the target, but he didn't say anything about the people offering him the job.

Remy only got jobs through two sources.

Me and the Post Office.

Time to dig into the back and see what was happening there.

CHAPTER
FIVE

REMINGTON

Three days of patient observation paid off. The nest was thirty floors up, on a floor under construction with no glass installed yet. The plastic sheeting provided ample cover. There was a bathroom one floor down.

As jobs went, this was almost like a room at the Ritz. Hour sixty-nine—good hour—the target arrived at his private apartment for an assignation with the mistress or call girl or whatever was the season's latest flavor.

The woman wasn't his wife. That was all I needed to know. She was also not a target. Collateral wasn't covered, but they would like a witness. So it wasn't just a physical assassination.

They wanted to kill the guy's reputation too. Then again, he was part mob sellout, part politician, and all around sleazebag. His numbers in the current poll were tanking but the guy hadn't lost an election in twelve years.

Frankly, I didn't care. The jobs came in, they paid the bills, some had some specialist shit they wanted done—like cutting out tongues or leaving their penises next to them. Those jobs were a little messy, but I'd done a few.

I preferred the distance work. I saw better from a distance. The more difficult the target was to acquire, the more I liked the job. It also meant the more I could charge.

Regular infusions also let me turn down the clean-up on aisle fourteen jobs. When the target turned out to be scum? That was just icing on the cake. He was dancing as he came in and he tossed her something. She had to be twenty years younger than him.

Nice tits and ass, but I liked them actually out of college at the very least. When she started cutting a couple of lines, I kept an eye on her for a moment.

Cocaine. She didn't look too buzzed right now. Maybe the next few minutes would scare her straight. Either way, she at least didn't have to worry about faking it for the limpdick who was already stripping off his clothes.

Fuck my life, I could have gone forever without having to look at pasty white flesh, apron belly, and flab that rippled when he swung his hips like he was some hot stud on a stage.

Only habits and training kept me from closing my eyes or giving in to disgust. I had a clean sight on his head, and when he turned to face the mirror—that would make a nice splatter target. It was also into a load bearing wall so it would be less likely to cut through him, then the wall, and into someone else.

The mushroom-tipped bullets were designed to shred once it was inside the body, but I liked to minimize the risk of pass-through shootings.

One breath.

Two.

In between the heartbeats.

I squeezed the trigger.

One round.

It blew the front of his skull off and he stood there, limp dick in hand like the body wasn't sure what to do before he collapsed. The rifle was muffled, but the shot had been loud on this floor. Might even have echoed down to the street, but the girl in the living room was riding her high.

Yeah, enjoy it while it lasts, birdie.

"You're welcome," I murmured. Snapping two photos to add to the collection of the others I'd taken. Proof of life snuffed out for the job. Then I broke down the gun and packed it away. Different pieces into different parcel boxes, all going to different locations where I could pick them up later.

Courier tags were already on the boxes. I separated out other pieces and tucked them into hollow crutches. In under five minutes, I'd policed the area of my nest and sanitized it.

Instead of the elevator, I took the stairs down four floors to where a customer service center was located and a trading company. They both worked weird hours. I dropped the boxes into the courier slot. Those went down to a lock box that was only opened by the courier service.

With care, I used the crutches to make my

way down the hall. The backpack over my shoulder and earbuds in my ears made me look like one of those traders wrapping it for the night.

"Oh, hang on," one of the guys stepping off the elevator said, he held the door open for me. "Heading down?"

"Yeah, parking garage."

"You got it, man." He hit P1 and then let the doors close. I tucked my head down, leaning heavily on the crutches while yawning. The tired rolled over me. Easier to play the part when you inhabit it.

Once I was in my vehicle, I scratched at the beard covering the lower half of my face. Damn thing itched. I started the old F150 up and rolled my head from side to side. At least the "broken" foot was the left one. Meant driving wasn't too much of an issue.

You needed to use a building badge to get in and out. Trevor Markowitz of Randolph Trading was the right height and build if you squinted and looked at him sideways.

Not that I had to worry, he was out of town this week and a couple of cameras had been on the fritz for the last few days. It all worked out.

It was just after midnight. The bars were still hopping. I took my time driving to another garage. It was a private one, and I dropped the truck off for clean-up, then walked three blocks over to pick up a different car.

Then I found myself at an all night diner for coffee and food. I ate in the car, firing off the proof to the client's dropbox.

I had a half-dozen fresh emails since the day before. Vetted files from Patch were at the top of the box. That was my girl, always on top of things.

Thumbing through her breakdowns, I grunted. She definitely found a lot more on the targets than my first go round. Probably should have taken it to her in the first place. I bit into the tuna melt.

Despite the ache of hunger in my gut, I ate slowly and deliberately. I tended to eat very little when on a job. The less I ate, the less I needed to take a shit.

The same with drinking.

Drink only the bare amount necessary. I'd hydrate before I got on my flight. In the meanwhile, I would eat my sandwich, sip my coffee, and do my research.

My email pinged three times while I read through the first file. I really did like how much detail she broke it down in from personal habits to online addictions. What I could never figure out was *how* she figured that out.

The comment that his background was *too clean* set off alarm bells. It meant someone had scrubbed him. Whether it was the government or whoever his criminal associates were, it was a very thorough job.

Thorough enough that Patch, the best goddamn operator I'd ever had, highlighted the discrepancies. She hadn't filled in the blanks. But I hadn't asked her to do that. It would be a much deeper dive and require a lot more of her resources.

Turning the information over in my head, I pulled out some fries and munched on those as I went through the next two targets' files. All scrubbed. Just like the first. Patch had left a note at the bottom of the last one.

Post Office should have better receipts than what they turned over. Suggests that they were part of the scrubbing. Be wary.

Part of the scrubbing. So maybe a freelance Eraser had taken the job. If that was the case, then Patch was right. Nothing that came out of the Post Office could be trusted.

Fuck.

I could turn the jobs down. I hadn't accepted yet. They'd come back with an increased offer. I'd declined the first time because they'd been cagey on the target and the timeline. I'd also been busy.

Now? Well, with the recent job done, I had plenty of time. The question was, did I want to deal with the fall out if it turned out to be a shit show? The coffee was dark and bitter, like my soul. So good.

Leaving the files, I flipped back to my mail to see the receipt indicating proof of death had been accepted. The next was proof of payment.

Oh, that would take care of a few bills. It was almost two in the morning, but it was after five in the Cayman Islands. My body had no idea what time it was, too many trips abroad. The internal clock was broken.

I slept when I needed sleep and that was fine.

When I finished the last of the fries, I put a call through to Isaiah.

"You better have blood or bone showing, I just poured my fucking coffee."

A grin crossed my face at the grumpy bastard's greeting. "Well, then I got you after you were out of bed. So bitch less."

"Oh," he answered with a grunt. "It's you. Hang on."

I waited as he probably switched locations. The soft click of a door closing and the beep of an alarm engaging confirmed the thought. Leaning back in the car, I stared down the darkened street.

I was close enough, I could probably drive down to the beach for sunrise. Problem was, I'd be facing the wrong way.

"Right, I'm at my desk. To what do I owe this honor of a before fucking dawn phone call? Do you need bail money?"

"You're a regular fucking comedian," I told him. "No, I don't need bail—today anyway. But it's time for you to earn that ten percent you charge me."

He chuckled. "I earn that ten percent plus interest every single day. You're up by thirty across most of your accounts. You also doubled your investments in that shipping company you took a liking to."

That happened when the CEO of the opposing business died while in the middle of a brothel in Asia. But I didn't judge.

At least not after they were dead.

"Glad to hear it. You should be getting a fresh infusion to the Carmichael accounts."

Didn't matter what jobs I took or what name I gave them. I spread out the payments to a wide variety of accounts. Every single account was designed to filter the money through investments, to clean it, then forward it on to where Isaiah could route it to my personal accounts, business expenses and more.

"Good. Probably close them after this payment. Unless you've already taken another job there."

I thought about the files I'd just read. "No," I told him. "Might be taking a vacation." I tried the words out. They seemed easy enough to say.

"I'm sorry, who are you and what have you done with Michael Remington?"

I snorted. "I can take a vacation."

"Name one you've taken in the last seven years." Then before I could comment, he said, "And Cabo doesn't count. When you're recovering from gunshot wounds, it's *not* a vacation."

I made a face. "Clean the money up, make sure you pay Patch first. Add a bonus for me, she's done some good work lately."

"You really taking a vacation?" Isaiah asked.

"Don't know yet," I said. "I'm thinking about it."

"Well, that's further than you've gotten any other time."

"You're an ass."

"That's why you like me," he retorted. "Let

me know if you take the vacay, I'll free up some cash and it'll be in the right accounts."

"Thanks."

"Don't mention it. In fact—don't call so early next time." With that, Isaiah hung up and I shook my head.

It was the middle of the night here, but I wasn't sure what time it was for Patch. I could call, but I didn't need to call. At least—not yet. For now, I checked in for my flight and got the hell out of Los Angeles.

It took almost half a day to get back to my place and it was afternoon when I pulled up her number on my work phone.

I'd made myself wait all day. I'd even come up with some questions about the files.

The only problem was, she didn't answer.

I frowned and tried the call again. It rang.

It rang and she didn't answer.

Patch *always* answered.

One more attempt, even if I already suspected the outcome. I was on my feet and had a go bag in hand while I waited for her to pick up. When she didn't answer that one, I headed to my garage. I needed to track that number and find her location.

That meant I needed computer access and I couldn't go through the Post Office.

Not this time.

CHAPTER
SIX

LOCKE

The museum gala was the perfect location to scout a few targets. While the wealthy guests—or at least their jewels—weren't on the shopping list for this trip, I still liked to keep up on my practice.

What I found fascinating were the abundance of treasures on display around slender necks, dipping between ample breasts, and dangling from ears. Rings, watches, and bracelets were out there along with some very distinctive cufflinks.

But those were rather hit or miss if a woman had on gloves or a sleeve covered the items in question. The mental game of evaluating potential resale value though was an old favorite.

It also gave me something to do while I waited for the right time to pick up the two items I'd come here to acquire.

"Good evening, Monsieur," Bellamy said as she slid up next to me and tucked her arm through mine. As both curator and hostess, Bellamy had been my ticket to get in.

"Mademoiselle," I teased her and she made a playful moue but her gaze was constantly on the move. "I am honored that you have taken the time to check on me."

Her snort of derision added some genuine humor to my smile. "Don't tease, you bad man. I have seen you eyeing up the clients and the guests. More, I have seen them looking at you..." She bumped her hip to mine as I navigated us around a cluster of women who were debating the depth behind the art on the wall.

"Really? Hmm... I hadn't noticed. Any suggestions?" The tease earned me a wicked smile and pinch.

"Play all you want, darling, do not get me fired."

"I would never." It didn't take much to affect being scandalized. Bellamy was one of my better contacts. Even better, she was a former lover who made a much better friend than bed partner. She preferred to be the one in control and I wasn't a shoe licker.

Still, I had to admit—she was definitely gifted in the sack. I seemed to have held up my end well enough she actually looked disappointed when we ended that part of our relationship.

"Champagne," she said with a note of command and one of the waiters deviated their course directly to us. When we each had a glass in hand, she raised it in a toast. "Monsieur De-Marcan has requested an evening with me after the show tonight. Do not be insulted if you leave alone."

"If I leave alone," I told her with a wink. "But thanks for the update."

She clinked her glass to mine. "It is the civilized thing to do. Now go back to your —perusing?"

"That's a good word. Perusing."

I rolled some of the champagne around my tongue as she strolled off. There was a natural slinkiness to Bellamy. She moved like a woman on the prowl, as comfortable with her beauty as she was intelligent.

Course, that also made her dangerous and probably why I'd been attracted in the first place. I still admired her, but we were so much better as friends and colleagues.

Out of habit, I tracked her path across the reception floor. She paused to speak to a couple here, a woman there, and an older man there. Sometimes she answered questions, other times she just exchanged greetings, but she was on the move continuously.

I tracked her until she reached a rather distinguished looking gentleman. He was maybe ten years her senior. They looked quite striking together. He gave her a smile so full of indulgence I had to shake my head.

Grinning, I turned away. The man was putty in her palms and seemed quite happy to be there. Good for them. The private museum was a popular venue in Nice, and I'd been here a couple of times in the past.

The art on display belonged to private collectors, most of them preferring to remain anonymous. The "donated" time here afforded them some financial returns both on their taxes and insurance.

I understood the whole financial morass, I just didn't care right now. Private museums meant private security. Also, they tended to deal with problems privately and not involve the police or international authorities.

It definitely meant leaving the country with acquisitions was a little simpler. Tonight's reception was for a popular artist from the sixties, made popular by their graciousness in dying the year previously.

A cache of heretofore unseen works had been discovered and were now on display. They would all be sold before the night was over, but would remain at the museum in the meanwhile.

The artist wasn't bad, but it was kind of like admiring the clean lines on soup cans. Clean, definitive—boring as fuck. Art should make a person feel and these barely inspired me to take a nap.

After "wandering" the collection, I made my way to the next gallery to explore along with a handful of others. We were hardly restricted to the one gallery. In fact, some couples were taking advantage of the exploration time to find some dark corners.

I found a group enjoying themselves quite lustfully in the impressionists wing. The man seemed to have both women in hand, mouth, and cunt. Good for him. The blonde bouncing happily on his cock beckoned me with a grin, but I just blew her a kiss and kept right on strolling.

In another corner, a man was on his knees for another. His partner didn't even notice me as his cock was swallowed over and over. Sex and sin could be the theme for the rest of the galleries. More than one little sex party was in full throes.

I drained the last of my champagne when I reached the medieval gallery. Odd, no one was fucking under the frescoes. Or maybe they just hadn't gotten this far. I took my time as I wandered from one display to the next.

The books housed here were all under glass. Ancient tomes lined up next to gloriously illuminated texts. Some of these were likely heretical, but they weren't here for their religious value.

It would be nice to think they were here for their artistic and historical merit, but no, they were here more for their monetary value. They were worth a king's ransom. For some, they were worth more than all the art in the impressionists wing.

Fortunately, I was not here to acquire one of the books. I had to admire the setup though. The weighted glass, the pressure plates, and the camera placements. It was all quite sophisticated.

A guard passed by as I wandered on to the next gallery. More paintings along with a drug deal. Those were always fun. I bypassed them. They ignored me. Useful for a distraction if I needed it.

Eventually, my circuitous path brought me to

the room of Greek and Roman Antiquities. Instead of the glass cases and pressure plates, it was laid out on tables under lighter glass.

The pieces were small, so several would be clustered into a display. Some had cloth backdrops, others had stone. There were neat little cards explaining each one.

Then there were the knives and the broaches which adorned the armor. I slid my hands in my pockets as I examined each one. I really liked the different pieces of jewelry.

There were a couple of truly lovely diamond bracelets adorning some of the guests. As exquisite and delicate as modern pieces were, I was far more interested in these chunky pieces of gold.

Specifically, the pair of serpentine armbands that featured a pair of tritons—one male and the other female. They each cradled a small, winged Eros. They were attached by the hoops on the back of their head to the formal dress of the Hellenic woman they had on display.

The clothing was a recreation, but all of her accessories? They were the real thing. I loved arrogance. The gold pieces weighed about six and a half ounces each. They were well over two thousand years old and right there.

Ripe for the taking.

An announcement came over the speakers, inviting guests to come and enjoy the words of the daughter of the painter in the main gallery. Not interested in that right now, I gave the camera in the corner time to complete its circuit then come back to me where I'd moved on to the next piece.

On its next circuit, I sidestepped. Replaced the two gold bands with the replicas and pocketed the originals. I was on to the next display when the camera returned. Eventually, I made my way back to the main gallery and caught Bellamy's eye.

She drifted back to me and I nodded to the painting of an old-fashioned switchboard. I'd been eyeing it earlier for other reasons. It would look beautiful in my Patch collection.

I liked to pick up items for her. Not that she would ever let me send them to her. But a man had to have goals and meeting her someday, bringing her to my treasure trove or taking it to her was at the top of my list.

She was my personal oracle. My good luck charm. Since she came on board as my operator, well—business had been much smoother and I got to enjoy myself far more.

"You're actually *buying* a piece?" Bellamy asked, her tone arch and I grinned.

"Think I can't afford it?"

"*Mon dieu*, I would never presume to insult you like that unless it proved true. Then I would take great pleasure in it." The funny thing was, she would absolutely give me hell if I embarrassed her with something as plebeian as a bounced check.

I could always come back and get it later. But the mood struck me and I had been thinking about the piece. I pulled out a black credit card and held it out to her.

"I will take care of this for you. Do you mind leaving it on exhibit..."

"I do, actually, I want it sent after the exhibit closes tonight. It's—personal." Did I really want to get that diamond bracelet for Patch tonight? Hmm. I'd think about it later. It wasn't really perfect. I wasn't even sure if diamonds were Patch's thing.

"I'll take care of it. Will there be anything else?" Amusement filled her eyes as I considered what I wanted to do next.

"I'll wait for my card," I murmured. "Or I can go with you and save you the return trip."

Chuckling, she led the way out of the exhibit and around the security checkpoint to her office on the far side. The paperwork took almost no time and the hundred thousand for the painting was a bargain.

After, I glanced at my watch and pressed a kiss to her cheek. "I'm going. Thank you for the invitation."

"Always. Don't be a stranger."

Then I was out on the street and I got myself a cab back to my hotel. The weight of the gold armbands in my pockets were a reminder that I still needed to deal with my haul.

It was still early in the States. Despite being near midnight here. She sounded American, so I assumed that was where she lived. I didn't ask, she didn't tell.

Though I had been looking for clues. The last

time, I'd told her I wanted to send a Christmas card and she laughed at me.

I'd figure it out sooner or later. Still, I made myself shower, pack, and leave the hotel to drive to Paris. I wanted to drop off the armbands with Felix so he could handle the clearance. Then I could get a drink at the airport before I flew home.

Professionalism kept me focused until the next day when I was at the airport and waiting for my flight. I called, and told myself it was because I was bored and not because I wanted to hear her voice.

She didn't answer.

That was weird.

I called again.

She still didn't answer.

Patch *always* answered.

When a third call went unanswered, I pulled up my laptop, turned on my firewalls and VPN, hopped on the airport net and went looking for an email. She *always* responded.

I'd found a way to message her in a game once and she gave me a way to send her a request to play. I had to agree to never use it for work and sometimes... I messaged her jokes.

Fuck, it was stupid to have a crush on a woman I'd never seen, but she had rules for a reason. Still, I sent her a request and waited.

The lack of any answer sent sweat prickling over my skin. Something was wrong.

Something was very wrong.

I was still more than ten hours from the

States. I needed someone on the ground and I needed a way to find her.

What if she wasn't in the States? Would I be even farther away?

Fuck.

I had a favor I could call in, but pulling the trigger would blow a lot of capital.

Fuck it. I needed to know where she was and if it turned out she was fine—well... like I said, a guy needed goals.

And I needed her.

SEVEN

MCQUADE

ockets lit up the night. The impacts sending plumes of flames, debris, and screams into the skies. Heat from the fires that were already burning left a sheen of sweat on my face. A half-broken sob from behind me had me shifting so I could glance at the half-dozen kids huddled with their teacher.

Seniors in high school on a trip of a lifetime. The last thing they expected was for a war to erupt all around them. The hot air ballooned out from the impact force. We were far enough away that it was just a hot breeze against my already sweaty face.

The choked sound of a sob reminded me that this was the last place these kids should be. The problem was, the situation had blown up from bad to worse to fucking insane in a matter of hours. Standard evacuation routes weren't available, civilians in country were in danger, much less out of country, and two hospitals had been hit in the forty-eight hours since I hit the ground.

"Listen to me," I said. "We have a plan. Do you guys remember the plan?"

The teacher, a guy who had his own asthma inhaler, but had rallied to keep the kids between us and kept them moving, nodded. "We do —Marcus?"

"We stick together, no one moves alone." The kid had athlete written all over him, but fear didn't care about your hobbies.

"Kendall?"

At the prompting, the girl with the glasses and the frizzy hair wiped at her eyes, sweat soaked her ruddy face and while she hadn't stopped crying since I'd arrived, it hadn't slowed her down.

She sniffled. "When Mr. McQuade moves, we move. When Mr. McQuade holds up his hand, we stop. When he drops his fist, we go low." A choked sound escaped her and she sniffled again. "Sorry."

"No need to be sorry, crying is a good stress reliever. It's letting you think. I'd rather you were teary and thinking than stoic and frozen."

Surprise flickered over her face. In the distance, a scream of rockets whistled through the air. Their impacts were followed by more heat, more wind, and the char of death on the wind.

The invasion was driving steadily into the more populated areas. The conflict was old, and it was colonial. Some said downright tribal. Right now, I wanted the civilians out of the way.

"Jonathon?" The teacher prompted the gamer in their little group.

"McQuade is point. Mr. Maxwell is rear guard. We are never to get ahead of Mr. McQuade or fall behind Mr. Maxwell. Move in pairs. Help each other. Watch each other's sixes and we'll keep moving northwest to the water."

Some of the spark Jonathon had for this had gone out of him. Grim reality was not a video game. Just being good at Call of Freedom didn't mean you could handle it when it was real bullets whizzing through the air.

I checked my watch as another set of rockets arced through the sky. It was five to six volleys, then it would go quiet for about six to seven minutes.

It was that six to seven minute window we would use to move.

Patch and I had gone over four different exit strategies. I'd memorized the maps, the road lay-outs, and the general security patrols. Every single one of those had to be discarded for the emergency extraction plan on the Mediterranean.

The safe corridors closed too rapidly. I'd feel better about it if I had Patch watching my back, but communications were cut off. Cell towers were down and I'd bet anything they'd cut cables so not even WiFi or hard lines would work.

Patch had given me options and we'd gone over it until I could move in my sleep. It was better to stick to the plan and knowing her—she was probably tracking me with a satellite or something. That woman had her ways.

"Solid planning," I said, sweeping my gaze over all of them before I went back to watching the road. We weren't the only ones hunkering down. I'd seen a family a way up the street.

Wars had no pity in them.

Another volley of rockets. I waited for impact and the hot breeze to get hotter. It was like noon in the summer out here. The air was almost too damn uncomfortable to breathe.

"Masks," I reminded the kids, dragging my own handkerchief up over my face. There was ash and smoke, and who knew what else out there. It was stinging my eyes and my face. We needed to shield our lungs as much as possible.

One more volley and it screamed a lot closer than I liked, hitting a building not more than fifty meters away. The detonation of the impact, and the sundering of the building facade, glass, and the crunch of metal as more of the building hit the road covered the girls' screams.

Terrified or not, though, all of the kids kept their heads down and when I raised my hand, they moved. Mental clock running, I scanned the street as I led them across it and through an alley. The stench of smoke, burning oil, and the acrid bitterness of munitions wreathed the air.

Breathing through the handkerchief helped, but it couldn't quite smother the foulness of it all. Movement ahead had me pressing flush to the building and I raised a fist. One hand touched the middle of my back.

A train, that was what I told them. They touched me when everyone was stopped to-gether, it would let me know we were all ac-counted for. The movement faded in and out of the flickering light and smoke. Then the dog trotted on and I blew out a breath.

Poor beast. Keep going, I urged it mentally. I spared one look back and found Mr. Maxwell splitting his attention between me and what was behind us.

Good man.

Normally, I wouldn't take on an extraction like this without backup. But no one expected the escalation to go as swiftly as it had. I was in country, and my backup wasn't.

If I'd been able to find a safe place to bunker down with the kids until a team could get to us, I would have. Nowhere was safe in the city.

Not anymore.

I checked the V Seven Harbinger. I had a Sig Sauer in one holster and a Glock - 19 in the other. Right now, Harbinger and I were going to be besties.

"We're moving," I said, raising a hand and we were going. "Keep moving. We've got to cross a hundred and fifty meters to the next cover."

There were abandoned vehicles, a burnt out school bus, and the husks of what looked like might have been shops once upon a time. Now they weren't much more than rubble with an occasional frame where a door might have stood.

I kept my head on a swivel, checking the kids, checking our perimeter, and ahead. One of the girls stumbled, but Jonathon caught her and kept her on her feet.

Something tickled against my awareness.

Something I noticed but I hadn't seen. I kept us moving. We still had another sixty meters to go.

Fifty meters.

Forty.

Thirty.

Twenty—

The man surged out from behind one of the cars. He had a knife in one hand and a pistol in the other. If I started a gunfight, we were going to draw attention. I couldn't give him time to either alert others or risk random fire hitting one of the kids.

I cataloged the options, sorted through my choices, then struck in the same breath as the man charged me. Yeah, I was the biggest threat. I struck him across the face with the stock of the Harbinger. It knocked more than one tooth out.

He sliced down my arm. The body armor took care of most of it, but the blade managed to cut my forearm. The blood and sting just reminded me I was alive. I twisted his arm, took the blade and then drove it right through his throat.

The fight was brutal, efficient, and over in seconds. It wasn't until I lowered him to the ground that I noticed the military clothing.

Yeah. I didn't want to hurt a civilian, but this guy came at me looking for the fight. I glanced around for the kids. They'd huddled near one of the stalled cars.

"Let's go," I told them. "Eyes up. Don't look at him."

For once, not a single one even tried to give a bravado-laced glance at the dead man. Mr. Maxwell's face was pale beneath the soot. The man rallied however.

We made it to the next block just as the rockets fired up again. Twenty minutes of raining hell that kept getting closer, before we got our next break.

The five hundred meters to the sea seemed to take hours, but the kids stuck with me. We'd encountered others fleeing the fire, but unlike the man with the knife, they didn't offer violence.

Live and let live worked for me.

The breeze rolling in off the ocean had never been more welcome in my life. The salty air promised something refreshing even if smoke still filled the dark skies.

The moonless night worked in our favor. The lack of cloud cover did too, it let the smoke keep rising instead of pushing it down. The inflatable was where I'd stowed it.

"We're going out over the water?" One of the girl's asked, teeth chattering. Her name was Jane, I thought.

"Yes." Another sweep, and I was pointing them to the water. The waves were low and slow. This was the perfect time to get out past them.

I secured my weapons.

"Stay together, we're going to push the inflatable out into the water. Everyone holds onto it. Don't let the waves push you back in. Once we're past them, swim and then we'll get you inside."

"I can't swim," Jane said, seemingly turning to stone.

"Everyone else can?" I checked with all of them and one by one they nodded.

"I mean, yeah in a pool," Jonathon said. "But —yeah."

"Okay." I peeled off a deflated lifejacket. I didn't have enough for all of them. "This isn't inflated, you tug here and here and it will. Don't do it."

I tugged it over Jane's head and secured it. She blinked up at me.

"Hang onto the boat. Jonathon, you're with Jane. Stay together, if you lose your grip, you can inflate the lifejacket, it will keep you above the water. We don't want the resistance getting out."

The terror crawling over her face was enough to give me pause but we didn't have any more time.

"You can do this, Jane. Trust me."

It wasn't a request.

The order did what coaxing wouldn't have. She nodded. We plowed out into the water. It was cool against all of us. Soaked clothing might be heavy but right now, we needed to move.

In the distance, the rockets started firing again. Past the break, I got them in the inflatable, one after the other and then I was in with them.

The motor wasn't designed for long term travel, but I had a compass and the stars. I also had a rough idea of the distance off shore to international waters and where a U.S. warship would be waiting.

When we were close enough, I pulled out a radio and checked the channels. As soon as we had acknowledgement, I passed it to the exhausted Mr. Maxwell. The kids were asleep, all of them except Jonathon. Exhaustion would do that.

"I was never here," I told them.

"But—" Jonathon said and I shook my head. Weapons still secure, I threw myself over the side. The swim back was gonna take time.

"Never here. You never saw me. Go home— live good lives." Then I was swimming. The current would help, but I needed to get back to land, then work my way out in a different direction.

The kids were safe. I saw the lights come into view when I was almost a mile away. It was another three days before I made it out of the war zone. I was tired, I was thirsty and I needed a fucking shower.

But I needed to check in with Patch.

Only problem.

She didn't answer.

I left my gear for cleanup to deal with, took a go bag and headed to the airport. I'd shower in the lounge.

Patch let it slip once that she loved Colorado. She'd been worried about the wildfires and possible evacuation. A warning she'd given me in case the call dropped.

It never did.

I checked on the fire—the only one at the time just happened to be northwest of Denver, near Rocky Mountain National Park.

In Estes.

That was where I'd start.

CHAPTER

EIGHT

REMINGTON

Three days.

Three unnecessarily long and aggravating days were spent cashing in favors, currency, and intelligence to get a lead that turned out to be a VOIP line. My informant had been sweating when they handed it over because it didn't seem like much.

The thing was, I didn't need much. Find a thread, tug on it, and it usually led to the next thread. Then the next. My next stop was a data broker. For a flat fee of a half a million dollars, he pulled the packets apart, then traced the IP address of the last four calls.

I kept calling Patch. Every few hours. Not once had she answered.

The last call routed to a disconnected message with advice to reach out for a new handler.

She'd been excised from the chain.

My data broker hadn't liked the disconnected message but it didn't slow him down. After far too many hours and energy drinks, he handed me a location.

It was in Colorado.

Another thread to pull.

"Donnie," I said as I headed for the door.

"You were never here, I have never seen you. And I just triple deleted the info."

"Thank you."

"Anytime, man. Anytime." The music cranked up as I closed the door. Donnie wasn't the easiest of men to get along with, but he'd worked for the NSA until he got himself booted for insubordination. Now, he freelanced for them so he didn't go to jail or the office, and they didn't have to put up with his crap.

I liked him.

For the most part.

He was no Patch.

It took time to get a flight to Denver. The whole time I kept turning over every iota of information I had on Patch. She'd been my handler for years. My operator. She could find anything, get me through so many doors, could and had bailed me out of situations gone wrong.

If she told me to duck, I'd be on the floor before the word cleared her lips. In all the time I'd known her, however, I'd learned very little about her.

She liked reality television shows.

Her favorite ice cream was strawberry.

Mornings were not her favorite time of day.

She functioned better at two in the morning

after being awake twenty-four hours than she did rolling out of bed.

Video games were a weakness she couldn't indulge when she was on the job.

Patience was a virtue she possessed in spades and nothing ever ruffled her. Whether it was talking me through security to get to a target or running the numbers and the routes to get me an escape path—she never tensed up.

The sexy, sweet voice wrapped around me like a lifejacket. As long as she was on the line, I was going to survive.

She hadn't answered in days.

~

THIRTEEN HOURS after getting the name of the town, I followed the directions from Denver, that took me on a northwest path toward the mountains. The interstate slimmed down to a highway then to a state highway, then a two-lane road.

Civilization seemed to fall away. With Denver not that far behind me, the road twisted through suburban areas before it became rural. Or rural enough that the homes clung to the sides of the mountain like goats on a perch. I couldn't recall a time that I'd been to this state much less the city.

I'd certainly never been in these mountains. Still, I followed the route that took me through Boulder, then higher to a place called Lyons, and higher still on a path that would take me near the Rocky Mountain National Park entrance in Estes Park.

The only thing I knew about the quaint town was it happened to be the location of the Stanley Hotel which appeared in the Stephen King novel *The Shining*.

Good book.

Interesting movie.

Not remotely why I was here.

My ears kept popping on the drive up and the temperature outside dipped the higher I went. Fair enough. Estes Park itself wasn't huge. Motels, hotels, restaurants, strip malls, and a quaint little "downtown" area with local shops and a Starbuck's.

Not bad.

I pulled into the parking lot, pulled up my computer and hopped on the "free" WiFi that I could reach. Engaging the virtual firewall, I cloaked my activities and then entered the IP address from the VOIP.

It wouldn't necessarily give me a street address, but it might get me close. Maybe. It was a long shot. Donnie had provided me with the program on a thumb drive.

The default window just sat there, cursor blinking as it said *searching...*

Attention divided between the screen and the area, I tried to see it as Patch did. Why here? Why would she base her work in a town that was higher up on a mountain, likely suffered from a lot of snow in the winter, and might even have to deal with supply chain issues.

Summertime probably brought a fuckload of tourists too. I suppose that wasn't just limited to summer, still... what attracted her to this place?

How did she even manage good internet up here? Fuck knew, she had to have excellent connection. The isolation might help keep her off the grid. It was easier to be lost in a crowd. A tourist destination meant that year round residents were probably protective of their own.

The computer dinged and I glanced down in time to see the browser opening a map window, then the screen zeroed in, again and again until it covered a handful of homes about ten minutes from where I was sitting.

Swapping the view to street level, I studied the collection of houses. Nice, suburban, upper middle-class, and a little cookie cutter. Nothing to really stand out.

A perfect place to hide amongst civilians.

Would they notice if she was missing though?

Noting the address, I put it in the GPS before shutting down the laptop and heading for it. There were roughly seven houses along that street. There were other homes in other clusters, but it had the feel of urban planning, keeping a lot of open green areas around the homes.

A few of them had fenced yards. Some had gardens, at least from what I'd glimpsed. Based on when the images were shot, that could have changed.

On a whim, I dialed Patch's number as I pulled onto her street. It went straight to the disconnected message with the advice to reach out for a new handler.

No.

Ending the call, I pulled over and studied the different houses. One had flowers out front. Another had perfect rows mowed into the lawn on the diagonal. Another house had hedges all across the front. The hedges were a good shield for windows. You'd get light but it made it hard for people to look in or get close.

Sight lines here were a mess.

Toys littered the yard of yet another house. While it looked like another home owner seemed determined to pull every non-existent weed in her flowerbeds while she watched another neighbor's argument through their very open dining room windows.

Husband and wife gesticulated wildly. He was red-faced and she was implacable.

Yeah, give that one up, buddy. Whatever line of bullshit you're trying to sell her, she isn't believing.

I flicked a look back to the nervous Nellie who'd actually pulled a few flowers while she watched the fight. Gossip? Neighborhood news? Or...

A car passed me and pulled into the driveway with the nosy neighbor. The way she jumped? Yeah, she was in on whatever that secret was.

Frankly, I didn't need an episode of *Desperate Housewives of the Rocky Mountains.*

More cars rolled in and I checked my watch. It was after five. People getting home from their nine to fives to their families. Cars pulled into four of the seven homes.

The only house with no movement was the

tall hedges. The lights snapped on at five-thirty though. Nice and prompt even if the sun was still up.

If I were a betting man—that house was Patch's. But time to do a little more sleuthing because with all the nosy neighbors around, I didn't want to draw more attention. Even if I wanted to be inside her place and figuring out where she was...

Maybe she had a cold. They did happen.

Starting the car, I pulled out of the little neighborhood and drove a few blocks back to town. I pulled into another fast food place to steal their Wi-Fi.

Sundown was another hour away. As soon as it came, I was heading back to check out that house. In the meanwhile, I took my time looking up each address.

Some searches pulled up the names of the residents. Others gave me phone numbers. A couple gave me two names.

The house with the hedges?

No names.

No numbers.

Nada.

Zip.

There wasn't even a realty listing for it.

That was Patch's place. It had to be.

The certainty brought impatience with it as I waited for sundown. I took myself inside the fast food place, borrowed their restrooms, washed up, and then got food before I headed back out to the car.

Burgers and fries weren't my favorite, but I did pick up a strawberry shake—just in case.

I ate one of the burgers and half an order of fries before downing a bottle of water. Then I washed my hands as the sun vanished behind the mountain. I'd have to admire the view later.

Once it was full dark, I headed for her neighborhood but I parked two blocks away next to a community center advertising bingo.

Dressed all in black, I wouldn't stand out and I made my way to her street. Then I moved behind them. While I hadn't clocked cameras on all the houses, I wanted to distance myself. Her place would have motion detectors, that was just a risk I'd have to take.

Her place also had a fence.

The eight-footer would definitely offer some privacy. But a jump and pull and I was up and then over. I went low and waited for any sign of movement.

You know, I could get inside and find myself face to face with a muzzle. She could very well blow my brains out before I get a chance to tell her who I am...

Patch knew who I was. She knew what I looked like.

Worth the risk. At least then I'd know she was alright.

Still, no visible movement from the house. The backyard was almost pretty nondescript. The grass had been mowed, the hedges along the windows blocked any decent sight lines, but like out front—they were neatly kept.

"Don't kill me without saying hello, Patch," I

murmured before I crossed the yard. A lot of people spent all their security on the front of their homes, trusting the backyard fences and the fact it was the back to discourage others.

A pair of deadbolts on her backdoor made me proud. She was going to make me work to get inside.

I always did like a challenge.

It took me three minutes to get the locks freed. They were definitely the sturdier kind. I approved. Another two to free the chain on the door. There had been a beep when I nudged it inward.

That was a sensor.

There was no alarm that sounded.

The lack of an actual alarm worried me more than anything. I almost gave into the urge to put my shoulder to the door and force it the rest of the way in, but I fought it.

Observe.

Explore.

Verify.

Act.

I needed to know what was happening. When the door swung inwards, I stared at the modestly decorated place. Tidy kitchen, coffee maker. Everything in its place.

Only one person lived here.

Definitely feminine. The lack of shoes near any of the doors surprised me, but I still slid my own off. I went to the garage first.

There was a car parked inside. The engine was cold.

Moving through the darkened house, I looked for any sign of foul play.

Nothing.

There also weren't any computers.

Or monitors.

I checked the three different bedrooms.

Two were clearly unused for anything. Based on the dust, no one went in or out. Or touched anything.

The third bedroom was done up in purple, but also neat. A stack of books decorated the nightstand. A television occupied the wall opposite the bed and there were a couple of tablets just laying on the bed.

Tablets.

But no computers?

This was Patch's house. It had to be.

That meant she had to have a computer room.

It wasn't up here, on the ground floor or in the garage.

Basement was the next logical choice.

I was on the stairs when the backdoor opened.

CHAPTER

NINE

LOCKE

Denver, Colorado. Not a city I could recall spending much time in. If at all. I liked bigger cities, Manhattan, Los Angeles, even Miami. I liked the culture of Europe. Denver had—a really big horse statue. A *blue* one.

No doubt there was a story there. I filed that away for later. For now, I opened up a piece of gum, slid it in to chew then kept watch on the assassin heading for his own vehicle. Dumb luck hitched me to Michael Remington's trail. Well, dumb luck and blowing a lot of capital.

I'd gotten nowhere reviewing all the old messages I'd stored on a private server. I'd also gone through a handful of information specialists— none of them the best because clearly that was Patch. Still, they didn't get anywhere either. Finding her was like looking for the most perfect needle in an infinite haystack.

All I needed was a starting point. Acquiring difficult to find items was my speciality. I didn't think I'd be able to snag an *address*. If I could narrow it down to a location, it would improve my odds. The only way I didn't find her was if I gave up.

My mother didn't raise a quitter.

She didn't raise me either, but still—my point stood.

Derrick returned my call when I left him a message that it would wipe out his debt to me and I might even owe *him* a favor. It was a lot of capital. Derrick was plugged into most of the information networks in the country. The man loved to eavesdrop on everything, it gave him good leads and he could be a fount of information.

But he was also a hoarder and *hated* to part with any of it. The more secretive, the more he liked to hold onto it. He only owed me because someone had "stolen" a mint condition rocket-firing Boba Fett prototype. Only a couple of dozen were ever made and they were never on sale.

The "thief" had outbid him. So, Derrick reached out to me and offered me three times the value of the thing to get it for him—a toy. Not that I judged, but it was still just a toy. The scarcity of it increased its value, but he didn't want it because it was so expensive—he wanted it because it was so rare.

And the only Star Wars rare toy he didn't own.

I jokingly told him I'd get it for him for the fee plus three favors.

He agreed without argument.

I delivered the toy four days later.

Despite him owing me the favors, I'd never felt the need to cash in before. Patch changed everything.

"Give me ten minutes," was all he said before he hung up. He didn't keep me waiting longer than five.

"Can't do it. Donnie's been digging for this guy Michael Remington. Dude has a kill count like you wouldn't believe. Sorry man. Not gonna happen. I'd rather keep my head and just owe you a different favor."

Then he hung up on me.

Hung up.

So, I dropped by Derrick's little bunker, took his hard drive, his backup drive, and his laptops. I picked up Boba Fett while I was there. I would have left it, but the little shit hung up on me.

For now.

I had a hacker who got into the drives and pulled out the info on Michael Remington. The number of kills to the man's name were enough to make the new hacker blanch. The man had a very well-earned reputation. Yet no charges. Because there was nothing to link him to the bodies would be my guess.

Suspected of the crime was nowhere near the ability to be prosecuted for it. Still, he'd been looking for Patch and while I might not be an assassin, I wasn't going to let him just kill her. Which brought me all the way to Denver. I landed an hour ahead of his flight, moved ahead to the rental place where he'd pre-booked a car.

Using an app, I did the same. It meant no talking to people and just getting the vehicle. I was already in place when he left the lot. Since there were lots of people leaving the airport, following wasn't a problem.

Heavy traffic worked in my favor as he headed through Denver and up the mountain toward Estes Park. It was really beautiful. While I preferred cities, the more rustic it got the more it made my shoulder blades itch.

For the most part, he didn't seem to notice me. I dropped back more than once, let cars get between us and I only passed when he accelerated more than the driver in front of me. Eventually, we were in the little town and I grabbed coffee while he was hunting on his computer.

Fortunately, his distraction let me drop a tracker on his car on my way out of the Starbuck's. Following from a distance was always preferable. I would know where they were and they didn't know I was here.

It wasn't until he sat on that street for the better part of an hour that I got the feeling, this might be the location we were both looking for. When he left, I made myself comfortable a couple of streets away and kept an eye on the tracker. I wanted to go walk the neighborhood, but I'd do that after dark.

Great minds thought alike cause he arrived and parked two car lengths away from me before he made his way toward her house. He moved like a shadow. My eyes had long since adjusted to the dark and thankfully, I could make out his outline.

I followed him all the way to the backyard, avoiding the cameras he missed. Not that those cameras were likely to pick up on him, but I'd rather they saw none of us.

When he went over the fence, I gave it a beat before I approached. Pulling myself up, I half-expected to come face to face with the muzzle of his gun, but he was at the backdoor, taking an epically long time to open the damn thing.

They were deadbolts.

My eyes narrowed. Three minutes.

Sloppy.

I let him vanish inside before I was up and over the fence. While I didn't doubt he was armed, I hadn't brought any weapons with me. I'd packed a knife in my suitcase, but that was more for utility than anything else. I didn't like guns.

I didn't hate them, but I wasn't a fan. At the door, I stood to the side and listened. The hedge placement didn't let me peek in the windows, or observe him. The door had beeped when he opened it so it would be a risk to let myself in if he was in earshot.

Still, no sounds drifted out from the interior. A couple of houses over, a couple was laughing and yelling at their kids. Nothing special. All normal, regular suburban sounds. I weighed my options.

I couldn't stay out here forever. If Michael Remington was here to kill her, I couldn't protect her from out here either. So, I pulled out my picks to work on the lock and stared in disgust.

He never relocked it.

Utterly unprofessional.

Pocketing them, I pulled out my knife then opened the door. The distinctive tone alerted anyone inside that I'd opened the door and I was already crouching as I slid in and shut the door. Crab walking, I made it behind the island in the kitchen, then paused to listen.

Where was he?

Did he hear me come in? The uneasy silence in the darkened house draped everything like a funeral shroud. Only the certainty I wasn't alone kept me in place. A creak of sound split the quiet like a gunshot. I glanced around the edge of the island in time to see the shadow of the man appear at the base of the stairs.

He was definitely armed.

Staying low, I tracked his movement or lack thereof. At the base of the stairs, he'd gone completely still. He seemed to meld into the darkness of the room except for his face. His face and his gun.

The hand wrapped around the grip was also indistinguishable. Probably gloves. Smart, he seemed to be waiting me out like I was him. Sweat trickled down my spine, but I didn't let his lack of action bait me into moving. His stillness and the lack of Patch's presence suggested either she wasn't here or he'd done something to her...

The second thought turned my whole world bleak at the very idea. No, I refused that notion.

Unless I found a body, just no. Suddenly, he just seemed to vanish from where he'd been standing. The distraction, swift as it was, allowed him to move and I couldn't see him.

Fuck.

Stay or go?

The choice ping-ponged through my head. Then the floor creaked to my right and I slid backwards, managing to crab walk to the far side of the island and slip around it before he appeared where I'd been planted.

I kept circling to get behind him and shot upwards when he turned. I got his gun hand pushed upwards and my knife angled toward his throat. Not fast enough because he had my wrist and we were locked in a strength contest as I kept his gun away and he fended off my knife.

The only sound formed between us were harsh breathing and grunts. He was taller than I was, broader built in the shoulders but I had more strength. I was slowly pushing the knife closer to his throat. Then his knee slammed into my groin and agony exploded through me.

One minute I was on my feet and the next, he flipped me, twisted my arm outward and pain radiated to my shoulder. I followed the twist, pivoting with him. The move caught him off guard enough, I pushed my shoulder into his gut and shoved upward. He had to let go of me to try and catch his balance and I ran him across the room and rammed him into a wall

He crashed his fist down against my shoulder, then my back, then where my back joined my neck. Each blow sent fresh pain to flutter after the rest and I snagged something from the table and swung it as I straightened. It knocked the gun aside, not that he let it go, but I caught him across the face with the metal plate or bowl or whatever it was.

Not enough to buy me the time to go back for the knife, so I used the metal platter to ram between his arm and body, then push upward. It sent his gun hand high as I turned, then rammed my elbow into his gut. He needed to let go of the gun.

The back door burst open and another man appeared, he had a gun and it was pointed at both of us.

Shit just went from bad to worse.

"Don't move," he snarled. "Where is Patch?"

Well, fuck.

CHAPTER

TEN

MCQUADE

etween getting back into the country and tracking down any kind of a lead on Patch, I was not in the mood to find these two jackasses battling it out in her house. I didn't know who they were and I didn't fucking care.

They were in the way. If they continued to be an obstacle, I would remove them. At this point, it had been over a week, seven days, since I'd last spoken to her. Seven days was an eternity in this business.

"Where the hell is Patch?" I demanded. They could be a pair of contractors, each taking a job to go after her and now fighting it out. "You have five seconds to answer me or I'm just shooting you."

I didn't even reach five, before the one in front dropped and the bald guy behind him shot my fucking gun. It flew out of my hand with almost bruising force, but I pulled out a second gun and then it was the three of us, in a triangle, each pointing a weapon at another.

Well, they were both pointing at me.

Fine.

Whatever.

"How do you know Patch?" The guy who'd shot my gun demanded. His English accent salted every word.

"How do you know her?"

"Fuck my life," the second guy muttered. "You're contractors."

That didn't mean a damn to me. "So are you," was my only comment. It was definitely not enough for me to lower my weapon.

"Locke." The second guy identified himself. Probably not the smartest move.

"Excuse me?" Did he have a point?

"Remington," the shooter stated in his crisp accent. Then they both looked at me.

"I don't identify myself, particularly to people I don't know." Not trusting people was an acquired skill that involved knives in my back.

"Then I can shoot you in the head and check your ID after you're down," Remington stated in the coolest of tones.

"Or we could not splatter blood all over her dining room without a damn good reason," Locke countered. "Killing people means bodies to deal with, I prefer to minimize the mess."

I blinked at Locke and it took a beat to realize that I wasn't the only one staring at him. "You're not an assassin then," Remington stated. To be fair, it wasn't a question.

"No," Locke stated. "You are. I've heard the rumors on the kill count."

Good to know. I liked the open sharing of information. Locke was less likely to shoot me than Remington. I reoriented my gun at the guy who had fired already.

"You followed *me* here, Mr. Locke," Remington informed him.

"Yep, because you were sniffing around for information on Patch. I wanted to find her too—but all my access points were shut down because you were looking for her. So, if you had the info, I let you bring me to her."

"Reasonable."

It also suggested they were looking for her *after* she disappeared. That meant they might be like me, aware that she'd stopped answering her phone. It could also be a covert ploy to get information.

Faking association was a common interrogation tactic. Then again, they hadn't known I was there before they tried to beat the shit out of each other.

I weighed the potential threat against the benefit of information. Particularly because they knew Patch's name.

"This is Patch's place," I confirmed why I was there and it arrested the attention of Locke.

"You know her?"

"Yes," I answered easily enough. I knew her. Clearly, they knew her.

"On sight, do you know her?" Remington asked.

And I almost smiled. Smart asshole.

"You don't," Remington answered his own

question before slicing a look at Locke. "Neither of you do."

"You don't either." That was the thing, if he could, he wouldn't be willing to wait out this discussion. "Are there photos here?"

They both paused, Locke with a frown, but Remington appeared more thoughtful.

"No," Remington answered after a moment. "I'd barely done one sweep when Locke walked in. No photos. Nothing of family or friends. If anything, it's been minimal in the way of personalization. It's *cozy* without being *warm* or homey."

I blew out a breath. The best covers to inhabit were usually those that were close to the person. She shouldn't need a cover though, just a—

"What about her call center?"

No surprise moved across their faces. No, they were definitely contractors. If I had to bet, then Patch was their operator too. My girl, stepping out on me with these yahoos.

Great.

"Not yet," Remington answered when Locke said nothing. Curiously, the cat had apparently gotten his tongue. Too bad. I had a feeling if he had more information, he'd have already shared it. "You're here because she didn't answer."

Again, Remington wasn't asking a question. Since the fact was pretty clear, it cost me nothing to confirm it. "The same as you, I would imagine. And Mr. Peace Lover over here."

"Never said I had a problem with violence,"

Locke responded. "I just don't see the point of dropping bodies if we don't have to."

I didn't roll my eyes, but Remington shook his head.

"Since we are all here for the same reason," Locke continued. "I propose a truce until we find Patch."

"You think something's happened to her?" Remington's whole focus swung from me to Locke.

"If she was fine, she would have answered her phone. If something hadn't happened to her, none of us would be here." Solid logic.

"I could argue that either one of you could be here because you are the problem." Then before either of them could suggest it, I added, "So could I for that matter."

The longer we wasted time on this...

"Look, we all want to find her. That gives us a common goal." Locke again. The man was almost too smooth. "We pool our resources, find Patch, make sure she's secure, then go our separate ways. No harm, no foul."

"If we don't find her or she isn't secure?" Remington's voice had taken a distinctly cold, unfriendly note.

"Then we secure her and eliminate the threats," I said. "By whatever means necessary." I held Remington's gaze and read the determination to exact more than a pound of flesh if necessary. With a nod, since we were on the same page, I transferred my attention to Locke. "Can you handle that?"

Locke pursed his lips. "I have no problems dropping any bodies in that quest."

Silence held sway for a long moment. Remington lowered his weapon first. He didn't holster it, but it wasn't pointed at me any longer.

Acceptable. I lowered my own.

Funnily enough, Locke was the last one to lower his weapon. Unlike us, he didn't keep it in his hand. "You searched the place already?" Definitely aimed at Remington since I just got here.

"Not thoroughly," the man countered. "You interrupted."

No apology was forthcoming, not that I could blame him. Instead, I studied the room around us. It seemed *cozy*, yet it lacked any distinguishing features or decorations. How did she make it warm without giving herself away?

The sharpness of her intelligence had always been a turn-on.

"Then we search it again," Locke said. "This is my area of expertise after all."

"Are you an expert in searching places?" I shot him a look that he shrugged off.

"Thief," he answered. "I'm very good at getting in and out of places people don't want others in."

"So you're good at locating these hidden places?" Remington sounded skeptical.

I didn't blame the guy, it smelled like horseshit. I moved through the kitchen then headed into the living room. Remington kept pace with me, neither of us giving the other our back.

Locke didn't follow, and I pivoted to find him

standing in the hallway just outside of the kitchen and dining room that led to a half bath at one end and to the garage at the other.

Head tilted, he seemed to be studying the wall. I kept him in my periphery as I scanned the room and its contents. There was a hiss of sound, like a door decompressing and I was a half-step behind Remington.

Locke stared at the door he'd just opened in the stairs to reveal another set of stairs going down.

"I'll be damned," Remington muttered.

"You're welcome," Locke said without a trace of irony. Nor did he wait for us as he descended the steps. Remington and I exchanged looks. Neither of us wanted the other at our backs.

But Locke was already down there and I wanted to know if she was here. So I took the risk, holstering my gun and descending the steps. Remington followed behind me.

There was another door open at the bottom of the stairs and there was a distinct lack of hum that would indicate running equipment. When I arrived, I discovered why. Locke had stopped just inside the door, and hadn't taken another step.

The room was a wreck. Easily a half-dozen monitors positioned at different angles. Two of them were broken. The desk was disheveled, a headset hung off the end, dangling. Blood decorated the keyboard. The actual machines were smashed, from the two boxes beneath the desk to the cabinet that had probably housed hard drives on the far side.

The chair was overturned. Papers scattered. A coffee cup lay on its side, an old brown stain pooled around it.

Was she taken in here? Or had they brought her down here for interrogation?

How the fuck had they gotten in here? I pivoted to study the room located down here. The stairs above us had closed. The insulation was remarkable. If she'd been all the way in and the door sealed—she'd have been secure.

A camera in the corner caught my eye. Another on the steps.

Cameras.

Were they throughout her house?

Easing past Locke, I made my way to the hard drive cabinet. There were wires going into the wall. I did a quick count.

Too many for just these drives.

"Patch would have backups," I said abruptly.

"She would." Remington moved with the same kind of deliberateness he'd had upstairs. He stepped around the mess, studying each angle. Locke, however, seemed fixed on her desk, at the destruction.

I moved back to him and tried to see what he was seeing.

"She let them in..."

At that, I raised my eyebrows and I wasn't the only one watching him.

"How do you know?" Remington asked.

Locke had on a pair of black gloves. At her desk, he slid his hand under the rim, then glided his hand along a short distance before he pressed something.

The click echoed through the room and the door behind us—the one embedded in the stairs opened. He pressed it again and it closed. He moved his hand, careful, then the door opening into this room closed.

I straightened abruptly at the whiteboard on the door. Remington beat me to it.

It was written in code. If I had a bet though, because of the grid, it was a calendar. The colors probably indicated different contractors. In all likelihood, that was us up there.

We weren't the only ones.

A crash sounded behind us and I pivoted even as Remington did and we both had guns out. Locke had yanked the hard drive cabinet away from the wall and he was working his hands against the bricks there.

One of them moved.

Oh, my girl was smart as hell. I'd bet there was a second rack of hard drives back there.

A glint of pink caught my eye and I glanced back at the board. There was something sticking out from behind it. I tugged it free while Remington crossed the room.

The slip of paper held fifteen digits.

It didn't mean anything.

Yet.

I pocketed it before I followed my new companions.

Locke had another door open and he was inside a computer room. The hum I'd been looking for earlier was present.

"We might be working together for a while."

I didn't argue with Remington, even as Locke worked his way through the room. The thief was handy.

Hopefully he knew something about computers.

"When we find who did this..."

"We scratch them off," Remington agreed and I nodded.

"Long as we're on the same page."

CHAPTER
ELEVEN
PATCH

The clank of a generator kicking on echoed through the wall and jerked me out of sleep. The jolt of alertness didn't do much to clear the fog in my brain. Piece by piece, reality sifted through me.

Numb arms.

Numb legs.

Numb ass.

I tried to lift my hand to wipe the drool from my face, but it was lashed to the arm of the chair.

Right.

I couldn't move.

Fuuuuuck.

Twitching my fingers didn't seem to work. Or maybe it was cause I couldn't feel them. I needed to look at my hands, but it was dark. No, not that dark. There was light against my eyelids.

Shit.

My eyes were closed.

Reality kept telescoping in and out. I was numb, tied to a chair, pain was right there, surging against my consciousness like the tide rolling in.

Open your eyes, I told myself.

Open them.

A part of me didn't want to and another wasn't even sure I could. I refused both and went for doing it anyway. If I couldn't move my hands or my feet, I had to be able to open them unless they'd been taped shut.

They wouldn't do that. No, they wanted me to see. Taped open for two whole sessions, I couldn't miss anything. Not their glee and satisfaction nor the way they leered. They'd stripped me down to my bra and panties. I supposed I was lucky to have those left.

While rape hadn't occurred *yet*, they made it clear that the option was on the table. Being cold, stripped mostly bare, and left vulnerable? It was assault all the same. It didn't matter what they stuck inside me.

Those images were imprinted in my brain forever. As if conjured by the thought, I could see both men. My interrogators. Tall, at least from my angle in the chair. One was swarthy with a scar that distorted his upper lip on the right side. Maybe a leftover from a fight or an accident where his teeth went through the lip.

He had dark, shaggy brown hair that desperately needed a cut. It didn't match the suit he'd been wearing or the air of cold authority that settled over both of them. Wild-eyed, I almost preferred his open cruelty and sadism to his partner.

The second man was all clean, pressed lines,

and perfectly manicured. Even his nails had been rounded and neat. Such a small thing to notice, but his suit was immaculate, so were his perfectly white teeth, almost too smooth skin. There wasn't even a suggestion of stubble.

He reminded me of a mannequin or one of those CGI monstrosities in the movies when they de-aged stars and they looked plastic. His eyes were cold, devoid of any emotion, and his manner was—clinical and detached.

When he took charge of the sessions, I screamed until my throat was raw. What little spit I managed to form wasn't enough to soothe anything. But my eyes opened, the sudden light, no matter how dim, stung until a suggestion of tears formed.

Not real tears. No, just a little extra moisture. I was dehydrated. I actually couldn't remember the last time I'd had water. Or food.

The room wavered in my vision. It was a plain room. The smell was rancid. Though that could be me. I needed to take stock of where I was.

Glancing down, I tried not to wince at the bruises on my neck. I'd pulled every muscle or they had. Even breathing hurt. I tried to move my fingers and the flicker of motion was my reward.

Okay, the pins and needles when I got free were gonna *suck*. I couldn't see my feet, but I could see my legs. I tried flexing my muscles. Yeah.

Pain rippled through me as the back of my thigh cramped viciously. Charley horses were awful. The fresh surge of pain ripping through me chased away the fog and brought clarity back.

Low potassium, magnesium and calcium could lead to cramps. Check. So could reduced salt, lack of electrolytes, and dehydration. Also check. Without water, a person could survive three days. Five or six days was possible, but it was also miserable.

Six days was the absolute limit. Most wouldn't make it that far. How long had it been for me?

A broken sound escaped me and I barely recognized the sound of my own laughter. Did I have a lot longer in these miserable conditions? I'd already pissed myself three times.

Good times.

It was only 3 times, right? I didn't have anything else to waste on urinating. I couldn't remember my last drink of water.

My last drink of anything.

Fuck, I would kill for coffee right now. I'd even lower my standards and take decaf.

I wanted to cry, but the lack of moisture had me closing my eyes again. They were so dry. No, I needed to keep them open. I needed to focus.

Eyes open once more, I studied my surroundings. Beige, plain room. Concrete floor. Drain in the floor.

That boded well for the future.

No sign of a door, but it could be behind me. I hadn't seen anything on arrival. They'd had a bag over my head. I'd been drugged too.

That had been wearing off though in the car.

It had been a car, not a truck. Cataloging what I could remember helped clear away more of the fog. It distracted me from some of the pain.

Some.

Not all.

I kept trying to flex my muscles to get the blood flowing and it just kept inciting agony. I rode out the cramps and the waves of discomfort that followed. Each time, I discovered a little more sharpness to my focus.

With the view so limited, I concentrated on what I could *hear*. There was a clang of mechanical equipment. Some kind of air conditioner? It rattled as it came on, followed by a humming whine.

Yeah, air con unit of some kind. A vague rush of air added to the soundtrack of my environment. It moved the mustiness around, but it didn't detract one iota from the foulness around me.

Great.

Focus, I said. Ugly beige room. Concrete floor. Air con unit. No windows visible from where I was locked to the chair. I tried to turn my head but it just added another set of muscle spasms to ride out.

Then a lock tumbled behind me.

Hey, look, I was right about where the door was. I braced for the arrivals. On each of the previous occasions, I'd woken to them being present. I hadn't actually had any time to myself.

How many visits had it been?

The scent of coffee drifted over to torment

me. The smell of too much cologne followed it and I had to concentrate on breathing through my mouth. Had one of them fallen into a vat of body spray? It was worse than Axe or Hai Karate.

Shaggy drifted into view with his unkempt hair and rumpled suit. Mr. Cold was with him. He was as neat as Shaggy was messy. They were like the Odd Couple. Fuck—what were the character names?

"Well, you're awake." Shaggy lit a cigarette after his announcement. Wonderful, he was going to add the smell of acrid tobacco to the powerful aroma wafting off of them. I almost wished I could go back to my own stink.

"Miss Brady," Mr. Cold said. "I will once again offer you the opportunity to cooperate."

I just stared at him. My options were limited. Cooperate and they would probably just put a bullet in me. Continue to resist and I might survive another day.

Granted, it would be painful survival. But living afforded me a chance to escape, maybe. Dying, well it was a one way ticket out just not necessarily in the direction I wanted to go.

"He asked you a question," Shaggy informed me, then backhanded me hard enough to send what little spit I'd managed flying out of my mouth.

I did cut my tongue and the inside of my cheek. The taste of blood filled my mouth. As gross as it was, I swallowed it. Moisture was moisture. Straightening, I managed to look up at them in time to get a face full of smoke.

"Actually," I said in a hoarse voice. "He made a statement, not a question. The implication being I could accept or decline."

Shaggy glared at me then slapped me again, this time the open hand of his palm knocking my face the other way. My neck popped and it was both painful and almost orgasmic. Oh, something went back into place.

"Everyone's a critic," I managed to mutter, but it sounded raspy as hell.

"Get her water," Mr. Cold ordered before he took a sip from the cup he held. Oh, the bastard had the coffee. I really wanted the coffee.

"She doesn't deserve water." Shaggy's expression was nothing but contempt.

"I didn't ask for your opinion," Cold informed him. "Get her water. *Now*."

With a venomous look in my direction, Shaggy stalked out of the room and left me with Mr. Cold.

"Miss Brady, you must have reached the same conclusion that we have. Yes?"

"That you smell like bad aftershave with clinical depression and a skin infection?"

His bland look was not amused.

Granted, it wasn't my best work. Still, I didn't want to die quick. Living wasn't going to feel pretty. So...I needed to focus on not being here for a while. Sooner or later, they were going to make good on their promise of physical violence.

They always did.

He shook his head, then took a sip of his coffee. He walked behind me cup in hand and I concentrated on slow, deep breaths. I might not hear him or see him coming. So I needed to relax everything and slip away.

The mind was a wonderful thing. The code I was working on—it would be perfectly elegant. It would create the best environment...

A chair hit the ground in front of me and I blinked to find Mr. Cold had set up a chair and a table. He put his coffee cup on the table before he stripped off his jacket. Then he rolled up his sleeves.

I went back to my code. Line after line, if/then statements with perfect definitions ready to act. I liked coding, streamlining it, particularly when it would let me craft a tool or a setting or a world.

Maybe I needed to get out of the business and become a video game developer. The work paid well, and I doubted it came with torture beyond what I could do to myself.

"Open up." A splash of water against my face pulled me back to the present and I found Shaggy leaning over me. A bottle of water in hand.

I stared at him. He had a burning cigarette in his other hand, and the water bottle in the other. It could be drugged.

Sniffing carefully, I tried to detect something alcoholic or medicinal around the rotting scent of me and them. The cigarette smoke didn't help but it looked like water. I parted my lips a little.

A hand fisted my hair and yanked my head backward. Pain shot down my neck and pooled between my shoulder blades. I forgot about Mr. Cold briefly.

Lips parted, I wasn't quite ready for the water they poured into my mouth. It was water. It soaked my parched and bloodied tongue. I inhaled some before I could swallow the rest. I fought the urge to cough. I needed more water, if I give into the reflex, they'd take it away from me. Chances were I wouldn't get it again.

At least not for hours.

So I swallowed, and swallowed, until the bottle was empty. Only when they let go of my hair and Shaggy backed off a step did I give into the cough. My eyes were burning and so was my throat.

But that water had been like ambrosia.

"Good," Mr. Cold said, almost petting my hair. "I like when you cooperate, Fallon. May I call you Fallon?"

Oh, that was a question. "No," I told him. "You can drop dead though."

"Bitch," Shaggy said, but all Mr. Cold did was yank my hair again and haul my head backward. He locked his hand under my jaw, forcing my mouth closed. I could breathe through my nose, but that was about it.

"Hit her in the stomach."

This was going to suck, Shaggy didn't hesitate. His fist plowed into me and I fought the gag sending the water back up my throat. Was he going to drown me this way?

Mr. Cold kept me in place as I fought the struggle. He tilted his head like some scientist trying to figure out what I was.

"Now," he murmured, dipping his head closer

as if he were a lover. A shiver of revulsion went through me. "Are you ready to tell me where the files are?"

The files.

Don't think about them.

I didn't have any files here.

Just me and my brain and my code.

"No," I croaked when he let go of my head and my mouth. I wasn't ready. I would never be ready. Don't think about the files. Just the code. I rolled my head around while I had the time.

"Pity," he said. "It's a real pity, Fallon, cause we've been discussing what to do to break you if you won't cooperate."

Shaggy put out his cigarette on my arm and the pins and needles came to life even as the smell of burning hair and flesh hit me.

I swallowed my screams.

"You win," Mr. Cold said as he retreated to his chair. "We're going to do it the hard way."

That was when I saw the glass bottle.

Shaggy was reaching for my panties and I closed my eyes. This was going to hurt, but I needed to focus on the code.

Just the code.

Don't think about anything else. Just the code.

TWELVE

REMINGTON

Despite our agreement to deal with whomever had broken into her house, we'd found nothing *actionable*. At least, nothing they were sharing with me.

I'd left skin tracers on both. The trackers let me keep an eye on them and slip in to plant bugs when they were less on their guard. Aware they could have done the same to me, I made sure to use rubbing alcohol on all exposed areas of skin.

Then showered three times.

Most skin tracers didn't last past a second thorough shower.

Still, I didn't need them to last that long. I just wanted to approach from a different angle at a different time when their guard might be lowered.

Unsurprisingly, neither left Estes Park.

But more amusing was they'd chosen hotels within walking distance of each other, though I suspected neither was aware.

It let me pick a spot to park my rental car, listening equipment armed, with a cup of coffee and I began my observation. Locke had a lot of skills. The hard drives, despite being present, proved difficult to crack.

That did not surprise me. Patch would never let her work or information be compromised. The fact we'd all recognized the danger in attempting —and failing—to access those hard drives meant we'd secured them again without disturbing them.

McQuade had also set a couple of cameras up in her office, then more in the house. To keep an eye on it in case someone returned.

I managed to get a sample from the blood on the desk. Taking it to a lab to get it typed and to see if DNA could be extracted would take time. What interested me most—beyond finding Patch—was the absolute lack of personal items or personal identifying items in her home.

There hadn't even been paper bills. The only paper trash from her mail had been in the recycling and it was addressed to resident. I'd swung by her mailbox before leaving and it was empty. So did she just not get snail mail here? Or did she have other arrangements for it?

The paper shredders in her office and kitchen suggested she had a method for handling personal data. But they were frustratingly empty.

"Locke," the thief's voice came over the bug, as clear as if I were in the room with him. "Thanks for getting back to me."

Phone call.

"That's all you got from the property records?"

Too bad I couldn't hear the other side of that conversation.

"Really?" True curiosity kindled in his voice. "How far back?"

The silence was enough to make me grit my teeth.

"No," he said after a long moment, sounding more thoughtful than anything else. "Leave it there. I don't want to set off any alarms. I'll dig a different way." A pause. "Yeah, you too. Thanks."

Then the call ended or at least the conversation did. His movement around the room carried over the bug. The shower kicked on and there was rustling. The sound of running water didn't diminish though.

I dialed it down. I didn't need to listen if he was the type to jerk off in the shower.

McQuade had been almost too quiet. He might have discovered my tracker. It wouldn't surprise me. While I waited and watched, I'd also done my research. Locke had almost no internet footprint of any kind.

He might as well not exist, if Locke were even his real name. Patch's work would be my guess. Then a thief would be better off without a high profile. It was all a little too neat, but also logical.

McQuade, on the other hand, had a reputation to rival my own and a history that suggested I never wanted him as an enemy. While he wasn't an assassin specifically, he had been known to take wetwork jobs.

No, he was far more the grunt on the ground. He got dirty and went to places many others avoided. Nothing in his jacket suggested altruistic motives nor criminal. But the variety of jobs attributed to him over the past seven years were too chaotically chosen to not be the product of a somewhat disturbed mind.

A rescue operation in Angola. Taking out a drug lord and all the higher ups in a cartel in Panama. Months spent in and out of hot zones with no clear pattern. The most recent being a year in the Middle East. My contacts liked McQuade, found him useful and requested that I not take him out of play.

Interesting.

A knock on a door had me glancing at my own, but it was coming in over my earbuds. The hush of steps muffled by socks, but there was the faintest creak of a floorboard.

McQuade?

"Thanks." Definitely McQuade. The sound of paper bags rustling. Sounded like food delivery.

No response, just the door shutting then the combination of sound created by the bags being upended. So, he didn't order soup. There were a couple of soft thumps. A pair of harder ones, then the rattle of ice in a cup before he slurped the drink.

Shotgunning it from the sound of it. I grimaced. He finished it off with a lengthy burp that took a few seconds to complete.

Well, it fit his uncouth image.

Then there was ice hitting the sink or a bowl maybe.

"There we go." His words were so low, I almost missed them. More plastic ripping, then his laptop booted up.

Dammit, McQuade had gotten some information. This was the time I wished I had eyes in those rooms so I could see what he was seeing.

Instead, I just worked on cleaning my guns. I was on the third and last. It was something to do to pass the time. My bags were packed. I'd had a new rental car delivered as well. Four of them—actually—under four different aliases.

If someone was tracking me, and I didn't doubt someone was... If Locke could follow me, then clearly anyone with the resources, and the wherewithal could be as well. It hadn't been that long since someone tried to snare me in a trap.

Better to not take chances. I wasn't sure who'd gone after Patch or who'd taken her. Whoever they were, they were going to regret it. Based on my observations, McQuade and Locke were both on board. One or the other could also be a plant.

Of the two? I'd have suggested Locke, but he seemed less guarded than McQuade. Whatever, once we located Patch and secured her, I could eliminate them if necessary. I'd almost gotten my gun reassembled to the soundtrack of McQuade tapping his space bar.

No sound.

No reading or mumbling under his breath.

Just tap.

Tap.

Tap.

Irritat—

The soft shoe of motion in the hall had me flicking a look to my door. I'd stuffed a pair of towels at the bottom to block the light from getting in. It didn't really muffle the sounds of other guests and staff in the hall.

I didn't want it to, either.

Other guests passed by talking and laughing. Staff called to each other or their radios went off. Their oversized carts creaked and groaned.

This footstep?

Someone was concealing it.

I set aside the gun I'd been cleaning, it was almost reassembled and screwed the suppressor on the gun I'd already finished, reloaded and had it sitting on the table next to me.

The hush of the step hesitated outside my door. I pointed my gun at it as the lock ticked once.

Twice.

Then freed itself.

I had the security bar on, and the way the door opened, the only thing my visitor would be able to see is the bathroom, but I'd angled the mirrors on the closet to give me a view via the mirrors in the bathroom.

It wasn't perfect. But the woman on the other side of the door was actually wearing a maid's outfit. At least a facsimile of one. The colors were right, but her name tag was missing.

"Maid service." Yeah. They tended to knock

first, not just let themselves in. Especially when I had the "do not disturb" on.

"Oh, sorry," I called as if I'd just noticed the door when it hit the limit of the security bar. "Naked in here, gimme a sec. I had the sign on."

"My apologies, sir. I don't see it."

Bullshit.

I kept my steps light as I moved around the edge of the door.

"I can come back," she offered and I nudged the closet doors so the mirrored door was tucked behind the other. She couldn't see me and I checked via the crack at the hinged side of the door.

She had towels but only three and they were covering one of her hands.

Yeah. Not a maid.

"No, it's fine," I called as if careless of how close I was. She actually gave a little jerk. The dickish side of me enjoyed that. "One sec." I pushed the door closed abruptly, and only used my left hand to unlatch it.

If she decided to shoot through the door, I didn't want to take a hit. I had about ten seconds, maybe less to choose my course of action.

She was an assassin and she was here to scratch me off. No question. You didn't walk into a room with a man like me with your gun drawn if you didn't intend to use it. I could take her out as soon as she was inside, that would leave me with a body to deal with and no answers.

Alternatively, I could take her down and then remove her from the hotel to somewhere quieter for interrogation. A name would be ideal to let me know who sent her.

The door opened and she pushed it all the way back, keeping me in the closet. That was fine. "My apologies again for disturbing you," she said and I didn't answer.

She started forward and made it just two steps. The minute the door began to close behind her, she seemed to realize her mistake.

Smart.

Not that it would do her any good. I had one arm wrapped around her and locked over her throat as I gripped her gun arm with my free hand and kept it aimed at the bed. She slammed her head backwards, but I was ready for that move.

She impacted a few times against my collarbone. Definitely gonna leave a bruise, but it didn't affect my hold. I increased the chokehold. Squeezing tighter.

Even with the suppressor on, the gun sounded unnaturally loud in the room as she fired at the bed.

Four bullets before she slumped. I didn't let up until her hand spasmed and dropped the gun. Another thirty seconds, because playing possum would be smart.

With that in mind, I didn't waste time getting her restrained and tape over her mouth. I emptied my larger suitcase after sizing her up then stuffed her inside it. It was going to be a tight fit, but she was on the tinier side.

I had her packed, secured and my weapons

ready in under fifteen minutes. Checking my bugs, I could hear them, breathing, moving, and occasionally farting.

These men needed new diets.

That much gastrointestinal distress could not be good for them.

I was about to walk the suitcase out to one of the rental cars when a familiar sound of a door hitting a safety bar hit me.

"Maid service," a woman called.

"Not interested," Locke replied. "There's a do not disturb."

"Oh, I'm sorry—"

Yeah, I didn't believe in coincidences. I texted him at the number he'd given us with a warning and sent another one to McQuade, then invited them to the cabin I'd rented further up the mountain with or without their plus ones.

I had questions for mine.

The sounds of the struggles echoed in my ears as I headed out and down the hall—a *fresh* do not disturb sign on the door. The smell of gunpowder was going to linger in that room. I'd have to pick up a new bed topper thing and then just replace the sheets.

As long as they left everything where it was, the new mattress cover and topper should hide it. Long enough to disappear. The ID I'd checked in with would be burned, but a small price to pay.

I whistled when I hit the door for outside and because a complaint came from inside the bag. Another followed when I bounced it down three stairs.

No one was around though and when she landed in the trunk. I leaned closer to say, "I'd work on breathing, and keeping it nice and shallow. Not sure how much carbon monoxide this car emits. Could be a bit nauseating."

I patted the bag, then closed the trunk before I headed around to slide into the driver's seat. The sound of smashing glass, and grunting echoed over my earbuds.

They were going to be paying some fines on their rooms. Still humming, I pulled out of the parking lot.

CHAPTER

THIRTEEN

PATCH

Consciousness hit like a brick. Or maybe it was the bare stone floor I landed on. My arms screamed as feeling rushed through them once again. The buzzing of murder hornets determined to destroy me. A sob stuck in my throat because frankly, everything hurt—including crying.

The cold, unforgiving stone actually felt good against me. It wouldn't for long. I'd begin to shiver. Then stiffen. It seemed like a mercy. But there wasn't a merciless bone in these assholes bodies.

Not a single one.

I tried to lick my lips but there was no moisture in my mouth. As it was, my tongue wanted to stick to my lips. Yeah, that wasn't good.

They gave me water periodically. Sometimes food.

Right? They gave me something to eat now and—

Shit. I couldn't remember. I'd lost track of

days and I was losing the thread of what happened on those days. Whether I liked it or not, they were chipping away at my sense of self. No one was interrogation proof.

No one.

I'd done too many studies, seen the research. Talked to my clients after. Everyone broke— eventually. Breaking might be easy, at least then it would be over. I turned away from that tempting thought. Hating myself a little that it even sounded inviting.

The screech of metal ripped through the quiet. I flinched. It couldn't be time already. How long had I been lying here?

Slitting my eyes open, I tried to take in what I could in the gloom. The only light in the ugly little room came from the hall. The thud of footsteps accompanied by the rasping drag of clothing on the bare floor seemed unnaturally loud.

Then a body hit the ground not far from me. In the half-shadows I made out long hair, bruised face and then the door slammed shut with another scream from the metal. The dark was an unforgiving companion.

I hadn't recognized the new arrival, but I also hadn't gotten a good look at them. With agonizing slowness, I pushed my hands to the floor and gradually got myself up to my knees. It took nearly every drop of my energy.

Checking on the other woman was an option or getting away from her. I couldn't do both. I wavered, I had to make a decision. I would collapse again very soon.

With a mental apology to someone who might be an ally but was probably a ploy, I crawled over to the wall. Stopping only when I reached it. Panting, I sat with my back against it.

Like someone cut my strings, I sagged. My eyes closed and my chin dipped.

I MUST HAVE PASSED out because when awareness swarmed back over me, I could barely move. My head hurt and my neck was so stiff. My hands were curled into fists, and I couldn't seem to stretch out my fingers.

Something cold dripped down my face. Flinching away from it, I smacked my head against the wall. It barely registered beyond waking me up further.

"Sorry," a female voice said in a dry husky whisper. "Was trying to give you water."

There was moisture on my lips. I touched it with my tongue out of reflex. It was cold. Fresh. Maybe a little metallic, but that could be the cup. I wasn't sure I could talk... even if I wanted to, so I said nothing.

The few drops of moisture in my mouth were like a gift. I swallowed slowly, it was like downing glass shards. Right now, I'd take the blood if I could spill it.

"Want more?"

A warm hand touched my shoulder. I didn't

think she was that warm, just that I was that cold.

"Here." She didn't wait for my answer. She must have used her grip on my shoulder as a guide because she pressed the tin cup to my lips.

I shouldn't drink. It could be yet another trap. Or poison. Or…

What did it matter? It was either water and it would help or it was poison and it would kill me. I wasn't that far off breaking. Could you administer sodium pentathol via a drink?

I should know the answer to that, but it didn't seem to register. I parted my lips. The cracks in them stung, then relief raced over them as water spilled into my mouth.

Like a desert in the rain, I sucked down as much as she let me have. I swallowed with care, not daring to inhale it. When she pulled the cup back, I almost grabbed her wrist so I could keep it.

But that would take more energy than I possessed. Her hand left my shoulder then the soft gulps of sound indicated she finished whatever was in the tin cup.

A ploy to prove there were no drugs or maybe she was thirsty. I'd gotten a glimpse of her bruised face, but not how badly it was bruised. My cheek was swollen and I had three splits in my lips at last count.

I had cigarette burns on my arms. Cane marks on my back and my legs. Bruises criss-crossing my thighs and my abdomen. Even my toes were battered at this point.

The drag of sound as she moved to sit next to me filled the silence. Her breathing wasn't ragged or coming in short pants. I doubted she was in pain.

Her long sigh offered more proof. She could take deeper breaths, filling her lungs. I had to keep my breathing to shorter, shallower breaths. I wasn't sure if my ribs were broken or only bruised, but they weren't fans of oxygen.

Bastards.

"My name is Kathy," she whispered, like it was a highly classified secret.

How nice for her. Kathy needed to learn to conserve her energy. Or maybe she didn't. I was going to be careful with mine.

She shifted next to me. The cold water in my stomach actually made it cramp, but I ignored it. The water itself had been welcome in my mouth and throat. If I got too active, I might throw up.

Then again, they might come for me sooner and make me puke. So no, I would sit here and let my eyes close again. Maybe get more sleep.

"How long have you been here?"

The words came just as I'd started to drift. Reaching a mental place where I could rest much less sleep was challenge. I didn't appreciate being jolted out of it. It would be a waste of energy and moisture.

Head back against the wall, I turned half-slitted eyes to the slot in the door that let light in. It was dim and murky. Even as adjusted as my eyes were, it was impossible to make out any real details.

"Aren't you going to say anything?" Impatience flavored the tremor under her words.

No, I wasn't. But I kept the thought and the energy to express it to myself. Whether she was another prisoner like me or a plant to gain my confidence, I couldn't trust her.

Another prisoner might be used as leverage. Force me to endure her torture alongside my own, hoping it would break me. Or if she were a plant—she might want to gain my trust that way.

Whatever she was, I couldn't trust or rely on her.

"Bitch."

Probably.

The sniffle that came from the dark was pathetically obvious. Or maybe I really was a bitch. I'd lost track of how many days I'd been here. The longer I was here, the more I assumed I was going to die here. Escape would require energy and effort that I just didn't possess.

Eventually, they *would* kill me.

Eventually.

Every minute I survived, however, was a minute I could use to plot a way out.

Tuning out the sniffling, barely muffled sobbing next to me, I tried to picture everything about the facility I could remember.

It wasn't much... but I had to start somewhere.

~

HAVING company didn't deter our captors from coming to pull me out. I half-expected them to take her first to "prove" to me she was also here against her will. Instead, they dragged me back to a very familiar room and shackled me to a chair.

The handcuffs cut into my wrists. There was a cut in the wood of the chair, a deep groove probably made by a knife. The wrecked state of my clothes meant it bit into my skin. Kind of helpful for the focus, I supposed.

Instead of the Shaggy and Mr. Cold, a newcomer entered the room. How—charming. I took a moment to glance at the guards. I hadn't paid as much attention to them. Were they different?

I had no idea.

Wonderful.

"Miss Brady," the newcomer said, his tone was clinical and detached. He began setting out a series of vials and syringes. "The next few hours are going to be very unpleasant for you."

They set up an IV, inserting the port into my jugular. Dehydration was a bitch. There was a saline drip. Well, that was something, I supposed.

"Remember, when this begins," the man continued as he began to pull the contents of one vial into his syringe. There was a place for him to add it to the IV tubing. Well, at least it was one needle stick. "You have only yourself to blame."

Really pleasant guy.

He didn't ask me a single question. Then again, he probably wasn't going to until they loaded me up with whatever all of those vials were.

I had an issue whenever I tried weed—I tended to hyperfocus on whatever I was doing in the moment it kicked in. Happened with a lot of other drugs too and nitrous. I didn't get why my brain did it, but it did.

As he loaded the second vial into the IV, I thought about Taylor Swift's last album. What songs were on it? What story did they tell?

The pain began like a thousand angry bees swarming me, stinging violently. Even with tears running down my face though, I was coughing out the Taylor Swift lyrics.

Yep, totally my fault.

THE NEXT TIME I woke up in my cell, I swore I had a hangover. My mouth tasted like cotton, my head hurt, and my eyes burned. There was a bang as the lights came on and the cell door opened.

I turned, curling over with an arm over my eyes to hide myself from too much light. I got a look at the woman. She was blonde, ratty looking hair, torn shirt. There was a fresh bruise on her face and an older one swelling her eye.

The guard hauled her into the cell—the one across from mine. Recognition began to bleed into my awareness. This was different from the last cell I'd been in. The dark hole had become an actual cell with bars. There was a walkway between my cell and hers.

After the guard dropped her on the floor, her wheezing groan said she was awake enough to feel it. Or maybe it was just her body's automatic reaction. The man closed the other door and the locks tumbled into place, then he strolled out.

I closed my eyes and pretended to be unconscious even when the weeping began again. Eventually, that sound died off and it was just quiet. Eerily quiet.

Another door opened down the hall and I watched from under my arm as a new guard approached. He had a tray of food. The doors weren't keyed—they had keypads. I saw two of the numbers he entered on her cell but not the other four.

Still, six digits.

He put the tray inside her cell, then turned to mine. From this angle, I could see where his hand hit but I only had a vague idea of what the numbers would be. The last two digits were on the bottom third I would bet, just based on his motion—and the fact the first two digits were three and one.

That gave me a few combinations to run. He put the tray down and then left. His bored expression never changed. He pulled the door shut and it auto-locked.

So—the newcomer had moved my cell, brought my new roomie along, changed the rules entirely—including adding brutal drugs to my interrogations and now *food*?

Yeah, my stomach cramped at the thought of

it, but after everything else—I wasn't hungry. The saline had helped to rehydrate me so—yay?

I closed my eyes and sought out sleep. I'd wait and see if I caught the code again. I needed it to be dark when I moved. But if the code worked and I could get out of this cell?

I was going to take my chances. I'd rather die on my feet and running from these guys than curled up in a cell.

Not that I wanted to die.

Pushing away the latter thought, I clung to the former. I might not be that brave, not really. But I could pretend. I'd gotten *really* good at pretending.

FOURTEEN

LOCKE

"Yeah, I'm not feeling that answer either." Remington pulled the plastic bag over the woman's head again and tightened it. She went from stoicism to struggle in ten seconds.

McQuade leaned back in another chair, whittling wood or some shit. He'd brought some piece of wood in when we arrived and he'd been shaving the wood down ever since. Remington had been asking his prisoner questions for several minutes.

He'd been suffocating her for the last fifteen on and off though. Just as her struggling weakened and seemed to stop, he pulled the bag off her head and then took a step back. Like a bored man, he picked up his coffee and took a sip.

I'd half-expected something like bourbon or maybe something stupid expensive, instead, he just drank black coffee. Black *instant* coffee. But this cabin was hell and gone, with no one around for at least three miles. She could scream all she wanted and no one would hear her.

Aware of the clock ticking on the wall, I waited for the sixty seconds since he stripped the plastic bag to pass. Then she let out a cough and choked, pitching forward as she sucked in air.

"It's funny," Remington said in a tone that was anything but humorous. In fact, his accent had taken on a distinctly British lilt. Maybe Irish. More London than north country. It wasn't specific and he waxed between it and sounding like a native American.

So what was that deal?

"Nothing about this is funny," McQuade said, pausing in his carving to reach for his own drink. "Unless you have a bizarre sense of humor."

"Bizarre sense of humor or not, I don't see anything funny either." Not that they'd asked me.

"Oh, I meant her." Remington said, motioning to the woman currently glaring daggers at him. "Clearly you're part of a group. Three female assassins? Not everyone runs women as a unit. So you were most likely all hired by the same client. You were all hitting at the same time, that says coordination."

Still wasn't hearing the humor, but I sipped water rather than coffee. My would-be assassin had ruined a perfectly good suit. She hadn't survived the encounter. I apparently "lacked the skill" to incapacitate and not kill.

At least that was McQuade's opinion. He had some ideas on body disposal. That was good, I didn't want to have to pay more than I already would for a professional cleaning.

The fact he had his own would-be assassin

had kind of sealed the deal. Remington warned us, so after cleaning up, we used the address he sent to get up here. Separate vehicles, of course. We hadn't completely lost our minds yet.

"Yet, not only did you fail—you failed spectacularly." Remington rubbed his jaw almost thoughtfully before taking a seat in the chair a couple of feet in front of the dark-haired woman with her dark eyes and sullen expression. She was *pissed*. "Not a single one of you got a target. Far as I know, you didn't even get a scratch on a target. That's—that's pathetic. You could get your assassin's card pulled for that."

"You get cards?" I wasn't entirely sure what his play was here, but I figured I'd join in.

"Bloody damn right we get cards," Remington said with a roll of his eyes. "The more punches in the card, the more hits you've made. When the card is gone because of all the punches... you become a legend. How sad for you," he continued, his whole focus on his target again, "that you targeted a legend."

She spit, the glob of it flew through the air and landed against Remington's cheek.

"So, not only an amateur," he said, pulling a handkerchief out of his pocket and wiping away the spittle. "But an uncouth one at that."

"We're really getting some miles out of this particular line of interrogation," McQuade said, raising his knife. "Let me have a go. Skin shaves nicely and we can take her apart piece by piece... though you might need another plastic sheet for the floor."

Game or not, the banter wasn't having any effect on the target. She wasn't afraid of pain or torture. That didn't bode well for us. Whomever hired her wanted someone who wouldn't break.

Made sense, I looked back at the equipment we'd stripped off the women. There were three phones, all burners, no GPS chips in them and the SIM cards were relatively blank save for one message "go" from another burner phone that was not one of these three.

If we had Patch, I could plug her in and she would give us the asshole's shoe size in no time, not to mention where he was, what his favorite color was, and how long it would take us to get there.

Or maybe I was being a misogynist and it was a she. I didn't really care, I just wanted to know who sent three assassins after *us*. Particularly right after we arrived where Patch had been taken and had actually been in her house.

Remington stood and dragged a hood over her head, then he put headphones on her before he pressed something on his laptop. She jerked, almost struggling in the chair more than she had been earlier. The hood was cloth and she wasn't going to be suffocating.

"Thrash metal," Remington explained to me when I lifted my eyebrows. "I don't think they'll talk and not because they are resistant to torture."

"They don't know," McQuade said. "Amateurs. Probably first timers. Maybe a way to get them wet…"

"You don't send an amateur after me." Remington sounded positively insulted. I almost laughed because he was *really* offended. "I've been killing longer than she's been alive."

"Maybe if you started when you were eight," I retorted. The girls were young. But not *that* young.

"Who says I didn't?" The bland expression coupled with the deadpan delivery seemed to suggest he was serious. Yeah, I wasn't going to focus on that part.

"So they send amateurs after us to what end?" I asked. "She didn't have a chance in the hit on you. McQuade over there would probably have been fine. I'm pretty sure I would have made it—but likely wounded."

I could be generous in my assessments, but I preferred honesty.

"Now, the chances of one of them surviving the hit exists." I rubbed my chin. Hunger twisted my stomach. "No matter how minuscule, there's always a chance. The fact that two of them did is a credit to you two, not their skills."

I was the one who killed my would-be assassin. Mostly because when it comes down to a them or me situation, I always pick me.

Period.

"Your point?" Remington asked.

"Well, my point is, these assassins were not sent here to succeed."

"Mother. Fucker." McQuade's growl punched through the room. "They were sent to be distractions."

I mimed a gun with my forefinger and thumb, then clicked my tongue as though firing it. "Exactly."

Sadly, the amusement proved fleeting. Remington's expression had drained of all animation. Even his eyes went dead. Only he wasn't looking at us. No, he was staring at his hooded captive.

Yeah, I'd feel guilty about pointing this out but she had tried to kill him. Don't ever start a fight you don't want to finish.

"Three bodies is a pain," Remington muttered.

"We'll take care of it. Cut our losses, use their tech or what there is of it, but we need to move again. Especially if they are trackable in any way." McQuade put away his whittling and rose. "Wrap it up with her, then we'll deal with the other one and get them out of here."

"We're just—gonna off them?" I grimaced and earned two bland looks. Yes, I sounded like an idiot, sue me. However... "It's one thing in a fight, it seems a little overkill, I guess, since they are prisoners."

"Are you planning to stay here, babysitting them?" McQuade asked.

"Or sit on them until you have to let them go and let them come after us again?" Remington drained his coffee. "Because I'm not on either front."

"Same," McQuade said. "If you're a little squeamish, go ahead and step out. But leaving them behind is leaving them to come after us again."

Would the threat of death make them talk? I studied the hooded figure with the headphones placed over her ears.

"Pain wasn't making her talk," Remington said. "Death is a release, not a threat."

Yeah.

"Okay, I'll go make more coffee. We need to plan our next steps." It wasn't until I collected their cups and climbed up the stairs from the basement to the kitchen of the little cabin that I realized what I'd said.

We.

We needed to plan *our* next steps.

I guessed we were working together. The house had power thanks to a generator. There was also some tinned food in the pantry and other supplies that were designed to keep without power on. Made sense.

I used the first pot of hot water to put together an easy meal of rehydrated mashed potatoes, canned corn, and peas. Not my favorites, not even remotely gourmet. Apparently butter wasn't something the place came with, but it was hot and it would be filling.

Second pot of water hit boiling about the time the pair ascended the steps—sans bodies. Not my circus or my monkeys. Body disposal could happen later. The temps up here were not going to do much more than freeze the bodies anyway.

All three of us made do with instant coffee, powdered creamer and some fake sugar shit. Whatever, it helped with the bitterness. Once we were seated at the rickety table, bowls of mashed potatoes and vegetables in front of each of us and with cups of coffee, I eyed them.

"Who starts?"

Maybe the putting our heads together thing came from me, but these two had something planned. Most likely individually. That said, I'd rather get a feel for it on all fronts before we launched into this. However, neither seemed willing to offer up the first morsel of data.

"Look," I said, lowering my cup of coffee and looking from Remington to McQuade, then back to Remington again. "We don't have to like each other or be buddies. We're not all that likely to hold hands and skip. What we are, is very dangerous and each of us possesses skills the others may not. We all have a similar goal..."

"Patch," McQuade said with a grunt. He didn't like it, but he didn't try to avoid mentioning it.

"Exactly." I tapped my finger against the table. "She's *our* switchboard. Someone *took* her. The longer we play games with each other, the more likely it is for them to keep getting away with it. When we went to her place, we got noticed. These distractions are to let them do what—"

"Clean up behind them in case they forgot something." Remington's eyes narrowed.

"Might be too late for that." McQuade pulled out a slip of pink paper. "Not sure fifteen digits is what they wanted but...I found this sticking out from behind her white board."

"Could be nothing," Remington commented.

"Could be everything. But from this point forward, we work together. I've got a setup that will let me do some research. I'm not Patch and I don't pretend to be, but we can at least dig in deeper."

"Or we can set up here and wait for the scratch off team," McQuade mused. "They are going to want to know if their people were successful."

"That's just more grunts," Remington said with a shake of his head. "I want the head of the snake, not the worms that slither below it."

He had a point. I dug into my food as the two of them eyed each other with cold, distant expressions. Yeah, we were definitely not going to be the bestest of buddies.

Totally fine with that. I didn't have to like them to use their help.

"If I had to guess," McQuade said. "This is an account or wire number. If we can track it to a bank, we can figure out who it belongs to..."

Could still be nothing. I finished my food then pulled out my phone. When I beckoned for the slip of paper, he hesitated. I didn't push or demand, I just waited.

Finally, he handed it over. I snapped a picture of it so I could keep it. Then I typed the numbers into a notepad. The signal up here was shit. "We need to move down the mountain again," I said. "And deal with the bodies."

"We're not splitting up." Remington rose, fingers pressed against the table. "We're going to become very familiar with each other."

"Can't wait," I said. "But I don't do dead bodies kind of like I don't do dishes. So I'll stick close, but you two get to do the fun shit with the dead people."

"Pussy," McQuade commented.

"Pussies push out babies. They are a fuck ton stronger than any of us, so I'll take the compliment." I smirked and his dirty look was worth it. "But I suggest, gentlemen, that for brevity, we get a move on."

"Brevity..." Remington shook his head, a smudge of disbelief on the word.

"It means a short time, keeping it concise." I tucked my phone into my pocket before draining my coffee.

"I know what it means," Remington said. "McQuade, back your truck up. You have more space in it. We'll ride together. I can send someone up here to get the other rentals."

Oh yay, I got to ride in the back with the dead people. "I'll get my equipment." Not that either of them were listening. Still, we had the beginnings of a plan.

Might not be much but I'd done more with less.

FIFTEEN

MCQUADE

Body disposal in winter was not my favorite thing. Add being in the U.S. to that and I was even less of a fan. Still, we all knew people. We just had to take the time to get to them. Locke bitched for about half the drive until we were in Boulder and finally heading out of the mountains. Then he had a signal and didn't say a word.

Periodically, I'd glanced back to see him squinting at his laptop screen and typing. He must have been using his cell for signal. It was an *actual* dump, but we had a contact who would take care of the rest of the cleanup. They also had a very nice incinerator. It took a lot of heat to destroy a body completely.

A lot.

True to his word, Locke just got out of the way and let us hustle the bodies out.

Dick.

Once we were done, though, he identified the

numbers. "Bank account," he said. "Part of the wiring info for MD Professional Resources."

MD. "That's a Mad Dog outfit." They had a few of them MD Outsourcing was another one. Bland, neutral names with boring profiles that masked their actual work. "They're shady as fuck, have zero morals, and they're basically thugs for hire. Calling them private military contractors is a joke."

"You sound like you've worked for them," Remington said, studying me.

"I did for about five minutes. Then I found out the type of jobs they take. I blew their bullshit op and got the fuck out of there."

"So," Locke said. "I'm going to guess they aren't your biggest fans."

"Nope." They'd been part of the warning Patch gave me about that job offer. It was a trap, likely done by an MD subsidiary.

If those motherfuckers laid a finger on her, I was going to end every single one of them. There was an MD not far from here in Denver.

"Question," Remington said, seemingly unperturbed by the icy breeze blowing around us. We could get in my truck and drive, but he made no moves in that direction. Locke had his laptop tucked under his arm. "What would they accomplish in taking Patch?"

I rubbed my hands together before I dragged my gloves out of my pocket. The last thing I needed was frostbite. "No fucking clue. She's my operator. She funnels most of the jobs through to me, vets them when I ask for it."

She was the quiet and the reason in the middle of a storm. She kept me sane when missions went sideways. More than once...

"She's saved my life. So I don't really give a fuck why they took her. I just need to know who so I can get her back."

"We," Locke corrected me. "That number could mean anything. But it is a lead."

"Then we explore the lead and see how far it takes us."

"Great, everyone in the truck, I know where we can pick us up a couple of MD's contractors."

Locke made it to the front passenger seat before Remington. "No more dead bodies back there, so you can ride in the back."

The man barely seemed to notice. Once we were all in, I glanced back at Remington. "They good here? Or will we need to come back to cleanup?"

I would prefer to not do a mop-up. I'd had to do them in the past when someone doing a job decided to get greedy.

"They're well paid, and they like their work. We'll be fine," Remington said. "The next closest body removal specialist is two states away. At least as far as one I would trust, so I would very much like to leave the Garner brothers where they are."

"Right-o, mate," I said, firing up the engine.

"Don't call me mate," Remington said. "How far is it to our destination?"

"Probably an hour," I told him. "Sleep if you can, I'll give you a heads up five minutes out."

Remington didn't say another word but when I glanced back, his eyes were closed. Locke had his laptop open and I caught flickering from the corner of my eye. He was doing some kind of search.

"So, we're just going to roll up to this place—MD Outfitters—and what, knock on the door and see if anyone is home?"

"I have a plan."

"You going to share it?" Locke asked.

"Nope," I told him. "Better to be in the moment."

"Uh huh." The skepticism was powerful on those two syllables. "Not sure that works for me."

"Well, since I don't either, I don't care." I could have given him more, but I didn't have it yet. While I had a plan, it wasn't fully fleshed out and had a lot of potential for going sideways. So, I focused on what I had with me, weapons, tools, and people.

Remington would be useful.

Locke should probably stay with the truck.

We were going to have to bag, tag, and work our way up the ladder. I doubted the grunts would know anything. "Tell me if they have any managers or area supervisors listed on their website?"

"You want me to help after that?" Locke didn't quite scoff, but since he was typing, I let it go. "I have four names."

"Excellent, our plan is to get to those four. Find out where they are and any other information they might have online."

"Right, that's more likely to be in their employee files but I'll look." He didn't sound confident. That was fine.

"Good thing we're on our way there then."

"Yeah, good thing." Again, with the doubt.

"You don't like to work on instinct, do you?" I had a hunch, but Locke didn't strike me as a go with his gut kind of guy.

"Not really, I like the specs and time to plan."

"I can drop you off if you want out." Not that he sounded like he wanted out, no matter how many doubts he expressed.

"Shut up and drive," he told me.

Yeah, I had his number.

Needed to figure out Remington's.

THE NEW DAY dawned on our way to MD Outfitters. It was gray, cloudy, and smelled of rain. But the forecast didn't call for it. Fine by me. For now, I focused on the building where MD Outfitters was housed.

"A half-dozen cameras," Locke said, "just focused on the lot and the front of the building. The glass is tinted to mirror so they can see out, we can't see in. Double-bars on those delivery doors. That's just what we can see."

I took a swallow of the coffee I'd picked up. The greasy, fried breakfast sandwich and hash browns went a long way toward quieting my stomach's complaints.

"It's early and there's what, forty cars in that

lot?" Locke shook his head. "This is a bad idea to just walk in, especially if they are all armed contractors."

"Got a better idea?" I asked. "I've taken down bigger places with less. You can stay out here, Remington can be eyes in the sky..."

"Really?" The absolute disdain in Remington's British accent would amuse me save for the way he looked at me like I was stupid. "Where do you propose I set up? It's flat for at least four miles around us and there's no good lines of sight to the interior."

"Fine, you can cover my ass the old-fashioned way by going inside with me. I'll run point. I prefer being the first one through the door."

"Hmm, more likely to get your head blown off." Not that Remington sounded like he objected.

"It's gonna be fun," I told him. "Maybe we'll get lucky and she's in there."

"We're not that lucky," Locke said.

"Man, you have got to learn to look on the brighter side of life." I patted his shoulder. The plan was pretty basic, but like I'd told them—I'd done more with less. Besides, after hours of waiting and looking, I was more than ready to crack a few heads open.

Ten minutes later, I drove us to another spot where we had some coverage. Then we'd approach from the open land rather than the road. They had fewer cameras back there. Fewer didn't mean none.

Once we were parked, I got out with Remington to check the weapons we wanted. Locke followed, then started off toward the trees.

"Where are you going?"

"Hitting the head," he told me over his shoulder. "Want to watch?"

"Don't take too long," I said and he raised a middle finger back at me.

As he disappeared into the trees, I kept one eye on that direction. Remington stripped down a Sig Sauer then put it back together.

"You're not taking it on a date," I told him and he ignored me. Not that I blamed him. I wouldn't walk into a fight with a weapon I hadn't checked unless I was in the middle of one already.

Still... five minutes turned into ten and Locke wasn't back.

"Where the fuck is he?"

"Maybe he needed to evacuate his bowels," Remington said. "We'll need to move sooner rather than la—"

At his breaking off, I pivoted to see Locke strolling back toward us with a bag over his shoulder.

"He didn't leave with a bag, did he?" I really hoped Patch wasn't fond of Locke. I might end up killing him.

"No." Remington managed to make that single syllable sound like an indictment.

"You wanna explain where you went?" I asked when Locke was in earshot.

"You had a plan," he told me, setting the bag down in the back where we'd been going through weapons. Then he flipped it open to reveal hard drives. "I had a better plan. Patch gave me a couple of programs for cracking drives on my last job. If these guys took her, she'd be in their files."

"So," Remington said slowly. "You took all their files."

"Yep and this…" He held up a keycard with a smirk. It had a red stripe on it. "Level One security should also help us get past some of the encryptions."

"You were gone for ten minutes."

"Technically fifteen," Remington said. "Accuracy is preferable. You didn't start counting until it annoyed you that he wasn't back."

"Work smarter," Locke said. "Not harder."

Lips pursed, I eyed the hard drives, then Locke and finally looked back at the building. The drives were nowhere near as satisfying as kicking in doors and cracking skulls. At the same time, they might net us a target sooner.

"How long?" I asked.

"A few hours," Locke said. "We need a place for me to get everything set up and plugged in. But I have what I need."

"I have something similar that Patch provided," Remington admitted. Ice licked every single syllable. "We will need to retrieve it if necessary, but if you have yours—then I say we do it your way *for now*."

I agreed with that caveat, particularly because I wanted to get eyes on Patch yesterday. "Fine, let's go. There's a couple of hotels back near the interstate."

An hour later, we were split between two

rooms with the adjoining door wide open. Locke worked on plugging the hard drives into a case, then plugging something else into them.

We got more food, and coffee, then waited. Locke was methodical, he loaded and searched each drive individually. The encryption programs took time and it was tedious to watch the screen as it ticked past.

Remington took a shower. When he was done, I took one. Locke waved it off. He'd shower when he was finished. It wasn't until he was on the seventh drive that he found the address for her house.

"Fallon Brady," Locke murmured.

"What?"

"Her name, it's listed as Fallon Brady. I didn't know Patch's real name."

Nor had I and based on Remington's tight expression, neither had he.

"It's a directive to acquire her alive, with no fanfare. Black bag job, very quiet."

"Alive is good," Remington said. "And bad."

'Cause it meant they wanted something from her.

"Where did they take her?" I asked.

"I'm hunting," Locke said and the screen flickered and changed. I fought the urge to pace. "This bit of encryption is harder and it's different —the programs are working." It took another ten excruciating minutes.

Then we had an address.

"It's a few hours away," I said, checking the GPS. "We need to get there and scout."

"We also need medical supplies," Locke said. "Weapons, gear, and probably stuff to break in and break out. The address doesn't exist on Google Earth. I don't even want to know what you have to do to get yourself scrubbed."

"Shower," I told him. "We're leaving in fifteen."

"Good job," Remington said to him as Locke went into the bathroom.

He was right. "Yeah," I said. "Good job."

Locke gave us each a look then shook his head. It had been a good job. We had a location.

"We do this together," Remington said. "Once we have her secure and these people burned down, we can deal with everything else."

"Including who from that outfit was sent to get her," I said.

He merely nodded. There wasn't much else to say. Locke was done with his shower and in fresh clothes in under ten minutes. We headed back to the truck with our gear. The hard drives were still with us. They might be useful later.

Hang on, Patch.

We're coming.

I had every intention of bringing hell with us.

CHAPTER
SIXTEEN

PATCH

Voices.

Boots on the ground.

I slid my eyes open, not totally, just a fraction. Two guards stood outside of my cell. The first one entered the code. I followed the track of his fingers. I had the first three and the last two. I just needed one more number.

The squeak of the cell door opening registered. I didn't react though. They were coming in whether I liked it or not. The past couple of "sessions" had been brutal. They'd gone to drugs for questioning. If I focused enough on songs, it worked. I didn't do anything other than sing and scream.

I'd half-destroyed my voice. This morning, like the past couple, a pair of guards strode in without a word and dragged me upward by my arms. They hauled me between them like a pair of silent ghouls all the way down the hall.

The click of their boots against the tiled floor played like some countdown to my next horror-filled hours. The room they pulled me into was painfully white.

The light seemed to reflect off every surface. I squinted, then had to close my eyes. The brightness assaulted me with sharp jabs at my eyes and lancing cuts to my eyelids. Even squeezed closed, I couldn't escape it.

They slammed me into a chair, the bruising went up my spine and forced all the air out of me.

"Good morning, Miss Brady," my tormentor greeted me as he strode into the room. I could barely slit my eyes apart. They hadn't lashed me to the seat and it was taking way too much effort to not just fall over.

My tormentor dressed in a buttoned down shirt, and tie. His shirt was pale blue. His pants were a darker shade of blue. A contrast for his white lab coat.

"Are you feeling more cooperative today?" He cupped my chin and lifted my face up so he could examine me. I didn't bother with responding. The only answers he wanted were not answers I would ever give.

Playing at being broken was not all that difficult. The pain was almost constant now. The pain in my extremities. In my chest. The cramps. They barely fed me. Fluids were regularly given during these sessions, but only to make feeding me drugs easier.

I had no idea where I was. What time of year it was or day.

Hell, I wasn't even sure how long I'd been here.

Time no longer had meaning. I stared at my tormentor without seeing at him. I barely flinched when he shone a pin light in my eyes. This room was so damn lit, how else was I supposed to react?

"Hmm..." He continued to flick the light from one eye to the other. I just kept them unfocused and staring into the distance.

It was impossible to miss his tense expression. The salt and pepper of his hair gave him a distinguished air. But his face was narrower, his cheekbones a slash. Worst, he had the palest blue eyes. So pale they might as well be colorless.

I hated looking in his eyes.

If they really were the window to the soul, then his was utterly absent.

"Problem?" A second interrogator entered the room. This one didn't usually speak. Though he had been the one working over my neighbor. I'd seen him slapping her repeatedly.

The fact he didn't enter my line of sight kept me from getting a better look at him. Every other time he'd been present, he'd been behind me. My would-be Tomás de Torquemada dug his fingers into my chin. The bite of his nails threatened to break the skin.

Leaning closer, he exhaled his coffee breath all over me. There was a fresh new hell. I hadn't had coffee since I'd woken up in this hellish place.

I missed coffee.

My eyes watered when he angled my head

back so I ended up staring at the lights. A single tear tracked down my cheeks.

"Maybe we should just give her to the guards," the second man suggested. "They can have a bit of fun and she'll finally accept that we can and will do whatever we want with her."

Tormentor number one gave my jaw a shake then let me go. I just let my head drop. It hurt the back of my neck, but I didn't care. Now my vision was fixed on the floor. The tiles hadn't changed. There was still a drain near the center.

If there had been blood from earlier interrogations, it was washed clean. Everything sparkled. Sanitized. When they killed me, they'd do it again. Erasing any sign of me from the world.

Then I would just be gone.

Like I never existed.

The second interrogator appeared in front of me. He shoved my head up and stared down. Right. I didn't need to have a memory of his face.

There was something inherently cruel in his expression. A scar bisected his upper lip and down through the lower at a diagonal before disappearing under his chin. Pock scars marked his cheeks, and his eyes were dark and sunken in. The shadows under his eyes added to the impression of darkness.

His slap ripped across my face and set my cheek on fire. I just let my head flop. When he straightened me again, he stared silently. His next move involved backhanding me, it toppled the chair and I hit the floor.

It hurt. Another bruise atop a layer of bruises. I refused to react though. It took everything to not try and save myself. But why bother?

Maybe if I pissed them off enough, this would just be over.

"This could be a problem," the first interrogator said and his companion kicked my leg. The blow rocked through to the bone and shoved my leg to the side.

"You think, we still don't have the answers we need yet. If she's shattered then we won't get them. Failure is *not* an option." They weren't talking about me so much on that last one. There was actually a kernel of fear in the second man's voice.

Huh. Well, I hope they didn't expect sympathy from me if they got killed over this. Too bad, so sad, and I wouldn't be mad. A laugh escaped me. A titter of a sound.

It yanked their attention back to me. Their scowls were almost mirrors of each other. Where tormentor one was buttoned down and cold, tormentor two was dark, unkempt, and violence seemed to just eddy around him.

Of the pair, he scared me less. Nothing about him offered safety. In truth, nothing about the first guy did either—but he played perfectly pleasant while filling my veins with drugs that set my skin on fire.

At least the second guy didn't pretend to be nice.

"Take her back to her cell," the first one said.

"We're not getting anywhere like this. We need a new plan."

The guards seized my arms in their bruising grips and dragged me back out. They didn't turn me around, so I had full view of the room as they walked away.

For some odd reason, the trip back to the cell didn't take near as long as the trip to the room. More warping time in my perception. At my cell door, one of the guards let go of me and I half-twisted, just hanging by an arm.

When he entered the code, I repeated the numbers and my guess for the missing digit had been correct. Door open, they dropped me inside and locked it. Then they left via a different door.

Same code.

Different door.

That was useful information.

Over my head somewhere, there was a bang and clank. Then another before the air began to move. Air conditioning of some kind. Didn't do anything for the cold floor I lay on or the rapidly stiffening bruises on my leg and side.

My face also hurt, but the pain wasn't that bad. Not when you considered all the other shit that'd happened. I listened for any movement or comments, but my neighbor hadn't been in her cell.

Had she been there when they came to get me?

I really didn't remember. Every time they took her to be tortured it just—felt wrong. Performative. When she came back, she had real injuries, so why didn't I believe her?

'Cause everything was a lie. Everything and everyone.

Instead of forcing myself up, I closed my eyes. I needed to conserve my energy. The more they thought I was through the less they'd watch me. They already thought I was useless.

Let them continue to think they'd broken me irrevocably. Then when dark came, I was getting out of here one way or another. I had the code to get out of the cell and to open the door. If I escaped, they would more than likely try to kill me.

Either way, I was out of this cell.

SEVENTEEN

LOCKE

Louisiana.

I fucking *hated* Louisiana. My nose started running the second we deplaned in Shreveport. It was like I was allergic to the air. The route would have taken twelve to fourteen hours to reach via vehicle. McQuade had another plan.

He *knew* a guy.

Honestly, I didn't ask for more information. It would probably have added heartburn to my allergies. Remington spared me a look when McQuade drove us to a private airport. The small plane didn't look sturdy enough to take a hard draft of air, but McQuade just strode away from his SUV and tossed his bags inside.

No one was there to greet or challenge us.

"You certified to fly a plane?" Don't ask me why I had to utter that aloud. Surely, he was. Or he would have had a pilot meet us. A pilot was another witness, another person who could be turned or conversely, turn us in. Not something I wanted to keep one eye over my shoulder on while we were tracking down Patch.

Fallon.

Her real name was Fallon. It was such a *soft,* almost lyrical name. Elegant.

McQuade didn't say a word until he was in the pilot's seat. "You staying on board if I say no?" He was already flicking switches after putting a set of headphones on.

Remington stowed our bags as I stared at Mc-Quade. The man was just fucking with me. Right?

"He's a mercenary. He undoubtedly has many undocumented skills." Remington's crisp accent didn't make that option sound like an improvement.

Undocumented could also mean unproven.

"Just don't crash before we find her," I'd suggested before pulling the door closed and securing it. This part I was at least familiar with.

"So crashing afterward is fine?" McQuade smirked. "Good to know. Buckle up." He was already talking to someone on the headset and ignoring us. Did I want to sit up there and see what he was doing or sit back here and pretend?

Remington settled into a seat and pulled the cross straps on. I mirrored the action. Then Remington kicked a pack over to me. I eyed it, then him.

"Parachute," he said, a faint smile on his face as the plane began to accelerate.

Everyone was a funny guy.

A little over two hours later, we were touching down at another airport outside of

Shreveport. My allergies were incensed, but I ignored them as I checked the maps for the coordinates of our destination.

The facility, if any, didn't show up anywhere except in one old, time-stamped map from about ten years earlier. It had the look of some kind of factory, but there was nothing registering it anywhere.

As of now, it didn't exist.

"Black site," McQuade said over his shoulder as I briefed them. "We have as much as we're going to get. This is going to be an on the fly operation. Locke, you're going in with me. Remington, you're on overwatch."

"I'm also the exit plan," Remington stated.

"Once we have Patch, we're going to extract on the run. You are definitely the exit plan, we'll need you to bar the door once we're out." McQuade had barely glanced at the photos I'd been able to find. "Everything we know about the facility says it's located right at the edge of a swamp. Our exit strategy needs to involve not going through it. Particularly if we don't know Patch's condition."

"No arguments here. I don't like stagnant water or alligators." Most of my jobs didn't involve getting physical with others, or worrying about being shot. I liked the mental exercise and the challenge of overcoming the obstacles in my path without alerting anyone or anything.

This was not going to be the same.

"Your primary job will be getting us past security. If I have to shoot our way out, I'm fine with it." McQuade sounded more like he was discussing meal plans for after the theater than a raid. "I don't want to alert them on the way in. If they have orders to kill her rather than letting her escape, I don't want them to have the heads up."

Made sense.

"I'll bring my gear," I said. "It also means you might have to be patient. If we can snag someone on the way in who has a security card I can slice, that would be better."

Without more information on what waited inside there, I wouldn't know the challenges until we hit them. Didn't mean I couldn't get past them—just meant it might take a little more creativity than my usual methods.

"Understood," McQuade said. Then there was nothing to do but drive.

This kind of operation should have at least three months to plan. Ideally, we could map all the security routes, and the layers. We'd know the schedule. I'd have access to internal cameras, or at least get cameras on it so I could see the comings and goings.

We were going to try and pull off what in the best of circumstances should take months in minutes? Hours?

I went over a mental checklist of what I had in my bags. Better to identify missing pieces *before* I needed them. The focus couldn't distract me from the one truly troubling part of this operation.

We had no idea what Patch looked like. Her voice? Yes, I knew exactly what she sounded like and what her voice did to me. But I had no description. No age. No hair or eye color. I suspected Caucasian but that was just bias on my part. Picturing the woman that went with that voice.

But even that was reaching.

After what seemed an interminable amount of time, we finally arrived at the facility. It was worse in person than what I'd been able to see on the map. It still looked a lot like an abandoned factory. There was nothing coming out of the smokestacks.

A mosquito stabbed at my neck and I slapped it even as I studied the drive leading up to the place. "Three points on that road that can be choked."

"Four," Remington corrected. Like me, he had binoculars up and studying. We'd parked two miles back and hiked in, skirting the edge of the swamp. Getting her out that way if she was wounded would be more than problematic.

I switched my study to the vehicles in the lot. Anything I could hot-wire fast? An old beater would be ideal. Anything pre-90's would be a great start. The chances of Patch being uninjured after what? Ten? Twelve days of captivity? They were slim.

Very slim.

"Can you handle this?" McQuade asked as he thrust a Glock-19 at me. I didn't comment, just checked the weapon, the magazine, then secured it in a holster located on the bullet proof vest he'd thrust at me when we got out of the car.

Sweat trickled down my back, even as the

rough humidity left my face sticky and uncomfortable. The grip on the Glock wouldn't slide out of my hand. That was something, I supposed.

"Not a lot of good sight lines here," Remington said as unruffled now as he'd been since I walked in on him at Patch's place. "I'll set up in the grass, twenty meters east. It's taller there. Better cover."

Probably had snakes too. Another mosquito took a bite out of me and I slapped it dead too. Mosquitos. Dragonflies. Midges. Ticks. Alligators. Snakes.

It was a fucking paradise.

The heat of late afternoon sun added to the scalding, armpit temperatures.

"We're not moving until dark," McQuade said, raising a pair of his own binoculars. "Get comfortable."

Right. Because hunkered down in the weeds near brackish water while being consumed by bugs was comfortable. I kept my comments to myself, however, while keeping an eye on the facility.

"Mr. McQuade," I said, keeping my voice down and my eyes trained ahead. "You have a strange idea of comfortable."

For his part, McQuade snorted. "You're not bleeding and no one is shooting at you. It could be worse."

"You're not comforting either," I mentioned, tilting my head from one side to the other. The crack of vertebrae releasing tension helped. Some.

"I doubt you want him comforting you." The clipped intonation from Remington's accent gave the words an air of formality that his faint smirk decried. Fucking Brits always sounded elegant even when they were telling you to fuck off.

Biting my tongue was not my favorite activity. First, it fucking hurt. Second, it was boring. Staring at the building I tried to picture the security, the layers, and the locks. The sting of a mosquito biting me again earned another slap.

Why didn't the little bastards bite Cool Duck McQuade and Remington, Brit Remington?

"You should consume more garlic," McQuade said. "You eat too much damn sugar."

"Well, I have to maintain my sweet personality somehow." The quip flowed easily. I could spend months stalking the right information to acquire a piece or casing an installation in order to get inside.

"Well, you might want to try something else," Remington suggested. "Your diet is atrocious."

"Everyone is a critic," I muttered. I dug out the small pack of gum mashed in my pocket. The wintergreen cold released from my first bite was a violent contrast to the mugginess.

"You don't like quiet much," McQuade commented, never taking his gaze off the building. "Do you?"

"Civilian," Remington stated as if it were the answer to everything. That snagged McQuade's attention and the pair shared a look of commiseration.

"Kiss my ass, Lord Rochester of the Household Cavalry Blues and Royals. Not all of us signed up for the honor guard."

Okay, probably a bit snappier than it needed to be, but Remington merely smiled. McQuade's snort of laughter rubbed me the wrong way.

"What are you laughing at? You could have been Delta Force until you received an 'other than honorable' discharge." Which beat the hell out of Dishonorable Discharge. Course, I only knew the bare facts.

"You trying to swipe right on me, Locke?" McQuade's tone remained unruffled.

"Nope. Just letting you know, I do my homework."

"So do I," Remington commented, the clipped British accent in no way disguising his humor. "You don't care that we're military, you just want to see how we'll respond to disdain for the profession."

"Were," I corrected him. Neither was on active duty of any kind. McQuade may go into every kind of hellhole he could find, but he wouldn't be doing it on Uncle Sam's dime. As for the good Lord Rochester, he wasn't in it for Queen—or King for that matter—and country anymore.

"Were, are," McQuade said. "It doesn't matter. What matters is we all do our jobs tonight. That we get Patch back."

"And after?" Because mercenaries and assassins didn't usually stick around after a job.

Then again, neither did thieves. Right now, there wasn't anywhere else I wanted to be.

"Let's get her back first," Remington said.

"Deal with the problems, get her secure, then we see."

Or not, I would suppose. Once we had Patch in the clear, there was no reason for us to work together. Probably better to keep it that way.

"You good with that?" McQuade asked, sparing me a look.

"Yes. I want her back." I slapped another goddamn mosquito. "I'd also like to not catch malaria."

That earned me a huff of laughter from both of them. Then we went quiet and watched. The quiet grated. Because I wanted to move. I wanted to throw caution to the wind and get in there. Break in and steal her back...

I didn't want to compromise her though. Our odds were better after dark.

Didn't make waiting any easier.

Not much coming and going for the next couple of hours. As sundown crept closer, a handful of people left the facility. Not many, but a few.

A couple in suits. Nearly everyone else looked more like a lab rat or tech.

They'd climb in their cars, the vehicles would start, and they'd keep doors open or windows for a couple of hot minutes to let the sweltering air out while their air conditioning kicked in.

Then they would leave.

All in all, by the time the sun had painted the western sky a burnt reddish-orange, and highlighted the scattered clouds in shadows, of the forty some-odd vehicles in the lot, about twenty-five were still there.

"I'm moving," Remington said. "Comms in, but keep them off for now until you're on your way out."

"Copy," McQuade answered. I ignored them both. I got not using comms until we were in the clear or needed clearance. They didn't need me to respond.

Sweat soaked my shirt and I swore I was going to have swamp ass for days. There was no way anyone would miss smelling us if we tried to stay out of sight. Lowering the binoculars, I glanced to where Remington had vanished.

The growing darkness and the ruffling of the grass in the breeze betrayed nothing.

"Get ready to move," McQuade said in a low voice that barely seemed to achieve whisper. "You stay on on my six until we're at the doors. You'll open them, but I go through first. Clear?"

"Clear." No sense in provoking him.

Anticipation sent a chill licking through my veins. I was ready to get in there and get her out. The day of sitting out here in the swelter while we watched had left a profound itch under my skin.

I pulled my pack on, then the crossbody bag with a wide variety of tools. I didn't know what I would need until I needed it.

When the last drops of reddish-orange were barely a line on the horizon, McQuade tapped my arm. "Let's go." He moved like a phantom, but also on a straight trajectory. I'd half-expected lights to turn on in the lot.

They didn't.

Security feature? Malfunction? Didn't matter. It was to our benefit.

I hoped, unless they were motion sensor triggered.

Clasping McQuade's shoulder, I stopped his forward momentum. As he dropped to a crouch, I went with him. I leaned close and mouthed the words more than vocalized them. "Possible motion sensors on the outdoor lights."

Why else have them installed?

McQuade tapped two fingers against my hand. A short-hand version of Morse code.

Understood.

I let go of his shoulder and when he rose, I was right behind him. We took a circuitous route around the lot toward the entrance we'd marked. The whole afternoon, we'd only seen one way in and out.

Not ideal, but it would have to do.

It also gave Remington one spot to mark and clear if necessary.

McQuade was good, I'd give him that. We didn't trigger a single light. Motion sensors or not, we made it all the way to within five yards of the entrance. We were going to have no choice but to pass by one of the lights.

Only instead of continuing forward, McQuade paused and there was a pop of sound. Then another. Then a third. Glass cracked and then came down in a shower of fragments where the pieces bounced against the cracked black pavement. Bullet resistant glass on the lights?

Definitely not an ordinary facility.

He waited another minute then we were on the move again. We passed right by the pole and no lights came on. Hard to turn on when the bulbs were shattered.

All right, I could admit it. McQuade had some talent.

Not that I planned to ever tell him that.

At the door, he gripped the handle and gave it a tug. It was a standard exterior door. No special security. No visible cameras.

That gave me a bad feeling. Still, the interior room at least had something resembling air conditioning, a much heavier door with a keypad and retinal scanner.

Right.

Time to go to work.

EIGHTEEN

PATCH

Resting was a misnomer for lying there on the floor. Yes, I dozed. More because my exhausted and, at this point, depleted body demanded it. The cold stone had no forgiveness for the bruises I wore like a full body tattoo.

Someone came along at one point and splashed water on me. At least I hoped it was water. My sense of smell was pretty skewed. The splash had done what probably little else could have at that moment. It got me to drag myself up, inch by inch, until I made it to the cot next to the wall.

The cot was hardly softer than the floor. I just didn't have to fall as far to land on it. Eyes closing, I dragged an arm up to shield my face and eyes from the overhead lights that they never turned off.

My first hole had been permanent darkness.

This one was permanent light.

Keep the prisoner off-center by creating an

inhospitable environment. I'd tried keeping track of days by the meals. The inconsistent schedules, the long sessions of torture followed by my own collapses, had made time so insubstantial it just slipped through my fingers.

I sagged against the bed. Deep breaths were hard, particularly with how sore my ribs were. The chances they weren't cracked had long since disintegrated to zero. I probably wouldn't notice, except laying flat made it feel even worse.

Hard or not, I needed to work on regular, deep breaths. Maybe if I rolled onto my injured side. That was what they told me back in high school when I cracked two ribs in a car accident.

Seatbelt saved my life, and hurt like a bitch.

Man what I wouldn't give to trade that for now. That had nothing on this. With a groan I couldn't quite suppress, I rolled toward my left side. Since everything was injured, there was no one side that was better than another. I just went with the side that put more of my injuries higher than my heart.

Could help with inflammation.

Maybe the stone had too.

It also angled me toward the bars, where I could observe from beneath the shelter of my arm.

My neighbor had yet to return.

Interesting.

A niggle of guilt crawled out of the debris left by the interrogations and the torture. What if she was a victim in all of this too?

Was it possible?

Yes.

A certainty?

Absolutely not.

Could I afford to risk my freedom on the idea of rescuing her?

No.

I wasn't even sure I could rescue me. If *I* got out, I could possibly contact help to get her out. I had—connections. Maybe not friends, but I had connections and those I could ask for assistance from. But to get that assistance, I needed to be out of here.

I hadn't spent the last few years all alone, isolating myself, only to die in a cell.

I might die on my way out. They could kill me. The escape itself could kill me. Risk I was ready to take. At least the dead told no tales and I wouldn't be able to answer the questions they kept asking.

Laying there, I allowed myself to doze again. Real sleep was impossible. I could pass out. Pain had taken me out a few times. But going to real sleep while I was already vulnerable?

Not an option I was willing to explore. Dozing, however, let me rest and track who came and went. One guard appeared with what looked like it could be a meal. Maybe. In some rustic, far away, fantasy land where they served bread and water.

Wasn't that against the rules of the Geneva Convention?

He didn't say anything or offer me anything, just slid the tray in and left. As dry as my mouth was, I didn't move. On the handful of occasions they'd fed me, that seemed to be a midday meal.

After another interval where I'd lost count of how many seconds because I dozed again. The guard returned. He had another tray with him. I couldn't see the food, but I could smell it.

Meat. Maybe.

I didn't care. He stared at the tray on the floor then over at me before he left without a word. Each time he came and left via different doors, but he used the same code. At least as far as I could see.

This time, I didn't go back to sleep. I started to count the seconds again. Until seconds turned into minutes, and those minutes morphed slowly into an hour.

At the hour mark, I eased my way off the cot. I could have gotten to my feet, but I crawled over to the food and the water. The trembling in my limbs required no effort on my part. Gripping the water, I lifted it to smell. It smelled clean.

No taint.

Still, I stuck a finger in it, then took it out and waited. If there were drugs—I might get a skin reaction. The bread was just—never mind. Crusty and stale, nothing about it was appetizing. Bread and water used to be considered a humane form of punishment.

A step up from flogging.

How...nice for me.

As it was, I finally rinsed the water around my

mouth. Just enough to help moisten and then as much as I wanted to drink it, I spat it out. Well, let it dribble out.

I hadn't spotted any cameras, didn't mean they weren't there. But I could only hope watching me had been exceptionally boring enough that my audience went to sleep.

If not, then I needed to move.

Once I got to my feet, there was no stopping until I was free or I was dead.

I rinsed my mouth twice more, then let it dribble out. It soaked the bra I wore. I'd been in my office when they came for me. My clothes had barely survived them taking me. They hadn't survived my incarceration. They'd torn out the gusset of my panties, but these were still on. So weird and I really didn't care.

Nudity was the least of my problems.

When I hit twenty minutes in my head, I "knocked over" the water cup and spilled the rest. Then I crawled over to the cell bars and bit by bit, pulled myself up.

When I reached the combination lock, I entered the code with shaking fingers. The faint buzz as it released made me want to sob.

One down.

Moving slow as hell, I headed for the door on the far side. They always took me left for interrogation. I did not want to go that way. The lack of windows meant I had to rely on what I could remember for navigation.

The code entered into the keypad next to the door. It buzzed and the locks released. I'd probably be crying for real if I wasn't so dehydrated. As it was, I couldn't even feel the tears forming.

The door pushed outward and I stared into the hall. Cooler air rushed in and it gave me the first taste of something fresher in days. There was a cold bite to the rush of air. Fresh enough that my own stench threatened to bludgeon me.

Tiles like ice beneath my feet helped numb the pain in them, even as it kept me awake and on the move. The hallway was so damn ordinary and unremarkable. No symbols. No addresses Nothing to betray what was here or where.

The first door had a window to glance through in order to stare into the room. The other side was dark, no movement, no light. Nothing.

The next one had a light. It was a cell.

Okay, so I'd probably been in one of these before they took me into the other room. The room was all odd misshapen stones, like it had been carved out of the rock. The door probably looked different on the inside.

Right.

Couldn't care about them.

I was almost to the end of the hall when I heard the sound of an elevator. Adrenaline flooded my system. There was the pick me up I needed.

With nowhere else to hide, I tried the nearest door *after* a swift glance inside. It was empty. The lights on low.

Inside, I gripped the handle to keep it from re-securing then pressed myself against the wall.

The doors cut off most sound. But a shadow of their passing flickered over the window.

I didn't remember a window in the door to my cell. It might have been there, but I had no idea.

Heart thudding, I counted to sixty then stole a peek through the window. I couldn't see anyone.

Didn't mean they couldn't be in the cell right next door.

The thunder of my heart gonged like a bass marching drum. The beat increased, the sound so loud in my ears, it was making me lightheaded.

Another sixty seconds was all I could give myself. The surge of adrenaline helped, but the crash was going to be so much more brutal. Testing the door, I pulled it open slowly. A peek out revealed—no one.

I could have wept. Closing the door as quietly as I could, I hurried up the hallway in the direction of the elevator I'd heard. The hall continued past the elevators toward—whatever.

Did I need to go up or down?

I had *no* idea where the hell I was. I could be a mile underground or in the top of a skyscraper. Not for the first time, I'd kill for an actual window.

Up?

Down?

Fifty-fifty chance of being right.

I flipped a mental coin.

Tails.

I hit the down button.

Now, I just had to pray no one was in the elevator. The faintest sound of whirring had me twisting to look back. There was a camera. The red light on top of it was on.

Yeah. Couldn't care about that.

The doors opened and the empty elevator was frighteningly anti-climactic.

Inside, my breath coming in shallow pants, I looked at the control pad.

We were on level three.

There was a one and a four.

There was also a G.

Ground.

I pressed the G.

A keypad lit up.

Entering the code, I closed my eyes as I pressed enter. It wasn't like closing my eyes and looking away would make it work any better than if I just hit enter. Didn't matter. I needed it to work.

"One more time," I murmured, clinging to the wall. "Just one more time." I entered the number and hit enter.

The elevator moved.

Holy shit. My heart was in my mouth, but we were descending toward G.

G had to mean ground. What *else* could it mean?

Get fucked?

Some dark, macabre part of my brain enjoyed delivering that a little too much. A shiver raced over my skin as the elevator slowed to a stop. The hesitation before the doors opened seemed to last an eternity.

The soft "chime" was so innocuous and yet I still jerked when it sounded. The doors opened to another floor that looked like a lobby, but they still didn't have windows.

Fuck, I hated these people.

Charging out, I headed for what I hoped were the exit doors. The quivering in my soul reverberated through my frame. I half-stumbled as I left the elevator. There was nothing to catch myself on.

An alarm bleated to life overhead and all the lights went red.

No.

No. No. No. No.

The sound of the klaxon threatened to split open my skull. I made it another staggering step and there was a man there. A guard.

No.

He seized my arm and went to wrench it behind me. I twisted with the movement. I didn't have the strength to shake him off. So I just let gravity work, as I tangled my legs with his and tried to pull him down.

Not that it proved successful, he caught me with a backhand before he wrenched me to my feet. I swore I was dangling with just my tiptoes touching the floor. When he shook me, I wanted to scream.

Another blow, then he slammed me against the wall. The impact knocked all the air out of me. My ribs screamed. My body screamed. My voice died.

Nothing came out as I raked my jagged,

broken fingernails across his face. He swore, one hand locking around my throat as he banged my head on the wall. He drew back his other fist...

Then a bullet ripped through his skull, tearing it apart and spattering me with blood. The fist on my throat went slack along with his expression and then he collapsed.

I still couldn't make a sound as the klaxon kept shrieking and I turned my head to where the bullet came from.

Impossible.

"Get her," McQuade snapped as he strode forward, gun raised. Then it was firing. The sound a staccato counterpoint to the wild beat of my heart. Men coming out of the elevator went down, blood speckling the walls behind them.

Or at least I thought it was blood. The red lights made it hard.

A hand brushed my bare arm and I turned to find Locke standing right there.

Locke.

McQuade.

What the hell were they doing here?

How were they here?

"Hey, Patch," he said, flicking a glance past me before sliding my arm up and over his shoulder. "My turn to watch your ass."

They were really here.

This wasn't a trick?

Then a faint smile curved Locke's lips. "Talk to me?"

"Later Romeo, get Sugar Bear and let's get the fuck out of here." McQuade was in front of me again. His dark eyes swept me over from head to toe. "Then I'm coming back here and killing every single one of them."

Good plan.

"I'm going to pass out now," I managed. "Sorry."

Then I dropped.

CHAPTER

NINETEEN

REMINGTON

The patience of the sniper lay in the ability to wait minutes, hours, days, and weeks if necessary for the shot. I could wait an eternity if necessary.

There was a moment of perfect peace found in the seconds between heartbeats, in lining up the target and squeezing the trigger. Profound tranquility that lasts microseconds.

As the hot sticky air wrapped around me like a cocoon, I settled into place. My gun was cool against my fingers. The scope let me isolate my field of vision as necessary. One by one, I cataloged the night sounds and began to eliminate them.

The buzzing of the insects.

The croaking of the frogs.

The singing of nightbirds.

The faint lap of the water.

A distant splash.

Each one identified, then muted. If the sound

changed or shifted in some way, I'd notice then. Until then, I didn't need to be distracted. Sweat trickled down my face. A thin line of Vaseline across my brows kept the perspiration from finding its way into my eyes.

While I settled into place, McQuade and Locke crossed the cracked, dilapidated parking lot that seemed more suited to a strip mall along an interstate than some secret installation.

Then again, black sites never looked like black sites. That was the point.

I studied the lot through my scope. The cameras. They had to have them, just camouflaged well. Nearing the muddy yellow glow cast by one of the lights illuminating the lot, McQuade fired three times before the glass broke and the light went out.

He wasn't that bad of a shot. Bullet resistant glass used for outdoor lights? If we weren't already certain the sketchy nature of the location, that would have confirmed it. They were in the first door swiftly after the glass came down.

I debated going ahead and taking out the rest of the lights, but the destruction of the first didn't seem to alert security. I marked the locations for ease of targeting later, then went back to overwatch on the door.

My awareness submerged, letting me process the sounds around me as I eliminated the ones I didn't need in order to listen for the ones I did. A car motor approaching? A shift in the breeze? Movement in the water?

Anything that could interfere with me doing my job—I was their exit plan. Time ceased to have any meaning for me. I didn't need to count the seconds or worry about the passage of time.

Not yet, anyway.

McQuade was excellent at infiltration as well as search and rescue. He had enough skills to assist should Patch be injured. It would do the other occupants of this building a favor if she was in perfect health when she was found.

Locke might not have the weapons training, but he possessed computer savvy and the ability to bypass *locks* and other security measures. Based on an assessment of our skills, they were the ideal partnership to go in.

Just as I was the one who would make sure their exit was not compromised. Minutes trickled together. At the fifteen minute mark, I registered it and gave myself a brief thirty seconds to roll my head from side to side. Then resumed watch.

Just one minute before the thirty-minute mark everything went to hell. The distant sound of an alarm seemed muffled and the air even heavier. Skating my tongue over my lower lip, I held position.

The alarm could have nothing to do with them.

It could have everything to do with them.

We had one fallback plan if it went to hell. That involved me going for more backup to retrieve her since they would likely be dead.

Nice plan.

It would take too long. I also had more faith in McQuade than Locke did. Or maybe I just understood him better. Both men wanted Patch back. While we may only intersect on that one point, in the Venn diagram of our acquaintance, it was enough to make me trust them and value their retrieval as well as hers.

My internal stop-watch began the countdown. I barely made it past six minutes and the outer door banged open releasing the sound of the alarm which blared even louder, the pop of gunfire, and Locke moving at a dead run with a woman in his arms.

Relief flickered to life within me before I cut away from them to the door McQuade backed out of. He was still firing his gun, then he tossed something before he hauled ass.

The flash-bang went off inside. Seemed almost too easy to pick off the guards who came stumbling out.

Then again, they came *out* which meant they were going down. I had zero intentions of letting anyone recover to pursue them.

Pop.

Down the first one went.

Pop.

The second.

Pop. Pop.

Third and fourth.

Pop.

Pop. Pop. Pop.

Let them serve as a warning to the others

who might follow. The alarm suddenly sounded outside, the muddy light went spotlight bright and the lamps seemed to rotate position. They were going to use the light to reveal where Locke and McQuade went with Patch.

I thought not.

Pop. Pop. Pop.

The .308 worked her magic. The lights extinguished as fast as their flare could expand. One went down in a shower of bursting glass and hot wires. When the last one was out, I targeted the door.

Three men had made it out during the distraction. I winged the one farthest forward as he dove for cover before taking headshots on the other two. Their survival rate would go up if they halted pursuit.

The idiots inside seemed to finally get the picture that coming out through their single chokepoint was a dumb idea.

Excellent. I switched weapons, taking the reprieve to launch a few grenades toward the lot. They had to have other vehicles elsewhere or they were bussing in their guards. Cause they had way more people exiting than the vehicles would have accounted for.

My phone buzzed in my back pocket as I reclaimed my rifle. My winged man didn't let the grenades flush him out. Ice in his veins.

I could respect that.

Another two buzzes. They had Patch at the vehicle. Extraction imminent.

As much as I'd like to play with this shooting gallery, it was time to go. I broke down the guns and repacked them without breaking cover. Then I hugged the weapons bag and rolled down the slight slope toward the water.

I didn't go all the way, I didn't have time to deal with the local reptiles. Once I was lower, I rose to my feet and began to run. We'd parked nearly two kilometers away and used the local flora for cover.

They wouldn't leave the grove until I was in sight. With no lights from the parking lot and clouds having gradually rolled in during the day, I didn't need to move with the shadows. The whole world was a shadow and my eyes had adjusted.

At less than half a klick away something hot creased my side and I pivoted, siting the muzzle flash in the dark as another bullet whistled so perilously close to my head that I felt the heat of it.

I fired in rapid succession and heard the grunt and collapse of my pursuer.

Then I was running again. Adrenaline sang through me, giving me the speed I needed. McQuade had a gun pointed at me as I descended into the copse.

He nodded and then motioned to the passenger seat. Then he was starting the car. This was the moment where everything could go wrong. I slid my rifle bag into the back and flicked a look at Patch. I couldn't see anything except long hair escaping the blanket she'd been wrapped in. There was an IV in, already attached to her hand.

McQuade worked fast. Gun in hand, I pulled my seatbelt on. I needed to focus on shooting, not flying out of my seat. As it was, I put the shoulder strap behind me so the lap belt was all that remained. She was with us and safe. I could do a full assessment once we were clear of these assholes.

"Secure?" McQuade checked, his gaze on the rearview mirror.

"Secure," Locke answered.

"Stay down and cover her." McQuade said nothing else as he put his foot down and the vehicle climbed back onto the road. We had no headlights and all the interior lights were turned down.

A moving target was harder to hit, especially if you couldn't see it. The only problem we had was I *could* hit one I could hear. There was no muffling the engine.

Silence filled the vehicle as McQuade accelerated down the road. I kept one eye on the side mirror. The flames from the fires behind us quickly vanished, swallowed by the darkness.

That didn't mean they weren't tracking us.

Tracking her.

Fifteen minutes later, we transferred her into a different vehicle along with the weapons and gear before dousing this one and setting it on fire. I didn't care if the exterior survived. Destroying the interior would destroy DNA evidence.

It was also my first chance to get a look at

Patch. She seemed—tinier than I'd expected. Blonde hair tipped by dark strands like she was letting a dye job grow out added a hint of goth to her.

Or maybe that was the violent paleness to her. If not for the fact her chest rose and fell, I'd be more worried about her stillness. She'd already emptied one banana bag and Locke hung another while I watched.

Thankfully, our second vehicle was loaded with what we needed. The ambulance came fully equipped. The markings all indicated Crimson Stripe Rescues, a nonprofit that deployed to disaster areas in the U.S. These vehicles were familiar in flood zones, forest fires, and landslides or in the wake of hurricanes and devastating tornadoes.

The U.S. certainly possessed a creative variety of natural disasters. McQuade was behind the wheel again. Though he also now sported a red uniform. Troubling to be so brightly colored, but I slid into the back with Locke and pulled out the scanners.

"ETA?" I checked. We were leaving Louisiana.

"Four hours," McQuade answered over his shoulder. "I can make it faster, but we'll attract more attention than we want."

That didn't require a response, so I didn't answer. Instead, I ran the scanner over Patch and examined the injuries we could see.

Cigarette burns.

Ligature marks on her wrists and around her

throat. The ones on her wrists included deeper lacerations, and scabbed over wounds.

Bruises littered her face, one cheek was swollen and there was definite inflammation around her right eye. Her fingers were...

I reached for her right hand and didn't think anything about it as I popped the fingers back into place one at a time. Locke winced.

"Fuckers."

"Agreed."

She didn't even twitch. They'd focused their torture—dislocating rather than breaking. Burns instead of scalding. The bruises on her face? Painful but not debilitating.

"We'll need to check her other joints as soon as we're fully secure." We couldn't afford to do it right now. The scanner let out a little wah-wah as I passed it over her.

It wasn't until Locke eased her over to tuck her against his chest that I found it. The "clothes" she wore were mostly a collection of rags with a seam.

Her bare ass showed more bruises, long, deep stripes likely created by a cane. They marred down her legs too. I cataloged it and added it to the tab of the people who'd taken her.

"Found one."

"They fucking tagged her like an animal." Locke's knuckles were white, but he braced her with his arms and kept his hands off her.

That was exactly what they'd done. I got a small scalpel out and a kit with some lidocaine. I could at least numb the area before I removed it. I had no idea how deep it was.

The vehicle bounced as I drew up the lidocaine and I spared a glance at Locke who glared toward the cab.

"Keep it smooth and steady, he's got to cut something out of her."

"Understood."

He'd do his best. We all would.

"You got her?" I checked with Locke.

He nodded sharply, a little jerky in his motions.

"A little stick," I murmured to her. She deserved to know what I was doing. Injecting the lidocaine, I gave her some time for it to start working before I traced the barely closed incision line they'd left behind.

Fortunately, I didn't have to go too deep to get the tracker. I put it to the side, then closed her up, careful to use skin glue to seal it, then applied butterfly bandages before I taped it up.

Done, I stripped off the gloves before I helped Locke settle her back onto the gurney. She was out. Her expression hadn't even changed. With care, I checked her pulse. It was rapid.

That was good, right?

"What else is in the IV bag?"

"Not much, but saline," Locke said. "She looks dehydrated, cracked lips and open wounds on her fingertips. But we have no idea if she's allergic to anything."

I glanced to the lidocaine and sighed. "I probably shouldn't have used it."

"Maybe."

"Lidocaine allergies are extremely rare," Mc-Quade called from the front. "We have epinephrine onboard so we can do something about it. For now, it'll have to do."

Yeah. It would. I went back to work, packing away the medical supplies before I dropped the tracker into a thermos and sealed it up.

"We need to dump this," I called up to him.

"Already looking for a good spot."

Fifteen minutes later, we left a rest area with the truck pulling out behind us now carrying the tracker in a thermos secured beneath it. Mc-Quade didn't stay with that road and diverted more toward an interstate now so we could move faster.

Through it all, Patch hadn't even twitched. I found myself studying her again in the flickers of light now that we'd turned off the lights in the back. The slope of her brow where it wasn't beaten. The curve of her lips. The lack of expression—or at least the utter stillness of her expression—didn't sit well with me.

Patch was one of the most vibrant people I'd ever heard.

She should be the same in person. That her light had been so dimmed was on them.

"Did we figure out who they were?"

"No," Locke answered, in a voice that seemed as troubled as my soul. "We didn't have time. She was trying to get out when we got in."

I paused. "You're sure this is her?"

"She recognized us," Locke said. "I saw it in

her eyes—they're gray by the way, if you were wondering. But she knew who *we* were."

"She spoke," McQuade added. "She said 'I'm going to pass out now.'"

"It was rough and she hurts," Locke confirmed. "But it's her. It's our Patch."

Right. Good.

We had her.

TWENTY

PATCH

"You're a special kind of irritating," McQuade groused. "How has someone not shot you yet?"

"I assure you, some have tried. They missed." Locke sounded almost bored.

"You realize I don't miss, right? I could just as easily shoot you right now." The complaint in McQuade's voice was all bluster. As irked as he sounded, there was a kind of gruff amusement present too. I'd heard it often enough when he'd been in the middle of some firefight he actually *enjoyed.*

Odd man.

"I'm sure you know a wide variety of ways to injure me, Mr. McQuade." Locke's retort was all him, sass intact. "That doesn't excuse bad table manners or the fact you made a huge mess in the kitchen and didn't clean it up."

"The pair of you resemble one of those old married couples on television." Remy...

He's with them, too?

How?

"Married couples?" McQuade snapped. "What are you talking about, *mate*?"

"I'm talking about those old sitcoms where the couple bickers constantly." Remy didn't bother to hide his amusement, it filled every crisp syllable. "I told you, don't call me mate."

Surfacing from under dark water, I had to shove myself upward. I wasn't sure what hurt more, my arms or my legs. Why was I even swimming? I could just sink back below the waves...

"I think he means Odd Couple," Locke suggested. "Though for the record, they weren't married."

McQuade actually snorted. "The old black and white with Jack Klugman? Yeah, they acted married."

"Black and white?" Locke sounded puzzled. "How *old* are you?— Ow."

"Behave gentlemen," Remy said, his tone casual. "I don't want to have to separate you."

Their voices filled the darkness, chasing away some of the pain. If I woke fully, would I still hear them? Were these snippets of memories merely relics left behind to taunt me, a bait and switch as it were. When I opened my eyes, would I be right back in my cell awaiting a new day's torture?

I didn't want to wake up if that were the truth. It might be better if I were dead. They'd never get what they were looking for if I died.

"Tell you what, Your Lordship, we gave the Brits the boot a few centuries ago." You could practically hear the smirk in Locke's voice.

"Clearly," Remy stated. "It's why you Americans cannot consume enough media about the royals and crave all things James Bond."

"It's the accent," McQuade deadpanned.

"I'd think it was the gadgets," Locke countered.

The dangerous notes had dropped out of their voices, the humor and familiarity rushing in to replace them. The oddness didn't fit. They didn't know each other at all as far as I knew. They didn't know who my other clients were and I never shared information about them with the others.

So how the hell did they know each other...

Were they now in the cells too?

Fear galvanized me, yanking the shroud of sleep away as I burst upward and opened my eyes. The room around me was dark, though there were nightlights on at two different points adding a dim bluish-tinged glow that didn't bother my eyes.

I was in a bed. An actual bed and the air smelled like pine and lemon cleaner. There was that detergent scent you got from fresh sheets—like the one laying over me.

"The gadgets were cool," McQuade admitted. "Though the idea of a watch laser is fucking stupid. He had a gun, most of the time, he only needed the gun."

"I could think of times that a laser would be useful." Locke's musing aloud was him. "Still, I preferred Pierce Brosnan to Timothy Dalton."

"Brosnan was fine," McQuade said. "He did smarmy Brit real well."

"He's Irish," Remy corrected.

"Well, you'd know—*Remington*." Locke sounded downright gleeful.

"My name is amusing because of a character that Brosnan played. Well done," Remy said. "I would applaud you, but it wasn't that funny."

"Everyone's a critic," Locke exhaled. "Should we check on her again?"

They were here and I was in a bedroom of some kind. Was this some new torture? I pushed back the sheet and had to halt at the pinch and pull on my right hand. Peering in the darkness, I could just make out the glow of the lights reflecting on the hint of tape.

As my eyes adjusted rapidly, I explored the spot with the fingers of my left hand. It was an IV. They'd put an IV in. There was tubing stretching out into the darkness.

Moving in that direction, slowly, I found a metal stand that seemed to be serving as something to hang the IV on. As I traced my fingers up. I located the bag. Okay, so IV in, and there was a bag attached.

My bladder protested after a prolonged moment and I gripped the tape carefully. Then in one movement pealed it back and took the IV out. My hand ached from the contact and I needed to put pressure on it for blood.

Shit, there was nothing handy so I just pushed off the bed and studied the room around me.

Please have an ensuite bathroom.
Please have an ensuite bathroom.

The mental chant went up like a prayer, but there was a hint of blue light reflecting back at me and I almost collapsed as I let go of the bed. It was like every ache and pain in my body rushed in to lodge their complaints all at once.

Irritation shivered through me like a colony of ants spilling out of their hill. I half-stumbled, half-walked into the bathroom and pushed the door closed.

I flipped on a light and winced at the brightness. The image that greeted me in the mirror looked like a horror story. Not that my bladder gave a damn.

Right, I needed to pee.

I had on an oversized shirt that hit me mid-thigh. It was clean and soft. I also didn't have on any panties. I flipped the toilet lid up, semi-marveling that the toilet *had* a lid and then sat down a lot harder than I meant to as my legs gave out.

I winced when I hit the seat but then I was peeing and the relief...

Well that was next level.

Eyes closed, I bowed my head and tried to make sense of my thoughts. Wherever I was, it was not that cell or the one I'd been in before. This place felt like a house or a residence.

I glanced around. The towels were too thick and plush to be a random hotel. Didn't—smell like one either. Business finished, I flushed and then went to wash my hands. The feeling of water sluicing over my skin ignited an itch everywhere.

I needed a shower so bad. I stared at myself in the mirror again. Dark bruises overlaid faded ones. The mottled coloring of blue and black couldn't hide the green and yellow.

Hands washed, I reached for a toothbrush that was sealed in its packet. Opening it took a minute. My nails were a wreck of jagged pieces and missing altogether on two of them. Right, I couldn't think about that. There was toothpaste and a toothbrush.

Getting my mouth clean had never felt so good. I leaned heavily against the counter by the time I was done, but I wanted to shower. I'd just gotten the water started when there was a knock at the door.

I damn near jumped out of my skin. The sudden slam of my heart against my ribs hurt. Thankfully, I didn't scream.

"Yes?" I said. Oh good, my voice didn't quiver.

"Hey, Patch." Locke. "You're up."

"So it seems."

"How you doing, Sugar Bear?" McQuade.

"TBD," I said. "I need a shower. Bad."

"You steady enough to do that?" Remy. All three of them right there on the other side of the door.

"I don't know," I said, deciding against a lie or a quip. "But I need one and before this all turns into a nightmare again, I want to have one."

"You're safe," Locke said. "There's a shower

chair in there. Use it. One of us will stay right out here and if you need help, just call."

Reasonable even. I traced my fingers up over my face to my scalp. Everything was too sensitive. It either hurt, pinched, felt like a sunburn, or throbbed.

I was alive.

It hurt too damn much to not be.

But I was alive. I survived.

The shock of it rippled through me. Then before I could let anything distract me again, I stripped off the shirt and moved to climb into the shower.

There was indeed a chair and I wasn't too proud to not use it. I lingered under the hot water until I'd scrubbed my hair and conditioned it. There were knots everywhere. Some of it was missing in places—they'd yanked out whole hunks at times.

When my hair was done, I went to work running soap over my arms and legs. I had bruises everywhere. I could feel them too. The burns on my arms stung when the soap hit them. A blister had burst near my wrist, but I just kept washing.

I lifted my right leg to brace my ankle against my left knee to wash my foot and grimaced. The bottom of my foot looked like it had been hit with a meat tenderizer. It took more than a minute to wash cause everything stung.

Eventually, though, I had to have achieved clean skin, but I just sat there under the water, letting it rinse over me. Even though it looked clear, I didn't feel clean.

I wasn't even sure I felt better.

I couldn't hide in here forever. Drying off proved a whole new challenge. I'd opened up some cuts on my feet when I'd cleaned them and there was actually a bandage on my ass.

While I needed to ask about that, it would be later. There was a brush and comb in with the other toiletries awaiting me. I perched on the toilet lid wrapped in towel while I worked out the snarled ends. Not all of them came free but the conditioner had helped a lot.

Maybe it would work if I combed it with the conditioner next time.

I'd worry about that later.

There were no more clothes for me to change into except the shirt so I tugged it on and then had to grip the counter to get the towel hung up. Every step was fresh fire to my feet.

Dammit.

"Who's out there?"

"Just me," Locke said. "Told you I'd wait."

"Won the coin toss?" I swiped at the nonexistent tears on my face.

"Something like that. You okay?" Then he paused. "You know, that was a stupid question."

"No," I said softly. "It wasn't. It was a kind question. And no, I'm not okay."

As much as I wanted to walk out there under my own steam, I couldn't. I'd end up collapsing or maybe I'd do even more damage to my feet.

"Can you help me?"

The door opened and nudged inward before I'd even finished asking. Locke filled the doorway and I stared up at him. Knowing his stats and seeing him via surveillance cameras really didn't do him justice.

Justus. Justice.

I almost laughed at my inadvertent pun.

He frowned as he gave me a once over, then he narrowed his eyes. "You're bleeding again."

"Yeah," I said.

"Arms around my neck," he ordered, and while it came out a little gruff, he didn't wait for me to comply as he picked me up.

Warm amber and musk with hints of citrus filled my nostrils. It was pure seduction to my senses after too long in the filth, the blood, and the pain. I wanted to roll in him and just wrap myself up in that sweetness.

The bridal hold was almost sweet except now my naked ass was hanging out. With care, I held onto him. Even my fingers hurt. Every inch did.

"Please tell me there are panties somewhere."

"I'll find you something." He didn't pause in the bedroom, instead he carried me right out into what looked like an open concept living room in a log cabin.

Where the hell was I?

This was definitely *not* where they'd been holding me.

Remington left the kitchen as we came out, his expression fierce. "What happened?"

"Why the fuck is she bleeding again?" McQuade charged over from wherever he'd been. Locke answered neither of them, carrying me right into the kitchen and setting me on the counter.

Holy shit that was cold, but it was also bracing and sent a pulse of wakefulness to my exhausted brain.

"She's opened the cuts on her feet." Locke was already returning with a first aid box.

"Let me look," McQuade ordered, then wrapped his huge hand around my ankle and raised my leg. At this rate, I was going to be giving all of them a free show. "We can't stitch these," he said.

"Skin glue," Remington said, his tone firm and unyielding. While Locke and McQuade dug into the bag, Remington claimed my right hand and lifted it. "It's lovely to meet you finally, Patch."

The surreality of it all swarmed me. "How the hell do you guys even know each other?"

"Well," Locke said as he dragged a stool over to begin gluing the wounds on my foot closed. "That's a bit of a story."

"Care for tea?" Remy offered.

"She prefers coffee," McQuade argued.

"The right coffee," Locke said. "Which we don't have here. But the brewed stuff will do in a pinch. Right?"

"I can get that started," Remy offered, then kissed my hand gently. "You must be hungry."

I couldn't quite process all of it. They were all in action. Remy moved to brew a fresh pot of coffee, taking the warmth of his nearness away.

McQuade stood like a great big thundercloud,

arms folded as he glared down at Locke as though he were ready to end him should he make the wrong move.

Locke ignored him, treating my foot with absolute care like he'd shown when handling priceless, precious objects. I'd seen him in action, I recognized it.

They really were all here. Their presence filled the entirety of the space, electric and intoxicating. There was no escaping them.

"Please," I said.

"What do you need to know, Sugar Bear?" The smirk on McQuade's face was firmly in place, but his eyes—the honey color of them almost a promise—were intense and focused. He seemed to latch onto me with his gaze, an anchor in the turbulent storm I found myself in.

I was Alice, I'd fallen into the looking glass and plunged all the way through the depths of hell and now I was—where?

Wonderland?

Purgatory?

So many questions.

Too many.

"I need to know what's going on... How do you know each other? How did you find me? What...fuck, what day is it?"

CHAPTER
TWENTY-ONE

MCQUADE

The delicate warrior perched on the kitchen counter while Locke doctored the wounds on her feet demanded all of my attention. A storm brewed in her deep gray eyes. The kind of storm where most men would need to seek shelter.

For some reason, whenever we'd talked, I'd pictured them as blue. Like a summer sky, but they were the color of lead and steel. Dark, and turbulent. They absolutely suited the warrior whose gaze kept moving, assessing, and searching for answers.

She let out a hiss of sound and Locke flicked a look up. "Sorry, almost done."

"It's okay," she assured him, white knuckling her way through the treatment. She was in pain. Assholes had done a real number on her.

Locke used care and an economy of motion to tend to each cut before he layered gauze against the bottom of her right foot and sealed it into place. Finished with the first, he worked on her left foot.

"Are you hungry?" Remington asked. It was the question I should have asked. Dammit.

"I haven't had a lot to eat in days," she admitted in a voice that gained in strength each time she used it. A voice that normally held soothing strength, confidence, and sass to keep me in line.

That something broken had etched a mark even on her voice ignited a raw kind of fury in me. Remington seemed remarkably cold despite his dedication to finding her. Suited the sniper. Locke seemed to be managing to keep his temper in check.

Me? I just wanted to put my fist through a wall. Or better, go back to the installation and drop enough C4 down the shafts until it crushed everyone inside or flushed them out.

Either would work for me.

For now, I moved to the other bedroom. There were two beds in here and only one in the room we'd left for her. In the two-bedroom cabin, it was clear we would need to balance watch with rest. One of us could sleep while the other two kept watch.

Depending on how long we were here. But we couldn't keep driving without doing a full assessment of her injuries and treating them. Unzipping my bag, I dug down through the clean clothes until I found the heavily insulated socks.

Beneath those were a pair of old sweatpants with a drawstring that I'd cut the ends off of years ago. They worked for sleeping in. The fabric was worn to total softness. I liked the damn things too much to toss out.

Never really thought I'd need them for someone else, but they'd cover Patch's ass. None of us had anything resembling *panties*. The last thing it occurred to me to grab for her at her place was her clothes.

After stalking back out to the kitchen, I arrived as Remington set a steaming mug of coffee next to her and Locke packed away the medical supplies. She had just reached a trembling hand for the cup when I held up a finger.

I needed to not focus on why her expression tightened or her knuckles had gone white. Even more, I needed to not think about what they'd done to elicit this reaction from her. For now, I packed it away because her condition made me homicidal enough.

"Socks," I told her holding them up and setting the shorts on the counter next to her. With care, I pulled the thick socks over her feet and up her legs. She grimaced despite how gentle I'd tried to be. "Sorry." The gruff word popped out.

"You didn't hurt me," she said, her raw voice scraping across me. "I just realized my legs haven't been waxed in forever."

I paused, glanced at the baby fine hairs that I hadn't even registered. With a shrug, I flicked a look up to catch her weak smile. "They look fine to me."

Her skin was soft too. But that was a conversation for another day. Once I had the socks on her, I held up the cutoff sweatpants.

"Not quite panties, but they will cover your ass and the drawstring can keep them up."

The tremulous smile, while faltering, was the first real glimmer of improvement I'd seen.

"Will you help me?" The fact she even needed to ask told me more than anything, we had some work to do.

"Yes." I didn't dress it up in flowery words or dip it in sugar. She was already rallying, on her feet,—despite all her obvious injuries—and ready to plan. While I wouldn't be opposed to coddling her, I didn't think she'd appreciate it.

Rather than let Locke or Remington help, I tugged the shorts up her legs. When they were most of the way up, I gripped her waist and raised my brows. At her nod, I lifted and she tugged the shorts all the way up. Once she had the tie fastened, I carried her right out of the kitchen and into the living room.

"Bringing coffee," Remington announced as he followed us. He waited while I set her on the sofa and then Locke tugged one of the throw blankets over her legs.

I took a seat on the other end of the sofa. That left the guys with the pair of armchairs or the loveseat to choose from. I could have moved, but I didn't want to. After handing over Patch's coffee to her, Remington set empty mugs on the table then filled one for me, Locke, and himself.

"Thank you," Patch said and there was more ease there. Clothes helped. Showering helped.

Coffee would help. Reclaiming her sense of self and power would also help.

Vengeance would help all of us.

"You're welcome," Remington said, taking a seat on the chair nearest her while Locke took the loveseat. We were all circling her in gradually decaying orbits. It was enough.

For now.

"You wanted to be briefed," Locke said without preamble or avoidance. In our respective worlds, information was power, gossip was currency, and ignorance a death sentence. We did her no favors holding back.

"Yes, please." She took a sip of her coffee and it transformed her whole expression to something resembling orgasmic. Not something I should have focused on so I down a mouthful of the bitter brew. It definitely braced a body.

Glancing from Locke to Remington then to Patch, I realized they were all waiting for me to start. "I finished my last mission, took me a few days to get clear where I could call in. You didn't answer." I lifted my shoulders, because the fact she didn't answer was a clarion call to battle. "It took me some time to work up the transport, but I headed back—immediately."

"Similarly," Remington stated. "Your lack of answer alerted me to an issue. It took some time and resources, but I made my way to the States and Colorado."

"Same," Locke said. "Probably shouldn't admit that I'd been filing away little things you said and did, but—finding you was more important than personal privacy. I knew some people, had some sources. Did some tracking. The fact all three of us were looking though, created some conflicts."

While locating her place in Estes Park shouldn't have been so easy, I doubt it would have been without our personal knowledge of her. Our skills. The horror crossing her expression as we detailed finding her place and I found the first kernel of regret in having violated her privacy.

"I'd apologize," I told her. "But finding you was more important than maintaining distance. As it is, I am sorry it took us as long as it did to track *you*. First, we had to find out who'd taken you and that—required more than what we all knew. We found the signs of a struggle—and the drives you kept as backup."

"None of us were altogether keen on sharing, but the fact that potential assassins tried to elim-inate us on the same evening told me we'd irked someone." The faint note of smugness in Rem-ington's tone was deserved. We had, in fact, been targeted. He had also been the one who warned both Locke and myself.

"Chances were they picked us up at your house," Locke said with no more apology in his voice than I'd offered. "Makes sense that whoever took you would want to know if a cleanup team would come after them."

Expecting a trap and triggering a trap were two different things. The fact the trap had with-drawn to hit us *after* we separated also said they weren't prepared to deal with us as a group. It could also suggest they weren't clear on our alliances.

Wise.

We weren't clear on them. Except where Patch was concerned. As Locke picked up the threads of the story, including invading the MD Outfitters facility to get data and to search through their files, I kept my gaze on her.

She cradled the coffee mug in her palms, almost self-soothing if I were to guess. It was taking me some time to reconcile this damaged wisp of a woman to the vibrant warrior who'd tracked me through war zones. The confidence she wore like a cape, wreathing her voice in the kind of siren song I needed when I'd had to wade into fields of blood.

Despite the "fragility" brought on by the dark smudges beneath her eyes, the tautness to her lips, and the way her hands continued to white knuckle even as she forced herself to calm, I would never mistake the very gentle and feminine air of her for anything other than the definitive badass she was.

"That brought us to the swamp," I said, catching the threads easily. "We worked out a plan. Remy to cover our exit, I would go in and handle the muscle while Locke took care of their security—you managed to undercut that plan by already being on your way out."

"Sorry," she murmured with the wryest of expressions. "Not sorry."

No, I didn't expect her to be sorry. "Survival is

always the first rule." For just a moment, our gazes locked and I read the absolute understanding in her eyes. Of course she understood. She'd been my first call after I'd gotten out of a prison in some backwater where a miscalculation landed me for three weeks.

I'd been tortured then too.

I understood the shadows drifting in and out of her gaze. They would be there for a while. They might not ever go away. Killing every single person that laid a finger on her might help.

But it was a plan for another day. Right now, however... "We need to know who it was that had you. That was a black site. Covert. No identifiable marks. Tucked away from prying eyes."

The level of security alone suggested government if not military contractors.

"I'm more interested in why the three of you decided to work together," she said. "You are all far more likely to be loners..."

"You say that like it's a bad thing," Locke said, smiling for the first time since this conversation began. "We are civilized."

"Are you?" The challenge rolled off her tongue in a retort to Locke, but her gaze flicked to me.

"Sometimes," I answered. "Where you are concerned, however, no. As long as you were missing, I'd work with the devil himself to get you back. These two were hardly that bad."

Remington actually snorted and Patch couldn't hide her smile behind her coffee swiftly enough. "You know, I think Locke might take that as a challenge."

"Maybe," Locke responded. "Then again, we've clearly proven we'd work with the Muppets if we had to in order to get you back."

Muppets?

I glared at him, but Patch laughed.

My sugar bear *laughed* and it pissed me off even more that Locke had gotten her to make that sound.

"Food," Remington said abruptly as he rose. "You need to eat and then brief us on the ones who took you."

"I—" She started but the assassin didn't pause to let her deflect or distract.

"You needed extraction. That has been achieved. Now that you're safe, we require that you remain secure. That is our next objective. While I'm sure the three of us could figure it out on our own, it will proceed far more swiftly with you directing us." He fixed her with a look.

While she turned neither mutinous nor agreeable, I didn't think she'd conceded the fight yet. That was fine. I liked Sugar Bear with teeth.

"We'll eat first," Remington continued as though they hadn't just had some silent argument. "Because you need nutrition and to heal. Then we need a list of targets, tactical information, and threat assessment."

Just like that, he pivoted on his heel and strode to the kitchen. If I hadn't seen him stitching up a long slice along his ribs while she'd still been sleeping, I wouldn't have known.

I didn't think Locke knew, he'd been in the shower at the time. Somewhere during our excursion, Remington had been shot, but he didn't mention it or bring it up. He barely even moved like it bothered him.

Which was fine, I'd been shot plenty of times. Hurt like a bitch, but when the fight was still on, you didn't have time to fuck around. Of the four of us, Patch was in the worst shape. We were all capable of carrying her as needed. Hell, she didn't even have to point a gun.

What we couldn't do was replicate her mind or her thought processes. That—we would need from her.

"I don't know that I'm ready to talk about it," Patch admitted finally and it pulled my attention back to her. "I know what you need to know…"

"Then we keep it to a mission briefing," I told her. "It can be hard to divorce yourself when you were the one who suffered. We just need names."

I'd considered adding more to the list, but no, we really just needed names. We could figure out the why and the where later. The who—that was important.

Who they were. Then next would come the how.

How we would eliminate the threats.

The faintest of frowns tightened her brow and she looked from me, to Locke, then toward Remington in the kitchen then back to me.

Yes, Sugar Bear, you have three loaded weapons right here.

Just point us in the right direction.

Or any direction you want us to go.

TWENTY-TWO

PATCH

The coffee tasted divine. Dark and bitter, yet smooth and warm. It was, quite possibly, the kindest thing I'd tasted in far too long. I still hadn't quite figured out how long I'd been missing. Their check-in dates didn't all line up with the last date I remembered.

Trauma was not always a friend to memory. It could burn some into the psyche so deep that a touch or a smell could set it off. At the same time, it could blur them until the edges melted away and everything ran together.

I really couldn't decide which of the pair was more disturbing. The fact I could recall some of the tortures in high definition with almost crystal clarity, had me shying away from focusing on them too much.

At the same time...

"Fallon," Locke said and I jerked, snapping my attention to the room. Sound rushed back in like I'd been tuning out.

"What did you call me?"

Dipping his chin, Locke gave me a small smile without an ounce of his normally cockier attitude. "Fallon. Your name."

"It's been a long time since anyone called me that." The sound of my name on his lips was unsettling as hell. "A very long time."

"If you prefer I continue to use Patch, I will." A flicker of disagreement flashed in the way he compressed his lips. "But that said, I like your name."

Reconciling that name with our current circumstances was taking me a minute. Apparently, everything was going to take me a minute right now. Remy returned with a plate and a fresh carafe of coffee.

Remy had said very little, letting Locke and McQuade do most of the talking. Yet, the weight of his assessment seemed to press in on me. He said a great deal by saying very little.

The plate held a couple of sandwiches. They were thick with cheese and— "Ham?" The question seemed almost inane, yet I was curious.

"Something simple. You mentioned it once." The precise intonation in his accent was sexy as hell. "I believe you said you could slap ham and cheese on wheat and eat it dry if you had too."

It wasn't remotely funny and yet, another laugh tried to break loose from the debris inside. "I'm going to guess it's not dry?"

For a moment, it almost seemed like he wouldn't answer then he gave a fairly graceful shrug. "Take a bite. Find out."

I had set my mug down to take the plate and

he refilled it, then his own before he set the carafe down for the others. Adding nothing more to his advice, he reclaimed the chair closer to me.

They were all right there, forming this loose but attentive circle around me. Their presence seemed to elicit confusion even as it aroused a tempest of feelings in me I wasn't prepared to address.

Frankly, I didn't even think I was qualified to address them. Their presence compromised me on so many levels but *without* them, I would still be in that hellhole. Had I gotten out of the cell? Yes. Had I made it to the ground level? Also yes.

But I'd been fading fast and that adrenaline would only take me so far. I had no idea what had been beyond those doors. Exhaustion clawed at me despite the coffee and the hours of sleep I'd already had.

"Hey." McQuade's gentle verbal prod shivered under my defenses and I blinked at him much as I had Locke when the latter used my name. "Eat. You look ready to pass out again. You need fuel."

I did need fuel.

"We need answers," he continued as I lifted the sandwich to take a bite. As much as the reminder could have stymied my appetite, I didn't let it impede me taking a bite of the food. I needed the distraction as much for my stomach as for keeping my mouth full so I couldn't answer.

The first bite was almost too much. The flavors overwhelmed my abused palate. A little mustard, ham, and cheese. The ham was salty. The cheese was cheddar and very sharp. The mustard had a bit of a kick to it. The wheat bread was probably the blandest thing and even it seemed to tease my tongue.

What food I'd been allowed had been tasteless, textureless, and for the most part—disgusting. I'd almost forgotten how good a sandwich could be. I followed the first bite with another. Then another.

I meant to keep the bites small and proportional, but my stomach threatened to cramp. Even chewing every bite thoroughly, I still couldn't eat it fast enough. Finished with the first sandwich, I reclaimed my coffee cup and forced myself to take a sip.

The IV bags they'd kept me on had obviously rehydrated me. It hadn't done a damn thing to dampen my appetite. The silence registered a heartbeat later and I found all three watching me with varying degrees of amusement.

"The sandwich was quite good," I told Remy. "I really liked the mustard."

"Duly noted," he murmured, his deadpan expression not shifting in the slightest. "Though if you'd eaten it with that gusto and hadn't cared for it—I would absolutely go make you something else."

Another laugh worked its way free and the heavy pane of glass that seemed to be cutting me off from the world cracked. McQuade chuckled and even Locke laughed.

"To be fair," I admitted, the coolness in

Remy's hazel eyes almost dared me to respond. The brown was far more amber in color and there were gold flecks in his eyes that seemed to gleam. "Whether I liked it or not, this is almost a five-star meal compared to the last few—I don't even know if it's been days or weeks."

"At least ten days," Locke told me.

"I am leaning more toward two weeks," Remy countered.

McQuade shrugged. "Too fucking long is the correct answer."

Murmured assents came from the other two.

"Agreed," I said, finally. "I—I don't like how easily you found where I lived. It tells me I left gaps in my security." I grimaced. "Not that their breaking in didn't reveal that to me."

I still couldn't believe how easily they'd sprung that trap. It had to have come in via one of my deliveries. How else had they gotten inside without tripping my security? They'd been there when I opened the secure door.

"How many?" Locke asked and I frowned. The sharp cold dump of adrenaline as the fear struck and sent ice racing over my skin had swamped me even in retrospect.

"I don't know precisely," I said, trying to reconcile the men in the dark masks and clothes. They'd had on heavy Kevlar. Even if I'd been able to get ahold of my taser, I doubt it would have penetrated.

The moment I'd released the locks, they'd rushed in. I barely had time to hit the lock on my system. Even if they could get in, it would take them far too long to do it there. Nothing was absolute. Too long without my actual password though would kick in a default setting that would erase the drives.

Better safe than dead.

"Six," I said. "I think. Six men—" I tested the way that tasted on my tongue. All of them had been much taller than me. "Definitely men or very tall women." I wasn't precisely short, but I wasn't really that tall either. I was fairly average.

"Six men to bag you, Patch?" McQuade rubbed at his chin.

"Six men inside the secure perimeter of the house. They shouldn't have been inside. I had security and redundancies, particularly when I was on the line. I couldn't afford to be interrupted." It could cost them their lives if I was.

Even if a delivery came while I was in the secure room, the buzzer wouldn't ring through. Instead, they'd have to leave it on the porch or follow my delivery instructions to return later.

It wasn't usually a problem, I scheduled everything to prevent those kinds of disturbances. Eyes closed, I tried to replay those moments following the rush inside. But the only thing I got was acid crawling up my throat.

"I think they must have knocked me out immediately." My throat went dry and it took a couple of swallows of coffee to ease. "Six men. Moving in pairs. There were two just *right* there when I started to open the door. They shoved it inward, I stumbled back a couple of steps. I hit the lockout for my system. It was already shutting down for the night, but the lockout requires a series of tasks in order to get back into the drives."

The only person who could do all of them was me. For the most part.

"Two grabbed me as I hit the desk. One wrenched my arm. Two more came in right behind them and there were at least two in the hall. Six men." Yeah, that felt right. "I don't know how they got me out or what they did in the house. The next time I came to, I was in a cell."

"Did they identify themselves?" Locke asked. "I know they didn't when they rushed your office, but once you were in the cell?"

"No," I told him. It was a direct response. It also wasn't a lie. They never told me *specifically* who they were, but I had a fairly concrete idea. If not their identities, I knew exactly what they wanted. "They asked questions. A lot of questions. Questions I refused to answer."

"So they resorted to torture." Remy's soft voice belied the subject matter. "How is your stomach tolerating the food?"

The shifting topics didn't seem odd at all. "Yes and so far, I'm fine."

Another sip of coffee and I eyed the second sandwich. I kind of wanted to eat it, but I also didn't want to risk upsetting what delicate balance I'd already achieved.

"Pure torture for torture or were they interrogating you?" McQuade honed in too close on a subject I didn't want to discuss.

"Both," I admitted. "There were days when

my hosts seemed quite determined to just make me scream. Not that it did much good. If I denied them, they worked harder. If I indulged them, they prolonged it."

It was a lose-lose proposition.

"Torture is not an effective way of gathering information or intelligence," Remy stated. "You could have answered anything to make the pain stop. At least until they could verify it."

"I presume they *could* verify it, whatever it was?" There was something eerie in the way Locke picked up on Remy's lead and followed it so easily. These men weren't supposed to know each other, yet here they were, working in concert.

While they weren't quite to the stage of finishing each other's sentences. They weren't far off.

"Presumably," I deflected. "I didn't break... even when I did, I didn't. I sang songs and told them stats from high school sports."

"You know stats from high school sports?" McQuade looked more intrigued than surprised.

"No," I said, giving in to the smile tugging at my lips. "But they didn't know that and the numbers sounded good."

"They went to a great deal of trouble to acquire you," Locke pulled us back on topic. "How likely are they to try and reacquire you?"

Too damn likely.

That was the other problem. Even with my escape, all we'd done was delay their next attempt at acquisition.

"Is there a chance that they will go for another target to get what they need?" There was care in the way Remy phrased the question.

"There's always a chance," I said. What they wanted, however, was not available to anyone else. "Please don't ask me what it is."

"Okay," McQuade said. "For now." Acceptance *and* a warning. "Sometimes information is need to know…"

"We need to know," Locke said. "I'd prefer sooner rather than later. We already know the trouble they went to in order to get you and to keep you."

"You've already done more than I could have asked for," I told them. Or expected for that matter. I'd been on my own for so long, I knew how to do *that*. "I should probably go."

The moment the words left my lips, my stomach sank. Leaving them meant facing the potential hazards on my own—again. Only this time without the preparation I'd taken, the supplies, or even the cover.

Frankly, it was a stupid idea to separate from them. Especially while I was vulnerable. My mind produced a dozen different reasons to reject the plan before I could even formulate one.

"You can go anywhere you want," McQuade said. "We'll make sure you get there. However, until we've identified everyone involved in your capture, incarceration, and torture, we are going to stay with you—or at least I am."

"So am I," Remy said even as Locke added in the same breath, "Me too."

"It's not a new cage," Remy continued as though he'd been the one to begin the conversation. "It may seem like one because we are making this decision for you. We will continue to make it until we've dealt with the opposition and are confident that it is safe for you to return to your home or a new location—I'd recommend new location with improved security methods, which we can all vet for you."

They'd made the decision without even an aside between them. Maybe they had made it before I even woke up. While I didn't like being "informed" of what was going to happen, I could also respect the need for it.

Hadn't I nearly made an epically bad decision a few minutes ago? The cognitive dissonance was real. I trusted these men—I *should* trust them. I knew them well, or at least how they worked and how they kept their word.

That was enough to at least trust them for now. Remy was right, it wasn't a cage of iron bars, abuse, and pain. It was security and care—with ham and cheese sandwiches made with spicy mustard.

I lifted the second sandwich and took a bite. It lasted a little longer than the first had. The food was a balm to my blasted and battered soul.

"How long before we need to leave?" This didn't feel like a permanent location and interior decor matched none of the men I knew.

"Soon," Remy said. "We need to make arrangements, but we have enough time for you to get more rest."

It was an offer of escape, a life line as I floundered beneath the should I or shouldn't I question.

"That's a good plan," Locke said. "Do you need assista—"

McQuade had already stood and scooped me up without waiting for my comment. Thankfully, Remy saved the plate before I dropped it.

"I can walk," I informed McQuade.

"Of course you can," he retorted. "But your feet need to heal and you need to rest. We can debate the rest of it later."

He strode into the bedroom and set me down as gently as he'd picked me up. When he took a step back the air seemed colder somehow.

"Get some sleep, Sugar Bear," he told me, the barest hint of mirth in his grave eyes. "Tomorrow is coming whether we like it or not."

Well, that was a cheerful way to view it. Pivoting on his heel, he left me alone and closed the door on his way out. Unsurprisingly, the softest murmur of voices penetrated the closed door.

They likely needed to discuss what to do with me and the problem I presented.

Sinking back against the pillows, I put a hand over my eyes.

They weren't the only ones...

CHAPTER

TWENTY-THREE

LOCKE

N one of us spoke until after McQuade closed the door on the bedroom, leaving her inside. It made me itch to have her out of sight. It had earlier when she'd been unconscious. Letting her sleep had been the right call. Whatever doubts I may have had cleared away when we got a good look at her injuries...

"She needs a doctor," I said, revisiting a subject the three of us had been dancing around.

"Agreed," McQuade said with a shrug. "The problem is we need one we can trust, implicitly. I won't risk her."

"We may be risking her by *not* taking her. She needs antibiotics."

"We can get her those," the stubborn mercenary argued. "The only reason we haven't so far is we don't know what, if any, allergies she might have. She's awake now—we can ask her."

"When she wakes up again," Remington

235

stated. The assassin was on his feet and gathering up her dishes. I hadn't missed that he waited on her, but he just prepped stuff for us.

Worked for me.

Scrubbing a hand over my face, I turned over what details she'd shared. I hadn't missed how she held back. Why shouldn't she? I'd trust her with my life and my freedom. No question.

I *had* trusted her. No one had to tell me that Remington and McQuade were the same. We'd all trusted *her*. She was our operator. The woman we called when we needed anything and she'd never let me down.

Not once.

So of course we trusted her.

"She doesn't trust us." Maybe it was obvious to them and I was slower on the uptake. But I'd spent the past couple of hours hoping she would trust us, tell us who hurt her, and let us take care of it.

"We can hardly blame her," Remington said, turning from where he'd finished washing up their precious few dishes. Arms folded, he leaned back against the counter and stared out at me.

"I don't blame her," McQuade said, the gruff tone punching up the sobriety in his words. "She hasn't had a reason to trust us as we have her."

That was it in a nutshell.

"But, I think our actions will settle that debt soon enough." McQuade shrugged. "We can't do anything else. Who sleeps next?"

"Not tired." It was a lie, to a point. I was tired,

but I didn't think I'd sleep. Not while I was trying to figure out who was behind this and what we should do. "We could go back... two of us anyway. Clear out that site."

"If they haven't already erased it," Remington said. The measured delivery didn't betray an emotional involvement. The more I got to know him, however, the more I recognized the reserve was just a part of him. "McQuade and I have already discussed cleaning it out, and appropriating anything of hers they may have taken."

"If we can identify it," McQuade said, reclaiming his mug. The cup seemed too small for his massive hands. Almost dainty, but he didn't seem troubled by it. "Frankly, I don't really care what they took so much as making sure they aren't alive to exploit it—or her."

Couldn't really argue with that. Except...

"I want to just agree," I admitted. "But I don't. Because I don't want to invade where she doesn't want us."

"We're not planning on using whatever we find to hurt her." In fact, McQuade sounded insulted that I might even be suggesting it as a possibility.

"If I thought you would—I'd shoot you myself." It wasn't an idle threat. I didn't have their experience or training, but it wouldn't stop me from trying to protect her. Our gazes locked for a long moment, then he nodded once.

Acceptable damage.

"It feels invasive," Remington said, speaking

slowly as though he needed to inspect each word, "because she doesn't *owe* us any explanation. We *want* to know because we want to protect her. There is a fine difference."

McQuade glared. "None of us have the info we need to eliminate the threat. How are we supposed to get her secure and walk away if we don't know what threat to eliminate and make sure it's gone? We *need* to know to protect her."

"She didn't ask to come and she's never made us any promises except that she would be there when we needed her." Then she wasn't. It made all of us come running. "She's kept those promises. That she was taken at all—not her fault."

"Nor hers that we came." Remington seemed to understand me, but McQuade's irritation climbed.

"So what do you want us to do? Pack it up and walk away? She's out...we did our part. So we leave?" Every single word was a damn insult and he had to know it.

"No," I told him. "I'm not going anywhere. Not until she tells me to get lost and for the moment—particularly while she's hurt and in the field? I probably won't go away then. I'll stick with her until she's got control back."

I'd also attempt to change her mind. Now that I was here, I didn't want to be anywhere else. McQuade's scowl and brusque attitude didn't faze me. Apparently, grumpy was his love language or communication style—personality defect?

"I ain't budging till she's safe. End of story." Remington and I really were absolutely on the same page.

"I want to know everything," I told them, setting my cards on the table. "We're here now, we can be effective now. We might have helped to get her out, but she isn't safe—not yet. As long as the threat is out there, she'll never be safe."

"We can eliminate all the threats." McQuade gave a shrug as he stood. He was the only one who hadn't gotten any rest since we began the operation. It might be time for him to take some shuteye. "We just need to identify them."

Then again, he said he didn't sleep while on an op. Not more than doze, which was why he'd taken first watch. If he was that light of a sleeper, it would be easier on him than having to listen to us moving around.

"My point," I said before I downed the last of my coffee. There wasn't enough caffeine to keep me awake much longer. She needed to rest and heal before we got on the move again. I'd ask about her drug allergies and everything else when she was up.

Acquiring broad spectrum antibiotics was not a problem. We'd passed a few pharmacies on the way in. I just needed the names.

"We can't make her tell us anything." At the end of the day, that was my final word on it. "We can ask, we can infer, we wait—but we can't demand it. As we've established, she doesn't owe us. We need to earn her trust."

"That might take time we don't have." Mc-

Quade punctuated the mutter with a grunt. Then he rubbed the back of his neck. "We might not have another choice though. We'll make the time."

"Exactly."

It was nice to know that while he might be a grumpy bastard, he did see sense. I caught Remington's nod. We were all on the same page.

"You still need rest," I told McQuade. "I've had four hours and so has Remington."

"I told you, I don't sleep on a mission."

"Well this isn't just a mission anymore," Remington told him. "It's likely going to be a long-term op. You need sleep so that when you have to watch our backs, you can."

McQuade scowled. I got it. I really did, but... "Maintaining that level of alertness on no rest is not healthy for any of us. Not to mention, your sweet personality doesn't need any more reasons to get grumpier."

His dark look seemed permanently etched onto his face. Then the corners of his mouth twitched. When I raised my eyebrows, he let out another grunt.

"You know, I still don't get why no one has shot you yet." Grousing tone or not, he was almost smiling.

"It's just a hallmark of how much more likable I am than you are. Try smiling once in a while, it's good for your mental health."

The absolute *snort* he released at that statement made me grin. So many battles could be avoided if you knew how to talk a person down. Charm could disarm even better than a weapon.

Sometimes.

The door to the bedroom opened and I rose to my feet even as Remington and McQuade turned to her. Patch limped out, every slow, carefully measured step made me hurt for her.

It was why McQuade had carried her inside. The last thing she should be doing was walking out. I took a step forward and I wasn't alone, they moved as well.

Only the fact she raised her hand stopped us.

"I know you wanted me to sleep," she said slowly, reaching the back of the sofa where she planted her bruised and battered hands. Leaning there, she looked from one of us to the others then back. "I'm tired—I need sleep. But..."

Her lips compressed.

"You don't have to say anything," I assured her. "We just discussed that you owe us nothing. Right now—you need to figure out if you can trust us the way we trust you."

The tightness around her eyes deepened. The fact her hair was pale like cornsilk that had been dipped into chocolate at the ends was a captivating look. Maybe because I always expected her to be a little more buttoned down, maybe even prim and proper.

At the same time, it suited her. Off-beat, independent, and very much her own thing. She wasn't going to fit in anyone's box.

"I am so grateful that you came," she said, the rasp in her voice revealed another layer to the damage she'd taken. "You want to help me and that's—amazing. The thing is, no matter how grateful I am, I can't ask you for more. I can't ask you to fight this battle."

Because it was a battle. At least she wasn't pretending it was anything else.

"You didn't ask," McQuade said. "You never ask."

"Nor do you have to," Remy added. We'd say it as many times as we had to in order to make sure she understood.

"Maybe you don't want to answer because you have secrets to keep and to protect. I get it." Their silent nods added agreement. "But currently, you're injured and without us you're in the open. Not a place any of us are planning to leave you, whether you answer or not."

Blowing out a breath, I locked my gaze on hers. Charm wouldn't work here. Nor would brow beating. We had to keep this as logical and precise as possible.

The devil, as it were, was always in the detail.

"We came looking for you because you've *always* been there. When I needed you, you always answered. When I wanted a way out, you found it. When I needed a trace, you dug up the information. You are *always* there for us, no matter what."

"Then you weren't," McQuade stated, the gruffness seemed less sharp now as though he'd sanded it down just for her. "You weren't and I had to know why. I had to know you were alright."

"Same," I promised. "So you don't have to ask us. We're here. You know what we can do. Use us. Use our skills. Put us to work, Patch. Whether you are Fallon or not, or even want to tell us why or what, we're here now. We're not going anywhere. Use us."

"Yes," Remy said slowly. "Talk to us."

CHAPTER

TWENTY-FOUR

PATCH

Despite my exhaustion, sleep proved elusive. Instead, my thoughts were a whirlwind that circled back on itself over and over. As much as I wanted to trust Remington, Locke, and McQuade, how could I involve them any deeper than they'd already gone?

They had no idea who was hunting me or, worse, *why*. The information might be useful, but it would only endanger them. Hadn't they told me someone had gone gunning for them *after* they found my place?

The fact they'd come looking at all may have compromised them already. So what more harm could telling them have?

Around and around my thoughts went until even the idea of sleep became a distant memory. Analysis was what I'd done for years. Pull the problem apart, examine it closely, determine what actions can be taken and what should be done.

Even as I argued with myself about telling

245

them, I had to acknowledge this could all be another layer of deception put into play by my captors. They'd tried everything else to break me. What could sting worse than bringing in "real" friends to "rescue" me?

Of course, I would trust them.

As soon as that idea tried to take purchase, I discarded it. First, I wouldn't have labeled them as friends no matter how often we spoke. Second, if they'd cracked my systems enough to identify them as clients—well, chances were they'd have had enough information to get the answers they sought.

I'd given up a lot to…

I shuttled that thought to the side. Better to not even focus on it right now. The longer I lay here, the darker and more twisted the paths my thoughts traveled became. Sleep, no matter how vital, wasn't coming.

Outside that door, three men waited for me and I needed to decide what the hell we were doing. Cutting them loose wasn't an option. I wasn't in any shape to do this on my own. Not yet.

Easing my way out of the bed, I was careful before I even put my feet down. They were going to hurt. The bandages helped. They helped a lot. But it didn't change the fact that every part of my body was in pain of some kind.

Another reason I couldn't rush through abandoning my rescuers. The fact I wanted to believe every word they said as well as wishing I could savor actually meeting them had nothing to do with it.

Yes, I could absolutely lie to myself.

The borrowed clothes were soft, but currently every part of my body was irritated so it wasn't like it seemed to make much difference. Except... the clothes and the bandages and the food—they were all acts of kindness and care.

Something dreadfully lacking of late.

At the door, I debated attempting to go back to sleep one more time. Even as the thought crossed my mind, I discarded it. Without a decision, we were all in limbo. I'd been in purgatory for long enough that even this faintly improved state offered no real certainty.

Life, as my father used to tell me, offers you no promises. If you wanted something, you had to make it happen for yourself. That way, at least you knew you'd done everything possible if it didn't work out.

There was an odd kind of comfort in that.

Trusting that wisdom, I opened the door. The light in the main room seemed almost too bright versus the darkness I'd been trying to rest in. The blur of motion said I'd snared all of their attention with my return.

Folding my arms, I leaned against the doorjamb. They came for me because I'd always been there for them, until I wasn't. The revelation tore open old scars that had long since formed in the place where my friendships and family used to be.

Leaving my life as I had required severing all

ties. I'd cut them, then cauterized the open wound their absence created. That scar tissue pulled taut as my links to these three men burrowed in.

No, not burrowed.

They were already there. I'd let them in when I hadn't been looking. Growing attached when it was the last thing I should have done.

Dipping my head, I let their words roll over me. I wanted to believe them so badly. Eyes closed, I dragged in a deep breath of air.

"Yes," Remy said, the softness of his tone wrapping around me like an arm over my shoulders, or a hug. It provoked hot tears to burn in my eyes. "Talk to us."

Isolation might be safe but it was damn lonely. Blinking rapidly, I forced the tears back then lifted my head. "What I have are—"

Before I could even finish forming the words Remy's hand came up as did McQuade's. All three men moved. The lights cut off abruptly and then Remy reappeared out of the darkness right next to me.

McQuade was a half step behind him and he had a weapon in his hand. His nearness dwarfed me even as he dipped his head. "Go with Remy. Locke will be right behind you. Do what they say and stay with them."

"How are you getting out?" I understood extraction plans. He was covering our exit.

"Don't worry about me, Sugar Bear." McQuade's breath teased my ear and I was barely able to suppress a shiver that raced over me from the brief contact. "I'm extraction and cleanup. I'll find you."

The last three words were a promise. "I'll hold you to that," I told him as sternly as I could manage. It came out breathy but I meant it.

"Yes, ma'am." Then he shifted his attention to Remy. "Take care of her."

"Of course."

"Why do I feel like we're not getting my deposit back?" Locke said with a manufactured sigh.

"Because you're not a stupid guy," McQuade said. "Give me sixty seconds then straight out back and down the hill."

I didn't have any shoes...

Locke passed a bag to Remington then he closed the distance. "I need to carry you, Patch. Trust me to get you down that hill?"

"Yes." No hesitation was left in me. Not with the threat imminent right outside. Car doors closed. The slam of them increasing the danger with every second we lingered.

"Arms around my neck," he murmured then I was being lifted. Contact sent fresh alarm through me, but his touch was gentle. "Can you wrap your legs too?"

I licked my lips, suddenly grateful for the darkness because my face caught on fire. "Yes." I hitched my legs around him. His shirt was stiff—oh, he'd put on Kevlar.

"Helmet," Remy said then something tugged over my head and there was something draping my back, not a blanket but... a jacket. "Keep your head down and tucked against him. Just let Locke run, don't throw off his balance and stay as quiet as you can. We'll get you out of here."

The instructions all made sense. I lifted my head and pressed a kiss to Locke's cheek. The two of them went dead still. "For luck," I whispered.

"I'll take it." Locke's voice dipped to a darker place for a moment, then he cleared his throat. "Ten seconds, Patch."

I was glad they'd remembered. Hard to believe that was my job before. I'd get it back. Locke had one arm around me and he was moving. The position was extremely intimate, but he didn't take any advantage of it at all. If anything, he'd gone into mission mode as I liked to call it.

Their focus was on escape.

Glass shattered somewhere and I couldn't help the little jerk.

"Shhh," Locke said, hum of sound soothing over the jagged bits of adrenaline scraping under my skin. "I've got you."

His grip was firm, confident and then more glass shattered and the distinctive pop of gunfire erupted. We didn't linger, Locke was on the move. He went from slow and deliberate to running.

I tried to shift my center of gravity with him, obeying the subtle signals of his body as he increased his speed. I wanted to lift my head and make sure Remy was with us. More gunfire filled the night, silencing whatever creatures might normally be out here.

So weird. No crickets. No frogs. No birds.

Just bullets.

Trusting them cracked more of the glass between me and the rest of the world.

McQuade would find us. Remy would take care of any targets that appeared between us and their exit strategy. Locke would never drop me.

That certainty erupted from beneath the debris my capture, incarceration, and torture left behind. Enemies had targeted me, located me, and stolen me from the safe haven I'd carved out for myself.

That haven was gone. I'd have to build again. I'd have to do it better so they couldn't find me the next time. But the experience also proved to me there were at least three people who gave a damn enough to find me. They were still fighting for me.

The farther we raced from the house, the more distant the gunfire became. Something blazed bright in the distance. Even with my eyes closed and my face angled down, it made me wince away from the sudden flare.

"Definitely lost the deposit," Locke grunted as he slowed. He was barely winded. A door opened. I swore my heart had to be racing faster than his. "Putting you in the car sweetheart," he said, his grip shifting so he could rub my back gently.

It took a moment for the words to register like I was on some kind of internet delay, a few seconds behind when he said it and when it reached me.

"Oh." I should apologize but it took effort to

unpeel my grip from him. I was shaking violently. Adrenaline and reaction kicking in.

"It's fine," Locke said as he set me down into the backseat of what looked like a dark SUV. "More than fine. You feel good plastered against me."

Heat scalded my face, and thankfully, there were no lights on inside the vehicle.

"Go," Remy ordered and Locke moved to the driver's seat, then Remy nudged me over in the backseat.

"Will McQuade really be alright?" I trusted him to save himself. He'd gotten out of some truly heinous situations in the past, but this—this felt different.

"He's too much of an asshole not to," Locke said, his voice light. The car started almost silently. Remy reached across me and gripped a seat belt then pulled it over me before he pushed the shoulder strap behind me.

"I need you to lay down," he said, his touch light. "I want your head below line of sight."

I glanced at him and his lap then back up.

"Yes," he said. "Normally, I'd put you in the well but if we have to do offensive driving that will risk you getting hurt more. Once you lay down, I'll pull the blanket over you."

I licked my lips again cause we were already moving. Locke was driving straight out, no lights, nothing. There had been a lot of trees, I hoped he could see where he was going.

My heart slammed a bruising cadence against my ribs. We didn't have time to argue this.

"Okay," I said and then ignored my own bruises to lay down. Before I made it a single inch though, Remy caught my chin in a grip so gentle and light it was barely there—yet it seemed to burn its imprint on my soul.

"I'd like a little luck of my own," he whispered scant seconds before his mouth sealed over mine. It was swift, hot, and absolutely breath stealing. The swipe of his tongue left its own brand on me and my lips tingled in the aftermath as he raised his head. "Yes, definitely feeling luckier now."

He tucked me against him and I pressed my cheek against his leg all too aware of how even more intimate this positioning was. As promised, he draped a blanket over me and then touched a hand lightly to my shoulder.

"We've got this," he said. "You're safe."

"You have this," I repeated.

I'd keep repeating it mentally until I believed it.

They had this.

TWENTY-FIVE

REMINGTON

Planning ahead for an exit came second nature to McQuade. We'd removed the tracker from her, but that didn't mean there weren't more. Clearly, how the bloody hell else did they locate us so swiftly?

Aware of her cheek where it rested on my thigh and the helmet edge that dug into the muscle, I had to fight the urge to put a hand on her. I wanted to offer her comfort, but right now, I needed my attention on our surroundings. Especially when I could still taste her on my lips.

Sweet, yet intense. The heat was almost a cold sting and I wanted to savor it.

Locke and McQuade had studied this route both when they put the SUV in place and after. It was heavily wooded and they'd done markers—probably smart—to know where the path turned and twisted. The last thing we needed was to slam into a tree.

"Hospital?" Locke said over his shoulder as

we cleared the last bit of trees and he turned onto an actual road. It was empty, and he didn't bother with the headlights yet.

Smart.

"Yes," I said. We needed to find the other tracker. The scanner hadn't picked it up which meant it could be deep. The number of injuries she'd had—we hadn't really had the time to get her a proper check up with an actual doctor.

Time to change that as well.

"Got it."

The drive to the hospital took us the better part of an hour. Locke moved along the backroads until we were closer to a bigger city, then he switched to the highways.

The hospital he was heading for was one of the largest in the area. The campus included more than 3.1 million square feet of space, six buildings, and multiple specialties including a Level 1 trauma center.

We'd identified every single one within a driving radius of our planned stops. Overkill to some, perhaps, but I happened to agree with Patch. The only bad plan is the one we didn't make.

"We're close," Locke said. The drive had been almost too quiet, but hopefully McQuade hadn't left anyone *to* follow us.

I nodded and stroked a hand over her shoulder. She gave the barest of starts. Had she gone to sleep?

She stirred under the blanket and I drew it

back and found her tilting her head to blink up at me sleepily. "I fell asleep."

Surprise rippled over her expression as she smothered a yawn. She froze in the act of sitting up.

"It's fine," I told her. "We can take the helmet off now."

"Grab a jacket for her from the back," Locke said. "I'm dropping you here, it's not the main entrance, easier to get around and avoid the ER."

Solid plan. I had the basic layout, and we needed to head down to radiology, which the sign said was in this building.

I took the helmet from her and then held up the jacket so she could slide into it. The ground was mostly dry, and if I picked her up, it was going to limit my aim.

Still, she wasn't walking over the uneven ground. I spotted a wheelchair near the doors.

That would do.

Five minutes later, I settled her in the chair then put the blanket over her lap. She shot me a worried look as she glanced around.

"Hospitals have a lot of cameras."

"They do," I told her. "Mostly on doors, and medicine cabinets and outside rooms. Some run on cycles, others have human observation. This is a risk, but one we're going to have to accept because you were tracked."

I had no problem lining the halls with bodies if it came down to it. But we needed to find the tracker and we needed to find it now.

"I trust you," she said and the soft words pulled everything into sharp focus. We hadn't really had time to talk before we'd been so rudely interrupted.

The fact she said she trusted me. Trusted us presumably, but me specifically? I absolutely refused to let anything rock that.

"Relax then, let me do all the work." I gripped the chair and guided it down the hall. If the plans we'd reviewed were to be believed...

There it was. A locker room. The door wasn't locked. I pulled her into the room with me. It took me about two minutes to find a pair of scrubs in the clean laundry stack at the back of the room. I grabbed a set for me, then eyed Patch to pick out a size for her.

She might appreciate something else to wear.

"Watch the door," I told her as I stripped out of the clothes I'd worn and changed into the scrubs. Eight minutes after we entered the hospital, I headed down the hall. I'd acquired a chart from one of the desks and added some blank sheets to it.

"Know anything about doctor's paperwork?"

We were waiting on the elevator.

"Some," she said and I set the chart in her lap and gave her a pen before turning and backing her in.

The fact my clothes were stored in a bag at the back of the chair with my gun easy to access didn't make me relax in the slightest.

"What do I need?"

"X-rays," I said. "Possibly an MRI, but I don't think we'll need that."

She nodded then filled out the paperwork. I didn't glance at my watch. When the doors parted, Locke straightened from where he appeared to be waiting for us. Like me, he was in scrubs. He also had a different set of badges, one around his neck, and the other clipped to his waistband.

He looked like an orderly.

"This way," he said, then strode down the hallway. Even with Locke present, that didn't ease my concerns. Locke was very good at what he did, but he wasn't McQuade. His presence meant I had two to cover.

He used his keycard to open a pair of doors at the end. The air that exited the secured space was icy. Patch shivered, but she didn't say a word. Once we were through, Locke continued to lead us down to the last huge door. Radiation warning symbols marked all the doors.

He opened the last set. The equipment was vaguely recognizable.

"You know how to use this?"

"Mostly," Locke said."I think."

Comforting.

I kept my opinions to myself. It was Patch who pointed to the room with the computer. "Most hospitals require you to use your ID card to log-in. It allows them to track and trace everything."

"Yeah," Locke said. "Really annoying. Hopefully Mr. Fernandez doesn't mind giving us an assist."

"If we have to override it," she said. "I can help."

"You always do." Then he winked at her and I frowned. The ease of flirtation was something I'd enjoyed with Patch. I didn't care to see the evidence in Locke's expression or McQuade's "Sugar Bear," comments.

It took Locke a moment to login then he had the screens up. Patch leaned forward in the chair as he scrolled through.

"I think we can line it up to do the kind of imaging we want...most of it is the program, right?"

"Maybe," she said. "Depends on how new it is. Let me look at it."

Locke flicked a look at me and I nodded once.

"Careful." I helped her up then moved back to cover the door. The limp was still present. It took her about three minutes to bypass the main system, then she was tabbing through a series of screens.

"Got it," she said, explaining to Locke in swift tones.

"Sounds like a plan." Then he scooped her up and carried her over to the table. Most x-rays were done standing, but I didn't want her on her feet any longer than necessary. "No metal on you, right?"

"No," she said. "I don't think so."

He gave her a careful pat down, the extreme gentleness not even something I could object to.

Once certain, he moved the large arm on the equipment, then entered the numbers on the keypad.

There was a certain poetry to realizing she was providing the same kind of support right now she would have if we were doing this with her on the phone. It was selfish of me to appreciate her presence, even if I loathed the reason for it.

"Full body x-rays," she said. "Always a good time. You boys should be in that room, out of the way of the radiation exposure."

"We'll be quick," Locke promised her and then he pressed a kiss to her lips, it was swift, there and gone again. "My turn to say for luck."

Then he retreated and I debated just shooting him. Not that he deserved a bullet in the head for that, but maybe a kneecap. Setting that aside for now, I checked that the door was secured and moved the lock to occupied before I slid into the cubicle with Locke.

"Problem?" He shot me a look and I eyed him.

"No. You?"

The corner of his mouth kicked a little higher. "Not yet. Let's see what we see...here we go, Fallon."

She gave a little jerk at the use of her name and I frowned.

"Yeah," he said, his voice dropping after he hit enter on the screen and the machine arm began to move. It was cycling through a series of scans. "She isn't used to her own name anymore."

"Maybe the fact she hasn't given any of us

permission to use it should be your clue." She had a beautiful name. If she didn't want to be called by that name, then we shouldn't be using it.

I would like to know why, at some point.

"Maybe." Locke scowled as images began to pop up on the screen.

It rendered slowly. Too slowly. She'd broken her arm at some point. The stress to her fingers was also visible. Her ribs looked intact. Hips. Thigh bones. Overall, her legs looked fine. There might be evidence of old stress injuries or maybe mild fractures, but I didn't see any actual breaks.

Then we got to her feet. Her shredded feet. Some asshole had cut them up and done a great deal—

"Son of a bitch," Locke swore and I saw it a split second later. There was a tracker buried in her foot. Likely in one of the numerous wounds they'd inflicted.

Our discovery didn't escape her notice and I caught the flash of fear on her face. I hated it.

"We can get it out," I told her. "That's why we're here."

"But I can barely walk as it is," she protested... "If we do more, I'll just be a burden."

"Then I'll carry you," I told her before I glanced at Locke. "You or me?"

"I'll get one." He didn't wait to clarify for Patch, just left. We needed a doctor. One who had skills and knew what he was doing.

It would be nice if we could buy him off, but once he got the device out, we could stuff him in a supply closet if necessary.

Crossing to where she waited, I helped her sit up. There was something about lying flat in a room like this. It made you even more vulnerable than she probably already felt.

"I can't believe they put it in my feet."

"Hard to notice with all the soft tissue damage." As much as I despised the fuckers, it was smart.

Thankfully, Locke didn't keep us waiting. He returned with a doctor who couldn't be that many years out of medical school.

"I can't—" The man was saying then he stopped to stare at first me, then Patch, then back to Locke. "You shouldn't be here."

"Doctor," I said, raising my gun, because it was typically quite effective for cutting to the heart of the argument. "We need one thing from you and one thing only. Once you're done, we're out of here."

"I don't want to—"

"How much are you carrying in student loans? Would it be worth it to you to do a minor procedure to ensure paying them all off?" I could certainly afford a half-million easily.

The doctor glared. "I have to report all gunshot wounds."

"Then it's your lucky day doc, it's not a gunshot. Think of it as stepping on an extra-large tack." Locke tugged him into the observation room tapped on the x-rays still on the screen. Frowning, the doctor glanced from the x-rays to Patch. It made me like him a little more. He was assessing the situation and her condition.

"Ma'am...are you being forced or abused?"

"I was," she admitted, not shying from his gaze. "These guys saved me and if I don't get this thing out of my foot. The ones who did this are going to find me."

His frown only deepened as he continued to stare at her. Then he nodded once. "I need a suture kit and antibiotics. Do you have any allergies?"

"No."

"Good. Stay here. The rooms are shielded and it should hopefully jam any signal."

"Just like that?" It's Patch who asked, doubt in her voice.

The doctor paused, meeting her gaze evenly. "Yes, just like that. I can explain or I can get the kit."

Her reluctance to trust anyone was understandable, but I'd execute the doctor before I let him endanger her. "I'll be with him," Locke said. "We'll be right back."

At her nod, they left and she stared at me. "I want all of this to be real... and at the same time, I keep wishing it was just some nightmare that I could wake up from."

"We're real," I promised. "As for the nightmare—we'll deal with that too. If you'll recall, removing problems is something I specialize in."

An actual smile touched her lips. "You are very good at removal and erasure."

"Yes, I am." Facts didn't require arrogance.

Eyes closed, she sucked in a deep breath before releasing it. Then the door opened letting the doctor and Locke back in. He was carrying medications and a pouch. Her nose wrinkled as he moved to her feet.

"Ready?" Locke asked her. The earlier smile flickered back to life.

"Can't wait."

TWENTY-SIX

PATCH

Doctor Thana proved both kind and swift. His name tag was rather long and complicated. When I asked, he just said call him Thana. He also didn't ask for my name.

Understandable.

I didn't envy his working under the cool gazes of Locke and Remy. Though neither man stared at him, one of them had eyes on him at all times. Remy's gun was also resting in his palm. He was seemingly ready for anything. As unsettling a thought as that was, it offered an odd kind of comfort.

No one was going to throw open that door and cut into me again. No one was going to beat me up or starve me or pump me full of drugs until I drooled. Remy would kill them first.

So would McQuade. While Locke wasn't a huge fan of violence and it was never his first choice, he was also not opposed. That kind of security could not be purchased. If I hadn't already decided to trust them, I would have in this moment.

Doctor Thana kept a steady conversation going as he used lidocaine to numb the bottom of my foot before he examined and cut into the soft tissue. Unfortunately, the tracker was actually in an area that had begun to heal. Scar tissue would form over it and tighten it up.

Rock steady hands and a conversational style told me a lot about Doctor Thana. He was a good guy and his interest here was purely clinical. As he worked, he seemingly forgot about Locke and Remy. Good for him, he didn't need to feel the pressure of their glares.

If the guys were planning to kill him before we left, I was going to ask them to change their minds. We hadn't had to bribe or blackmail the doctor. He'd been inclined after one look at me.

That made him a *good* doctor.

With a pair of tweezers he worked on extracting the hateful little device. It required a deep sensation of pressure before he tugged it out. There was blood dripping from it.

More blood and flesh they'd taken from me.

Doctor Thana's dark look spoke volumes for his thoughts about the device. He surrendered it to Remy when the assassin held out his hand. With care, Thana returned to my foot and wrapped it to apply pressure.

"We're going to shoot another couple of images, I want to make sure there's no more surprises."

"Thank you," I murmured and he nodded once.

The x-rays of each foot revealed no more foreign objects. Relief spilled into me as the doctor returned. He added some small sutures to the incision he'd made then treated the rest of the injuries before he wrapped it again.

Without comment, he also treated my other foot. "I'm going to give you some pain meds, as well as medical supplies. You need to keep these wounds clean and dry. It's hard because of where they are located, but just dry and apply fresh bandages so you can keep it clean. The stitches will dissolve on their own. I did it loose because that area moves a lot. If you can stay off your feet..."

He trailed off a little at the end of that.

"Thank you." The fact I would not be able to walk a lot was—aggravating. But we'd manage.

"I'm also going to give you a number to call me on." He was already writing it down.

"Why?" I wasn't upset, but the guys were shooting him narrow-eyed looks, I was more curious than anything else. His focus was clinical, his manner kind, and his attention? It had been on the right things.

"Call me when you're safe," he said as he handed me the sheet of paper, "and I'll answer that sometime. If you can give me five minutes, I'm going to get you the meds and supplies. You don't need to be stopping at any pharmacies."

"Thank you, Doctor Thana."

"You're welcome." He left, stepping out briefly with Locke right behind him. Remy closed in and I slid the paper with the doctor's number into my pocket before I let him help me pull socks over my bandaged feet.

He glanced down at them then at me. "We'll sort it out."

I believed him.

"Do you want to change your clothes?"

I glanced at the scrubs he gestured to. "Yes," I said, blowing out a breath. "But later. Not right now. I have a feeling the doctor will be back soon and we still have to deal with the tracker."

He nodded once. Then helped me off the table and back into the wheelchair. He'd just tucked the blanket over my legs when the door opened to let Thana and Locke back in.

Locke's expression was far more relaxed and he gave Remy a nod. So whatever they were worried about, it was fine.

Good.

Once Thana had given me the supplies and the instructions for the meds, he turned to hand a card to Remy.

"The amount for my student loans. I'd have done this for free, but you offered."

Remy's expression bordered on genuine amusement. "I did."

"Take care of her, and remember what I said about staying off your feet as much as you can." Then the doctor left and this time, Locke didn't follow him.

We couldn't really linger. The doctor had done us a favor but that tracker needed to be dealt with and we needed to link back up with

McQuade. Remy handled my wheelchair. We left with as little fanfare as we arrived.

"Pick me up near the street," Locke said before he jogged off. I stared after him a beat but Remy didn't slow down. Instead of the SUV we'd arrived in, he helped me into a new car. This one was far more luxurious and it had a huge back seat. More like a limousine than an SUV.

Where did they keep getting these cars? And had they moved our stuff? Well, their stuff, I didn't really have any stuff.

Once I was secure and tucked in, he didn't make me put the helmet on, though Remy did suggest I could lay down if I needed it. Not once did we discuss the kiss or the fact I'd fallen asleep with my cheek pressed to his thigh.

Maybe later.

That made sense.

Remy climbed into the driver's seat and he opened the divider so I could see him. Five minutes later, he idled near a curb until Locke climbed into the front passenger seat.

"Taken care of?" Remy asked and Locke nodded.

"It's all loaded." He pointed to a cleaning truck that was pulling out of the lot. He'd dealt with the tracker.

"Good." Then Remy turned away from the truck and took us in another direction all together.

Curled up in the back, I wrestled with every piece of what happened. The danger. The torture. The injuries. The risks. Their arrival—them.

"You ready to trust us yet?" Locke asked and I glanced up to find him watching me.

Was I?

"My real name is…"

The words seemed to stick in my throat as though they would choke me. It had been so long since I said my name aloud or even let myself *think* it. Training yourself to not be yourself took a lot of mental effort.

How strange to think that my name had become something *alien* to me.

"My name is Fallon Amanda Brady." Saying it was surreal. More than surreal. Tears burned in my eyes as I shook my head to fight them back. "Sorry, I—I've been Patch for the past five years if I've been anyone. That's why when you called me Fallon…"

"It threw you." The rough sympathy inhabiting Locke's voice provoked more tears. I rubbed a hand over my face. I'd gotten so used to the bruised feeling that I didn't really notice until I added pressure. No wonder Doctor Thana seemed so worried about me.

I was a mess.

"Yes," I said. "More than I expected or could have predicted." I swallowed, or tried, but all the moisture had fled my mouth.

"Here," Locke said, twisting off the cap on the water bottle and passing it back to me.

"Thank you."

I took a long drink. It was pitch dark outside, leaving only a dance of shadows as the city lights flashed over us. I couldn't see Remy, because he was driving, but Locke's focus never seemed to wander far from me.

"I was recruited by a cybersecurity arm of the NSA when I was still in college."

"A?" Locke asked, his brows gathering tighter together. "Not *the*?"

"No, there are different areas and different focuses. Not everyone knows what everyone else is doing. It's very compartmentalized."

"Okay." He accepted it so simply. But then, why not? Government agencies, especially the more secretive ones didn't exactly list every department or job title on a website. No matter how *transparent* they might seem.

Another swallow of water. "I interned for a summer between sophomore and junior years. Then by senior, I was interning full time. I graduated early and with honors. They offered me a position. Also paid off all my student loans."

The minute they told me they were going to do that, I'd been shocked. My supervisor at the time had merely smiled.

"The lack of incurred debt helped with my security clearances. Made me less malleable to monetary incentives." How painfully naive I'd been at the time. "I got to work in a field I loved, while also paying off all my debts? It was amazing. I had to move, but I was fine with that. I also couldn't tell anyone what I did."

I'd had a cover story to tell my family and friends. Looking back now, I saw all the questions I should have asked. It wasn't like I accepted it all at face value. No, I'd asked plenty of questions. I just hadn't asked the *right* ones. Then I was installed in my new position in a new city, where the only people I knew were the people I worked with.

Isolated.

Dependent.

Buried in work.

"Patch?" Remy's gentle inquiry pulled me back to the present.

"Sorry," I said. "It's been a long time since I thought about any of this. I had top secret security clearance. I worked specifically on securing computer systems at various secure facilities and bases. It was my job to investigate and track any incursions. Particularly those performed by agents of foreign powers. It was a great game of cat and mouse. Sometimes...sometimes I helped out agents in the field when we needed to locate the operatives in question."

To assassinate them, although occasionally they had been recruited. The latter was far more common than I'd been led to believe. I sighed. So much I hadn't understood and the only people I could talk to had been others either in charge of our "discretion" or others in the same boat as me.

Looking back now?

"Anyway, I was with the department for almost four years. Eventually, I was tasked with running my own series of operators—a team who could back me up but also did similar tasks. They kept us in groups of five. The people on my team only reported to me. I reported to my supervisor. That supervisor reported upward—everything closely guarded and compartmentalized. A team working one floor up or down might be doing exactly what we were, but we would never know. It was just another form of compartmentalization."

Not always the most efficient. What happened if we doubled up on work? That wasn't something I was supposed to be concerned about, according to my supervisor. If two teams were gathering information on the exact same thing, they could serve as a check and a balance because you never knew what the other team was doing.

Absolutely rational. Pragmatic even.

And another lie.

"I was dedicated to my job. In fact, so dedicated that I didn't take a vacation, or see my family for almost two years. I can't even excuse it as they overworked me—I loved the challenge of it. The puzzles to break, the hunts to go on..." No, there were no excuses for the choices I'd made then. "That's not really important. My fifth year on the floor, I noticed actual patterns in the assignments. Not just what my team was given but the other operators. We weren't just hunting down cyberterrorists and hackers, we were hacking our own operations. Sometimes changing orders."

How could I have been so stupid?

"Clearly we shouldn't have been doing this, but it was presented as a test for another operations group... We would play the part of the intruders, sift information, and lift it. They were tasked with identifying the intrusions and stopping them. Every time we won, we got points then we were put on countering their incursions —allegedly."

"How long did it take you to figure it out?" Remy offered no comfort or sympathy, just a kind of understanding. He didn't make excuses for me or try to make me feel better about it, just wanted more facts.

That was better.

"That I was working for a shadowy government contractor with political and military ties that went far too deep for comfort and operated outside of the law?"

"Yes," he said and I could feel his gaze even if it was dark and I couldn't quite make out his eyes in the mirror.

I downed the rest of the water and then handed the empty to Locke. Then he handed me another bottle of water and what looked like a protein bar. "Thank you."

"You're welcome."

"Seven missions," I said, opening the wrapper with slow, deliberate motions. "Seven incursions, including one into the Pentagon and two separate military installations."

"Holy shit," Locke said with a slow exhale. "Patch..."

"I know. It was treason. I committed treason because I broke their security encryptions and duplicated the files." There had been worse... "Three days after I accepted what was happening, I recognized that there was no exit plan. No way out. All this time I'd been convinced I was working for a sanctioned NSA division and I wasn't. Some of the information we lifted was being sold to the highest bidder. The rest?"

I shook my head. Wherever it had been going, couldn't have been good.

"I had to build my own exit. So, I wrote the protocols that would begin cleaning out my own files, my own footprint. It took me a while, but I managed to mark every piece of intel I'd taken. Most of it was four layers deep in encrypted files, but the worm I developed could go in and tag them. Then it began to shuttle the files out, one or two at a time. It took me almost a month to get everything in place."

I took a bite of the protein bar, it was tasteless and dry. Yet the very act of chewing ignited all the grumbling in my stomach. They waited while I finished the bar, then washed it all down with water.

"The chances they would recognize what I was doing existed. Every single day that I went into the office, that I played the part, I knew it could be a day they figured it out. But I kept working, I needed to make sure I left nothing behind. When I left, it had to be scorched earth."

So I had. I'd taken everything and left them meaningless gibberish in its place. The terabytes of information funneled out by the worm had been stored in stacked servers all over the world. The worm wouldn't replicate, once it was done, it destroyed itself in their system. No trail was left for them to track electronically.

The files were out there in so many disparate packets they would never find them. Not without the encryption key. Not without knowing what to look for specifically, cause if they weren't recompiled in the correct order?

They would get nothing.

"You strip-mined all their data?" Locke sounded impressed and worried.

"Yep. I emptied their servers, leaving them nothing but trash data in its place. I infected their systems with a half-dozen viruses that would be kicked off when they started searching for what I'd done. Then I finished erasing myself before I got up and left. I left the building, I left my life, I left everything."

I'd begun building a bolthole for myself the day I decided to put the plan into action.

That was the day *I'd* died.

TWENTY-SEVEN

PATCH

Weariness swept over me in waves. Despite the exhaustion, however, the last thing I wanted to do was go to sleep. Sleep meant dreams, possibly nightmares. Worse, it might mean waking up back in that cell and discovering *this* was the dream.

There was a ribbon of light beginning to appear on the horizon, splintering the darkness into something that looked more like navy velvet. The sunrise was on my right, so we had to be driving north. I wasn't even sure what state we were in.

When we changed lanes and began to slow, I shifted in my seat. "Where—"

"Picking up McQuade," Remy said. "He had to make sure no one was following him."

Relief spilled into my veins like a plunge into icy water. I hadn't wanted to ask. We'd left him behind and then the hospital and my confession...

Then we cruised into what looked like a rest area along the highway. One of the signs indicated we were in Texas. Well, that was something. McQuade made his way from the direction of the restrooms.

Despite wearing a cowboy hat, there was no mistaking the dark scruff on his face or the length of hair he wore loose now. For all his military background, he never went with a regulation haircut. Not that I could fault him, there was something about taking your life back—one piece at a time that I recognized.

More, I'd done some of it myself. Only in my case, it wasn't about reclaiming a life but building a whole new one. I sighed as he dropped his bag into the trunk then slid into the backseat with me.

There were traces of dirt on his face. He smelled faintly of gun oil, graphite, and something earthier. The expression he wore lightened some as he gave me a once over.

"Sugar Bear."

That name. An involuntary laugh escaped me and I shook my head. "That name is not going to stick."

"You say potato," he murmured, then winked. "How you feeling?"

"Sore, but I have antibiotics, pain meds, and I'm a little lighter on the metal components."

The neutrality in his expression turned tense as he flicked a look to the front seat. We were already on the move again.

"A second tracker."

A second...

"The first was just under the curve of your

sweet ass," Remy said by way of explanation. "We removed it on our way away from the facility. I scanned you. Not sure why it didn't detect the second tracker."

"Could have been inactive," Locke said with a half-shrug. "But we did full body images. Active or not, we would have seen any others they may have inserted into you."

Inserted.

Tagged with trackers like I was an animal.

Bastards.

"Thank you," I murmured. "Thank you for getting both of them out." With a glance at McQuade, I summoned another smile. "Thank you for covering our backs so we could get away."

"Anytime," he said, rolling his head from side to side. "It was fun. Though, we need real food soon. And a gallon of coffee."

I sympathized.

"We're going to stop somewhere after the state line," Remy said. "Can you wait?"

Locke tossed back a protein bar that McQuade caught easily.

"Yep." He glanced from the snack to me.

"I'm good," I told him. "I ate one and they're —very dry."

He nodded once. "We'll find *real* food soon."

Neither Remy nor Locke told McQuade what I'd said, nor did they prompt me to continue. They were being very careful with me.

As much as I appreciated it, they were all still taking risks for me.

"I was just telling them about how this all began..."

While McQuade didn't fixate or stare, I was very aware of his attention as I brought him up to date with what I'd already shared. Weird, I hadn't vocalized any of it altogether. Not once in the five years since I erased myself.

I'd kept my secrets even from myself.

Here I was telling the story twice in a matter of hours. Remarkable or not, it was something he needed to know.

"So, you think they worked for the same department you did?" McQuade frowned.

I shrugged. "I don't know. I can't tell you exactly what I took, the information was vast. There are a lot of people who would do anything to get it back. The reasons I cleared out those caches hasn't changed. They were not using it to prevent disasters or incidents, but to control when they happened and sometimes even to trigger them."

"So, who do you think your captors were? If the people in your department were information hacks and operators, would they be capable of a black bag job and interrogation?"

"I don't think so." Then again, what did I know. "It was all highly compartmentalized and I gave up wishful thinking a long time ago."

"Not government," McQuade said, almost too fast then scowled.

"Maybe," Locke retorted. "Could be black ops, CIA isn't supposed to operate here but it could be Homeland. Since you took it from 'them'."

Them. "The department I worked wasn't likely sanctioned even if it was linked. Too much of what we were doing and taking..."

No, there would be no Congressional oversight that would let that go.

"Then that makes the people you worked for even more suspicious," Remy said. "They have no reasons to pull their punches. Whatever you took, they want back. How long have you been out?"

"Five years."

Years of hiding from my own shadow, locked away in my very comfortable, well-appointed prison where I could do the best I could while never stepping a foot outside my door.

"That's a long time to wait," McQuade said slowly. "What brought them out now? Or were they hunting you all along?"

"I don't know, I don't even know how they tracked me this time. I've always been careful. I don't use video. I don't post as me. I haven't even said my name in years before today." Monitoring existed everywhere. From cameras at the grocery store watching you do self-checkout, to cameras observing you at ATMs, crossing streets, because security cameras were everywhere.

The U.S. didn't quite have the CCTV coverage of some nations, but if you knew how to get into the private networks—we had almost as much coverage.

"The first couple of days I was in the cell, I kept hoping someone would slip and tell me how they found me. They didn't—just kept asking me where it was." When asking didn't work, they went for torture.

"You said you killed the worm that stole it," Remy repeated my earlier statement.

"I did. They can't get it without me. No one can. It's always moving, it's stored across a hundred different servers. It will never have one port or home or even a dedicated drive. It's all garbage without a decryption key."

If I'd died, then the information died with me. Maybe I couldn't survive their assaults in the long run. I accepted that might be my fate.

"But you can get to it," Remy said. "They have to know that."

Or they would have already tried to reclaim it all themselves. "I should have just destroyed it." I'd thought about it. If I destroyed it entirely then the risk was gone along with the exposure. But it also meant the people behind it all may never face any kind of punishment. "But... it would let too many off the hook. So, I made it inaccessible."

"You're the key," Locke said with a sigh and McQuade's expression darkened even further.

"That means they have nothing to lose in their efforts to get it back. They have to have you." He shook his head, admiration wound through his voice. "You really are a bad bitch, Sugar Bear."

I refused to get used to that nickname, no matter how much affection he punched it up with. "Why?"

"Cause they wanted to break you and they didn't"

No, but I'd been close so many times.

"The question is how do we handle this?" Remy had been circumspect in his comments since I began explaining everything. It was as though he needed to absorb all the data one part at a time. Now, he was processing it.

"We need to eliminate the threats," McQuade said. "All of them."

"We need to secure Patch while we do it." Locke's expression had taken on a narrow-eyed, focused look I recognized.

"To do all of that," Remy said, "we need a plan that gets us access, identifies all the players, and lets us build the right approach. Some of it we can steal. Some of them will need to be scratched off the board entirely. That will take time, resources, and research."

That pulled all of their attention in my direction. McQuade stared at me steadily, Locke twisted in his seat, but Remy just lifted his chin as though he flicked a look at the rearview mirror.

"You're going to need an operator."

They needed *me*.

"You up for it, Sugar Bear?"

I leaned my head back against the seat.

"I have to be," I said quietly. "If you are going to fight this war for me, you are not doing it without me."

I was their operator dammit.

"You need to sleep," McQuade said and he lifted his arm. "We're going to be on the road for a while yet. This doesn't work if you don't heal." The invitation was right there.

I should refuse. I should keep my distance. There were a lot of "shoulds" I could list. I chose none of those. Instead, I just eased over and curled up next to him and when he draped the arm around me, I closed my eyes.

Warmth wrapped me up tight, but it was more than body heat and the smell of pine, smoke, and gunpowder. It was three men who walked right into the unknown to get me free, and who kept standing between me and danger.

It was the fact someone was holding me. Human contact. More—friendly human contact.

Who knew how long it would last?

My eyes grew heavy.

"Sleep, Sugar Bear," McQuade said. The roughness in his voice every bit as soothing as Locke's sly sass and Remy's precise intonations given his accent.

Sleep should have been impossible, but it rushed up to meet me, bundling me up as gently as McQuade did with the blanket.

"We need to talk," Locke said.

"We will," McQuade answered. "Let's get her to sleep first."

"Agreed."

They needed to talk without me? A yawn stretched my jaw. I really needed to object but I really wanted the security of sleeping without fear for a little while.

Just a little while.

LOCKE

A WEEK LATER...

I checked my watch after loading the last item into the back of the Jeep I'd acquired. I preferred more luxury vehicles, but this one fit the area and blended in. Not standing out was ideal for the operation. The fact temperatures had been on a steady decline meant I could wear bulkier clothes too.

McQuade had taken care of sourcing a location. Remy had transferred funds so we could work with cash and reduce the traceability. That left me on supply duty. The only protest Patch had made was when we wanted her to rest.

While the operation would require all four of us, she needed to heal, no exceptions. Period. The cabin was a quaint name for a huge five bedroom place with its own security systems. Located in far north Michigan, it was almost in Canada, if you didn't mind traveling by boat. The address didn't exist beyond a route number and as far as we could tell, it didn't have a post box. Fine by us.

Snow had been a suggestion in the forecast for three days. Today, frost was in the air and flakes had begun falling steadily while I was in the store. While we didn't dare risk returning to her place in Colorado, not until we exterminated the issues, I'd found nearly every item she'd put on a shopping list from motherboards to video cards to processor chips and memory.

The monitors had actually been the easiest. But I'd made a point of picking up the pieces from multiple locations, including having a few pieces shipped to different locker locations.

Granted, I was still the one picking them up. I could still change my appearance enough to confuse facial recognition. I preferred a higher caliber of marks, but fooling Big Jim at the local Meijer took a little thought. If they didn't know you, you already stood out. So, I had to look local without being too familiar while also not standing out as a transplant.

Coming up from Detroit had evenly split the middle. Especially when I let comments like "military family" slip now and again. Those sharp assessing gazes had softened a fractioned to be replaced by grudging humor and respect.

Still, I didn't get too chatty. I wanted to reduce the impression I left behind. They could remember me as just some guy who stopped in, someone new, but not that new. The vaguer the descriptions, the better for all of us.

Patch had also warned me about cameras

anywhere. Didn't matter if they were innocuous or only present on the register at the corner bakery, I needed to clock where they were at all times. Profiles were much harder to match, so angling my face to keep it away from them while also not looking directly up was crucial.

"So," I'd drawled at her. "I need to look around without looking around and be vigilant while trying to act casual."

"More or less," she'd murmured and given me a faint smile. Those smiles had come more frequently this week, but they were still edged by pain and shadows. Each time I saw them, however, it reminded me of how I wished we'd known sooner that she was in trouble.

Known sooner.

Acted sooner.

Prevented it entirely.

Since time travel wasn't actually a thing outside of fiction, I would have to address it as best I could with care, consideration, and measures to make sure it never happened again.

A tracker placed on a person sounded like a great idea, that way we could always locate her if needed. But that also took us too close to what her bastard captors had already done to her. So as tempting as the idea might be? I discarded it without bringing it up.

If she volunteered or it came from her? Fine. I wouldn't be the one asking to do it. None of us would be for that matter. I didn't have to ask McQuade or Remington. The way those two watched her when she wasn't looking?

No, I understood their feelings on the subject completely. After picking up the last couple of pieces of hardware I'd ordered from one of the lockers, I took some time to stock the grocery cart with food and meds. The antibiotics the doc gave her had been helping.

We'd been treating the other injuries. But I wanted to have everything at hand if we needed it. As with everything else I'd been purchasing, I spread them out. Not too much of any one thing. The fishing and tackle box was ideal though to make a travel med kit.

It also didn't stand out. I bought a couple of fishing poles while I was at it. The fishing twine could be used for garrotes. I'd grabbed some rubber bands as well. They were good for popping off safety chains. Just a little of this and a little of that.

The Jeep was packed when I added the new items to the back. My last stop on the way out of town was a clothing store. I had all of her sizes and I'd called ahead and put in an order for my "sister" coming in from out of town. When I'd told the lady she was from Florida and didn't own anything that wasn't a flip flop or shorts, she'd said she'd put together warm weather gear.

Everything was ready when I got there. I paid cash and left with three huge bags. As much as she gave us shit for forgetting panties, I'd actually driven a couple of hours south to get her some nice ones. No way in hell could I order underthings for my "sister."

Firing off a message on my phone, I slid back

behind the wheel. The closest town to our cabin was still well over an hour away. Trading convenience for security made a lot more sense. I had a surprise in the back, a splurge. I couldn't wait to set it up for her.

I didn't care if we were only here a few more days. She'd accepted everything we'd needed to do without complaint. Even the instant coffee. The standard brewer had come with the place and it was a moderate improvement over the freeze-dried crystals and boiling water.

The most direct route to the cabin was relatively clear. Though the snow was falling steadily, it wasn't sticking to the roads. The farther from civilization and the closer to the cabin I drove, the more aware of being watched I could feel.

Remington had built a nice nest up in the attic. The angle and height gave him a good view with his scope. If I picked up a tail that I couldn't shake, I could warn them as I came in.

So far, I'd just sent all green messages. I fired off the last one before I hit the cell phone dead zone. The only reason we could use cells at the cabin was the presence of internet. The VPNs Patch had installed our first night there meant we could "change" our locations frequently before we went out skulking on the net.

The idea of skulking on the internet amused me. Unsurprisingly, McQuade waited for me as I pulled up to the building. We had other cars in the garage. Two of them were backed in and loaded with go bags for us.

We were ready to ditch if we had to. At least this place was on Remington's dime. If we lost the deposit again, I wouldn't be the one with the debt. I was still chuckling when I killed the engine and slid out.

"What's so funny?"

"Not much," I answered easily. "Got everything we needed and the last pieces she wanted."

"Good."

Between us, we made short work of offloading everything into the garage. When he pulled out the espresso maker, his smirk amused me.

"Suck up."

"You're just jealous you didn't think of it." I stripped off my hat, then tossed him the keys. "How far do you think you have to go?"

"Probably be out the rest of the day," he said. "I need to pick up ammunition and his lordship has some very specific requirements."

I snorted. "You like to be specific in your requirements too."

"Yeah, but sometimes, a bullet is just a bullet." He gave another shrug. "I'll be back after sundown. Keep the fire going."

I nodded. If there was a problem, the lanterns would be on the porch. They turned on automatically. We had to manually shut them down.

He was already in the car and pulling away when I shut the garage. Then I stripped out of the heavy jacket and muddied boots before I started ferrying everything in. The interior of the cabin was cozy, despite its size. The corner of the kitchen had become her workshop.

The first few days we'd been here had been all about her resting. While she slept, we conferred on what we knew and what we'd learned as well as what we could do tactically to identify, track, and eliminate the remaining threats.

McQuade and I split up the "hunting trips" as we called them. The only one who never left was Remington. His accent would stand out even if he could modify his voice, but also, he made it clear, he was the best to keep a ranged watch.

Right. He just didn't want to leave her.

I respected it. But if they were getting closer while I was gone, I couldn't tell. They didn't seem to talk more than they had previously. Based on McQuade's watchfulness, I wasn't the only one paying attention to any suggestion of a shifting dynamic.

Once I'd gotten a good chunk of the parts she'd asked for, she'd begun building her machine. Or should I say machines? I stacked the boxes with the latest acquisitions in her chair. When she'd first started putting it together, we'd all offered to give her a hand. The look on her face was like we'd actually offered to fuck her mother or something.

Right, I just raised my hands and surrendered that particular fight. Honestly, Patch was a study in contradictions. Shorter in stature than I expected, but full of fierce personality. The weariness in her eyes and her manner could evaporate in a split second if her temper was pricked.

She rarely complained about anything whether it was her wounds, the time it took to heal, or the fact that walking had to hurt. The fact she tolerated the three of us carrying her whenever we could said more about how bad her feet hurt than anything.

It also prompted me to find her the softest shoes I could with the thickest socks. The boots were advertised as slippers but they were very cushiony. I'd gotten her thick, fur lined socks as well. Between the two, she'd actually been able to reclaim walking around in the house.

The brilliance of her smile had been thanks enough. The grumbles from McQuade had also added to my personal enjoyment.

"Is that an espresso machine?" The surprise in her voice in no way masked her delight.

"Looks like it," I said, finishing my stock of the freezer and the fridge. "Huh?" I hefted the bag of whole beans I'd also bought. "This looks like espresso beans too?" I tossed it up once and caught it.

Her grin redoubled and for the first time since we'd rescued her, there wasn't an ounce of flinch associated with her smile. That was a win on multiple levels.

"I need to set it up."

"You can," I said. "Or you could let me do it while you go check out the last few items I—"

"You got the secondary motherboard." Delight transformed into genuine pleasure or maybe it was just a thrill. Fuck knew the expression and her breathy voice definitely did it for me.

"Got those memory cards you wanted and that—" She thrust herself at me and I had an armful of Patch. The ferocity of her hug made me chuckle. Wrapping my arms around her, I savored the contact. "If I'd known a motherboard would make you that happy, I'd have gotten you the second one sooner."

She pinched me before she withdrew and I grinned. Inch by inch, she seemed to be clawing herself back from the dark place that torture had left her in. The little signs were there. The way her gaze would duck away, or how she would suddenly ease back from contact.

For the most part, I initiated "nothing" if I could help it. Nor did McQuade or Remington. She didn't tell us much about what they'd put her through, but I could imagine plenty.

The evidence was right there in the injuries she still bore and the ones she was healing. There would be scars. No way to escape it. The burns on her arms were going to leave marks. I doubted the bottoms of her feet will ever be pretty.

"You said you had to order it separately and through a friend of a friend," she reminded me.

"Huh, I did say that." Then I winked.

Her smile widened again.

"Go on, go play with your stuff. You know you want to and I'll get this espresso machine set up before I go work on installing the last of these items in the mobile unit."

"Mobile unit." Her scoff lacked any real derision. McQuade had sourced the big rig we currently had parked in the barn. It was out of sight and let us work on it without anyone spying on us.

Remington had arranged for a private plane at a small airfield to be available to us when we needed it. McQuade handled the armory and weapons supply as well as ammunition. Once she had her equipment set up and ready to go, we would have everything we needed to start the operation.

"Would you like an espresso when I make it?" she asked, already heading for her workstation. Her movements were still a little hesitant, but easier. The stiffness in her shoulders had gradually diminished. The combination of thick socks and slippers helped her limp.

Better might be relative, but—she seemed better.

Maybe it was also incremental, but I'd take every inch we could beg, borrow, or fucking steal back for her.

"Ahh, I see the sneaky plan beneath the offer. You want the privilege of making the first cup."

Her laughter to the teasing remark was its own reward. "You saw right through me. Couldn't have been that sneaky."

"Well, I might have a little experience with sneakiness." The retort flowed easily and some of the tension locking my own back up seemed to ease. She could laugh. She could smile. She was *healing.*

When we had extracted every pound of vengeance she was owed, she would also be free and safe.

"But yes, I do want to make the first cup, but I was going to offer to let you drink the first cup."

I put a hand to my chest, letting out a mock gasp of shock that earned me another laugh. "Be kind, Patch. I'm a simple man with simple needs. You could overwhelm me."

"Bullshit," she fired back. "You forget, I know just how expensive your tastes are."

I snorted, but I didn't deny it. Of course, my tastes were expensive. I preferred the items that were unique and individual. Just like her.

She was worth every penny I owned and more.

"Now, stop staring at me and get that espresso machine set up."

"Yes, ma'am," I murmured and moved to do just that while I kept watch over her from the corner of my eye. Today was definitely a better day.

As I pulled the espresso machine out of its box, I allowed myself my own smile.

In a few minutes, it would be a better day.

CHAPTER

TWENTY-NINE

PATCH

Just getting the last piece of equipment didn't mean the system was up and running. But it was the final piece of *hardware* I needed to begin setting up the desktop. The little machine was a powerful tool, and it had all the memory and hard drive speed I could ask for to go with the internet connection we had at the house.

It did, however, open up a new series of tasks for me. As sore as my fingers were, they still flew across the keyboard. I had to start with the kernel and build it out. The first few commands I entered seemed to ease everything in my gut.

This I could control. I had power again. Confessing everything to the boys had cracked more of the deep glass between me and the rest of the world. But I was still relying on them for survival. On the one hand, it was perfectly rational, reasonable even to rely on them while I healed.

Didn't mean I enjoyed having everything taken out of my hands. I couldn't fire a gun with precision or take down a host of men as I fought my way through them. No question about breaking into highly secured facilities and lifting priceless objects with no one being the wiser.

No, I couldn't do *those* things. They weren't in my skillset. Though, arguably, I could get around electronic locks with a little time and planning.

But this? Building the kernel, then installing the programs so I could take back over my corner of the internet and hunt down my enemies? *This* I could do.

It took me the better part of three days to get everything where I was ready to start firing off bots to do my searching. I had to mask my internet footprint, but that was old hat at this point.

I would have been ready sooner, but the boys insisted on regular breaks and sleep. The one argument I'd had with them, I lost when McQuade just carried me off to my room and set me on my bed. Then he held up the power supply he'd taken from the computer.

"When you're one hundred percent, Sugar Bear, you feel free to kick my ass. Until then, you need to heal and you won't if you don't rest."

As irritating as his high-handed manner had been, he wasn't wrong. Not that I planned to admit it. Fatigue was my constant companion. There was so much I needed to do *before* I could get to work digging up what we needed.

Neither Remy nor Locke offered any kind of back up on that one. If anything, they'd merely given me sympathetic looks and suggested that I go ahead and rest. A part of me wanted to rage. But only part. Because the rest of me understood it. I really did need the rest.

On day four, however, with everything up and running, I triple-checked the firewalls before I fired off the first set of bots. They would skip trace across several servers, laying false trails for the information gathering.

If they were tracked by another program, their server hopping would give us another leg up on avoiding identification. Most programs would give up after the first server hop. The more specialized would begin to error out at three.

Government programs needed five or more. Even my trackers ran into issues after five servers. Course, you also risked information degradation with that many handoffs. It was why I used bots. Break the info down into smaller chunks, reduce the risk of corruption.

Reduced, not eliminated.

This was a test run. I was going after the military contractors that McQuade, Locke, and Remy identified. In addition to being a part of the black bag team that scooped me up, they worked for the highest bidder. They also had a bone to pick with McQuade.

Their business, like any good off the books operation, was highly compartmentalized. It also meant that their systems weren't all connected twenty-four seven. Instead, they opened up burst uploads to sync up their databases. Good plan, especially if you only did it intermittently.

In theory anyway.

Still left me with a route in. The best part of bots, you could send them out to "sniff" the information packets. They would find where the "pops" came from. Then they could be ready to act when the next "pop" happened.

Like I said, it was good security, in theory. But if you were familiar with the types of protocols they would use and how they would write them? Well, then it was like baiting a hook before you cast the line. You just needed the right bait.

Pretty sure my grandfather wasn't talking about computers or the internet, but the principle applied. Movement behind me served as a reminder that I wasn't alone. The guys kept their distance once I'd begun writing code, installing it, and building the tools I would need.

Not everything was proprietary, but a lot of it was. It was easier to make sure no one could trace my tools if I developed them on my own. Also, I was familiar with the trap and traces we used to run from my days in the department.

Chances were high they'd brought in someone else after me. It was also equally as likely that they'd worked to not only improve on the tools I'd left them, but retrofit them. Coding was pretty personal. You could learn a lot about a person based on how they coded.

How their mind worked.

What options they worried about.

What signatures they left behind.

What flaws appeared in their code.

Everyone had flaws. If you could find a pattern, you could find their code. If you could find their code, there was a good chance you could track them.

The next set of bots I dropped out there would be looking for my own code. Unless they'd rewritten it wholly, I still had some stuff out there.

Once the last of the bots were released, a timer began running in the upper right corner of my screen. Fingers hovering over the keys, I tracked the information beginning to feed back into my system from the first skimming attempt.

The bots were already returning. By the time it zeroed out, I severed the main connection between my machine and the internet. Isolating the data onto a partition with no access to anything at all.

Now my decryption programs could go to work, break it down and see what the first skim attempt netted us.

"Well?" Locke said after another long, pregnant pause. I could practically feel the curiosity swirling around him. It brushed over me like a breeze.

"Not sure yet," I admitted. The faintest of trembles revealed itself in my fingers and I had to curl them into my palms. The decryption would take as long as it took. The machine was a muscly little thing, but it didn't have near the processing power of the monster I'd had at home.

"No?"

Was he disappointed? I twisted to glance up at him. He wore a long-sleeved Henley in a deep cream color that gave him a a more tanned appearance. He wore it untucked from the faded denim jeans.

Everything about him was so utterly *human* and at odds with the cool thief who took insane risks. The dark hair he normally kept short but currently brushed his collar, was tousled like he'd been running his fingers through it betrayed an agitation he never showed on the job. While he'd been clean shaven this morning, there was a shadow of growth on his cheeks.

I couldn't deny that *this* Locke fascinated me. The other Locke, the all business one who rubbed elbows easily with aristocracy seemed almost too aloof. Too professional. Too unflappable. Or maybe it was the mannerisms. He lacked *this* Locke's warmth and ease.

Frankly, I liked Remy and McQuade here too. They were still themselves, but—more casual versions. No, casual wasn't the right word. They were just—easier versions maybe. I really lacked the right descriptions.

They were *more* than the men I'd talked through everything on the phone. They were just *more.*

"Patch?" Locke frowned, concern evident. Oh, I hadn't answered him.

"Sorry," I told him, waving off the worry. "I was thinking. No, this is just a first attempt." I motioned to the screen. "A test run, as it were, I wanted to see the strength of the bots against their security systems. I wanted to grab a pop of information as they did a data sync, then siphon it to here. Now—"

I touched my tongue to my teeth. Excitement shivered through me. Not everyone enjoyed the cat and mouse, which usually involved a lot more patience than a hunt of that kind normally indicated, of data acquisition.

He ghosted a hand over my hair to rest on my shoulder. The earlier shiver redoubled and it was like a current raced under my skin. It prickled over my scalp and sent a pulse up my spine.

The weight of his hand was barely there, and yet I was achingly aware of it. The brush of his thumb against my throat sent a jolt to my pulse. If he hadn't been right there, I might have sucked in a deep breath. As it was, every single inhale filled me with more of his scent.

"Now?" he prompted. The crinkles at the corners of his eyes deepened a fraction.

"Um..." What had I been saying? I tried to replay the earlier part of my conversation but it stuttered out the longer I stared up at Locke. Information. Skim. "Oh, I—got a lot of info, I just don't know what it all is yet. The bots returned the packets and I have them isolated on a partition where they can be decrypted without alerting anyone that someone else has them."

"So you have the box, essentially," he murmured. "But you still need the combination to open it and the time to do so without worrying about the alarm."

As analogies went. It wasn't a bad one. "Yes. More or less. I mean—definitely more, not less but yes."

The fact I couldn't seem to adjust the flow of

information escaping me registered on some level. I made a face and then nudged my chair back to stand.

Locke didn't retreat far. In fact, he barely retreated at all. He raised his hand briefly and the loss of contact was as keen to my senses as him putting his hand there in the first place.

I almost sighed when he slid his hand against my shoulder then around to my nape. There was an intimacy in this hold. A flirt with closeness we'd been developing but I hadn't wanted to read anything into.

They rescued me. Transference of emotion was absolutely normal. Textbook case even. I should remember to not act on these impulses. Clearly, it would be a terrible idea.

"Patch?" Not that I could look anywhere else when his voice dropped into that softer register.

"Yes?"

"I'm going to kiss you right now."

"You are?" He was? "Why?"

Why? I asked him why? The earlier tingles seemed to ignite like sparklers on fireworks as he stroked his thumb down the column of my neck. Why the hell had I asked him why?

Rather than answer me, he dipped his head. When his lips were nothing more than a breath away from mine, he seemed to hesitate. My pulse jackhammered, no way he couldn't feel it. The scent of him was an utter intoxication. I pushed forward, closing that gap.

I wanted to *know*.

His mouth was fierce and firm. Nothing

gentle inhabited the kiss. If anything, the moment I put my hand on his chest and leaned into his touch, he took over the kiss. There was a kind of raw demand that urged me to pay attention.

His tongue stroked against the seam of my lips, and I opened my mouth to him. There was no way to deny him. To deny me. He squeezed my nape firmly, the grip burned through me and left a mark far deeper than just my flesh.

Then he was sucking on my tongue and nibbling bites against my lower lip. From pressing the pedal, to hitting one-sixty on the speedometer, Locke's desire ignited my own and I had to grip his shirt to stay on my feet.

The drag of his teeth over my lower lip signaled an end to the contact. He didn't seem to be in a hurry at all, the lingering connection sent tingles vibrating through my whole system. Then he lifted his head. Thankfully, my breath wasn't the only one coming a little faster. The hammer of his heartbeat beneath my fist promised me he'd been every bit as affected as I'd been.

"Wanted to drop a kiss on that sexy mouth for years. Sorry it took so long."

For years?

My heart stuttered.

For...*years?*

He licked his lips then brushed his knuckles down my cheek. "I think your program is done with one of them. More coffee?"

"Yes," I said. "Sure." The words were perfunctory and then I forced my hand to uncurl from the softness of his shirt. He snagged the chair and pulled it over for me.

Right. Sit.

Finally, I broke eye contact and looked around. Once I was in the chair, he nudged me closer to the desk. Then he brushed his fingers against my nape and another shudder went through me that had my cunt clenching and my nipples taut.

Holy shit.

"I'll get your coffee," he said, the whisper a seductive promise or maybe my brain was just conjuring all of that. A moment later, he stepped away but I kept feeling his gaze when it touched me.

I couldn't focus for the array of shocks hitting my system one right after the other. Remy kissed me and I hadn't even spoken to him about it. I'd almost have thought he'd forgotten about it, but I kept catching him watching me.

With Remy, like now with Locke, my awareness of him seemed to take over everything.

Remy kissed me offering me salvation and freedom. More, it had been a cold kind of heat that warmed as it chilled and set my whole being on fire.

Now Locke?

Locke had absolutely blown my damn mind like he'd discovered the secret to crack me open.

Knowing him? He had.

I touched two fingers to my lips as I tried to focus on the screen in front of me.

Whatever was going on, I liked it.
I liked it too damn much.

THIRTY

MCQUADE

"How long has she been at it today?" I pitched the question in a low voice, though I doubted Patch would have noticed, much less acknowledged us. Since she assembled her new system, she'd been at the computer near nonstop.

The only way I got her to rest at all was to pull the power supply. The first night I'd done that, she'd been so pissed off she hadn't spoken to me for two days. She'd slept. So, I considered it a win.

Since then, she'd argued she had "modified" her schedule to include sleep. I could debate that part and would. More than once, she'd been up in the middle of the night. She didn't always leave her room, but I would hear her moving around. She also maintained that the level of research she needed to do involved a lot of search and skims that none of us could do.

"Almost ten hours," Remington stated in an ice dipped voice. His accent grew more pronounced when he was upset. Or maybe I was just projecting. The Brit didn't seem to get upset. Made sense. An assassin needed low blood pressure and a cool demeanor.

I wouldn't mistake it for indifference though. Nothing about Michael Remington was even remotely *indifferent* for our Patch.

"Ten hours," I repeated, then checked my watch. It was already after eight in the evening. "She was up early today." She'd gotten up during my watch. It was four that morning, but I would have sworn she was earlier than that. She just didn't leave her room until four.

"Sounds right," Remington said. "Locke told me she took a break around nine. But she was back at the computer at ten."

So she was up from four until nine working, then ten until now?

That was more like *fifteen* hours.

Even if she *wanted* to declare the break was enough, she was pushing it. The bruises had decreased from black and blue to green and yellow in most places that we could see. That didn't detail the hits she'd taken to her ribs or the deeper cuts, burns, and abrasions.

Her feet were still a mess. Everything Locke and Remington found to help her were useful, but they couldn't speed her healing. Particularly if she didn't *sleep*.

I scratched at the beard I'd been growing in steadily for the last few weeks. Normally, I kept it shorn for missions unless having facial hair was useful. But I'd been on the go and I'd worried more about getting her out than what my appearance was.

I'd finally trimmed it a couple of days previous when I realized I was getting length on it. A beard was fine, particularly when combined with a hat and sunglasses, it helped to muddy facial recognition. I didn't care for it being unkempt or dirty.

"Did she eat?"

"A sandwich," Remington answered in the same neutral tone I'd attempted to use. "It's been almost all coffee today."

I flicked a look to the oversized tumbler she lifted and took a long drink from before she resumed scanning the tables and tables of data scrolling in front of her.

"Got it." Folding my arms, I leaned back against the counter. "Get some sleep."

Remington slid me a look but I didn't tackle his unasked question. He'd had Patch watch for the last several hours. If he'd wanted her up and out of that chair, he should have done something then.

Me? I set an internal timer to count down to her next break, whether she was willing or not. The last thing I wanted to do was scare her, but kid gloves weren't doing her any favors either. If she looked after herself like this when we weren't around...

I scowled. It was absolutely her choice to do what she needed when she needed—and I would support her a thousand percent *after* she healed.

Stress, in addition to not eating well and not sleeping, was not remotely conducive to recovery.

The assassin continued to stare at me for another minute before he nodded. Instead of just heading to his room, though, he paused to put a hand on her shoulder. She glanced up, blinking owlishly as though she hadn't even realized he was there.

Or maybe she'd just forgotten. I added that to the mental inventory I'd been taking. Remington spoke to her in low tones. Clearly, he didn't want me eavesdropping. Rather than lean closer, I moved into the kitchen and started putting together a small meal.

It wasn't fancy like the dishes Remington made or even particularly specific like Locke's straightforward meals. I could grill, I could heat up an MRE and I could make sandwiches. The rest never seemed like something I needed to learn.

As it was, I sectioned the meat and the cheese into bite sizes and added some Ritz crackers and a little honey. She seemed to like the honey.

By the time I had it ready, Remington was gone. The lights were all low in the kitchen and the living room. The windows were covered with both blinds and curtains. None of us cared for the sight lines so we closed them all.

I carried the plate over to her desk. "Break time," I told her and she sighed, impatience edging the long exhale before she glanced up at me.

"I might have something." Not her best argument. If she actually had something, she'd tell me what it was instead of a vague notion.

"Then it will be there when you're done. You haven't taken a break in a while and you need one." When she would have taken the plate, I held it away from her. "Nope. A break means you get up and you eat somewhere that isn't in front of that computer."

That earned me the sourest look. Those gray eyes were pure steel. "McQuade, I don't have time to play games."

"Then don't play, Sugar Bear. Just get up and eat. You should get up and move around anyway, sitting for too long..."

She didn't even let me finish the admonishment before she pushed the chair back and stood. A grimace rippled over her face and I didn't miss how she put a hand against the desktop to steady herself. Inch by inch she straightened. She also tried to cover, but it was way too late.

Yeah, she'd been sitting in that chair for far too long.

"Come on," however, was all I said. "Something to drink?"

"Fine," she said on a long exhale then headed for the breakfast bar on the other side of the kitchen. There was a definite hitch to her steps. She wasn't *quite* limping, but she wasn't moving evenly either.

I didn't say a word when she leaned against the counter rather than sit. She'd grown paler while she moved. Away from the light of her screen, her pallor seemed even more clear.

"Drink?" I asked after setting the plate in front of her. She stared at the food with a kind of weariness I could feel in my bones. The faintly baffled look suggested she wasn't even clear on what the food was.

Yeah, someone had definitely been overdoing it. The pussy footing from the assassin and the thief was not doing her any favors.

None.

"I don't even know if I can eat all of this," she admitted. Well, that was a start.

"You don't have to," I told her. "But you do need to eat some because you need to take your meds, *including* your pain meds."

"I don't like them." Yeah, she didn't have to tell me that. She'd more than made that clear. I went to the fridge and studied the options inside of it. No sugar or caffeine. She needed rest.

I pulled out a cold bottle of water and opened it. When I put it in front of her, she stared at it for a beat. Then rubbed a hand against her face before she claimed it. It was like someone had pulled the plug and all of her energy swirled down the drain.

After piling some of the meat and cheese onto a cracker with a little bit of the honey, I waited for her to finish the long swallow of water then held it up to her. The confusion in her eyes took a little longer to clear, then she accepted the offering.

Rather than argue, I just kept feeding her in small bites in between her sips of water. When she waved off the next bite, I ate it myself and earned a faint smile.

"If you were hungry," she murmured. "You should eat too."

"I eat when I am hungry," I pointed out. "No one has to tempt me with food or honey."

"Really?" She shook her head, then drained the water.

"Sugar Bear, don't know if you've noticed, but you're the only one we have to coax. You don't see me waving cheese and crackers at Remington or Locke."

She chuckled, then rubbed her face again. Now that she wasn't leaning fully against the counter, she swayed.

"You're tired."

"We're all tired," she countered. "I need to work."

"It'll be there," I reminded her. We'd all been keeping our distance. The trauma signs were there. I'd seen them enough in the field. I'd kept a running catalog of every reaction. Every time the shadows slid through her eyes, or she jerked in surprise from contact—every single time, it just made me want to inflict that much more damage.

But right now, what she needed was someone to take care of her and not back away from it *or* her.

"C'mon," I told her. "You're exhausted and you hurt. Now that you've eaten, you can take your meds and get some sleep."

"I don't want to go to sleep," she argued. "I have work to do and—" She tried to push away from the counter like she would head back to her desk, and pain tightened her whole expression.

"Sorry, Sugar Bear." I told her as I intercepted and scooped her up. "That's enough. You've overdone it and you need to rest. You healing is non-negotiable. If that means I take more than the power supply, I'll do it."

She glared at me as I headed for her room. "McQuade..."

"Yes, Sugar Bear?" I grinned at her as her eyes narrowed. Riling her up was fun, it flushed her cheeks with a little color and gave her that snappy little tone she used to spank me with on the phone.

I liked it.

"You can't keep picking me up and just ordering me around," she argued as I shouldered open her door then nudged it closed with my foot.

"Okay," I said as I met the blazing anger in her eyes. "Stop me."

She blinked. "What?"

"You just said I can't do this anymore." I was still cradling her. "If I can't, then stop me."

She eyed me for the longest time while wearing the fiercest frown. "I can't kick your ass."

"Accepted."

"I could get Remy or Locke to do it."

I grinned. "They could try, Sugar Bear. But Locke's not a fighter. Not really. Remington? He would only do it if he didn't see the value in my interruptions."

Her groan shouldn't have been a reward yet it was. "You do not fight fair."

"There is no such thing as a fair fight. There's

the fight you win and the fight you lose. Right now, this is a fight you will lose. Not because I'm bigger or stronger, but because you are a lot smarter than you are stubborn. You could stop me with three words." I raised my eyebrows. "You know it. I know it. So, if you want me to stop—what do you say?"

"Stop it, McQuade."

The fact she didn't even pretend like she didn't know what the words were satisfied something deeply primitive inside of me. The lizard brain that understood the needs for fight and survive and for protect and defend.

With care, I put her on her feet and only kept one hand on her hip lightly to steady her when she swayed. "Three words, Sugar Bear. In truth, you only ever have to use one. I will listen. If you say it to anyone else while I'm there, trust me, I will make sure they listen too."

Pushing her wasn't a kind thing to do, but not pushing her seemed almost less kind. Because it meant letting her hurt herself.

When she tilted her head back, baring her throat, the restlessness in me settled. It wasn't a true surrender in the way of such things, but she was relinquishing this particular battle.

"I hate being weak," she muttered. "I hate being a victim."

"You are not weak and you are not a victim." I gripped her chin lightly, not letting her look away from me. "You were a prisoner of war. You were tortured. You suffered. Now you're free. Freedom —doesn't always fit after you've been through the kinds of things you've been through. That's okay. You work it like any other problem—one day at a time."

"I wasn't all that normal before," she protested, then she scraped her teeth over her already abused lower lip. "McQuade... what if I can't do it?"

"You will."

"But what if I can't?"

"Then you'll find a new way. Remember, what is the only bad plan?"

"Not having one." She closed her eyes and when I should have pulled my hand back, I found myself cradling her cheek. Then she rested her face against my palm. "I don't like to sleep."

"Okay, what can I do?" Because I would do whatever she needed.

"I need—I need to work. I need to have what I can control, what I can do—I need my power back." The adage that you just had to admit what a problem was to begin to defeat it annoyed me. On the one hand, it was partially true. But identifying it also meant letting yourself be vulnerable.

Right now, the very last thing Patch wanted was more vulnerability.

I dipped my head and brushed her lips with mine. I intended for it to be a quick kiss. A sip. A single taste. But the brief moment turned into so much more. She parted her lips, sealing my fate. I all but fell into the kiss like a dying man in the desert. She was the oasis and the promise of heaven all at once.

Devouring her would be so fucking easy and

my cock had gone rock hard at the first tentative touch of her tongue. I'd brought her in here to get her to sleep, not to seduce her. I forced myself to break the kiss because no matter how badly I wanted her, she wasn't ready for me.

She wasn't ready for that right now.

"You need a shower," I told her. "It'll help with the stiffness. Then into some pajamas and take your pain meds. Then I'll stay with you until you go to sleep."

She blinked up at me. The shadows in her eyes darkened the gray to something bruised and aching.

"Trust me," I whispered. "I know I just kissed you, but I promise, I'll be a fucking priest while I help you. No one is going to touch you without your consent."

Her silence speaks volumes and then she presses a hand over my chest.

"I believe you."

Three beautiful words.

"Will you help me?"

Four more. Raw. Vulnerable. Open.

"With anything," I promised.

Maybe I couldn't fight her demons head on, but I could back her up every step of the way.

THIRTY-ONE

PATCH

I rocked the pen back and forth between two fingers as I stared at the feed from the bots. I'd released far more this time, sending them on a direct harvest for information rather than just a skim. A timer ran in the upper right corner. Every second seemed to reverberate with my pulse, adding an extra dimension to it.

Movement in the kitchen behind me served as a reminder that I wasn't alone. The guys took turns. One of them was always awake. It had been that way since we arrived. The only two who left remained McQuade or Locke.

Remington preferred to be here. It was safer for me to remain out of sight and I was fine with it. With the exception of not being in my safe room or having the routine I'd once embraced wholeheartedly—

Had they noticed I was gone? Jimmy, who brought my groceries and Vince, who often brought up my mail or packages?

Would they have reported me missing?

The home was already compromised. In no world had I ever thought I could return there.

"Lunch in fifteen," Locke said from somewhere behind me. "It smells good, whatever it is."

"It's just a roast," Remington said. "I was bored with burgers. You like making them too much."

"Burgers are easy and they are quick. Also no one cares if you eat them cold." Locke shrugged. "Liking fine cuisine and cooking it are two different things."

"Clearly," Remington retorted, his tone dry. "However, I draw the line at the persistent servings of ground beef. Or haven't you noticed that the lovely Patch has not been finishing her burgers the past two days..."

"I noticed," Locke grumbled. "I just thought maybe we were feeding her too much."

"You two are adorable," I said without looking away from the screen. "I get that you want to engage me in the conversation, but I didn't finish the burger because I was simply full. I'd also had sandwiches about an hour before you made the burgers last night so I wasn't hungry."

A fresh set of numbers popped up on the screen. The first wave of bots returned. Quarantine programs immediately engaged. Someone had tried to attach a worm to one of the bots.

How sad for them.

I nuked that one immediately and kept it compartmentalized.

"If you want something different..." Locke began but I shook my head.

"Guys, this is going to go faster if we don't need to keep tallying the calorie log. I haven't eaten this well in a long time. I'm used to just cooking for one and—"

Bingo. I forgot about the conversation as the details began to unfold about MD Outfitters. They'd been on my radar while I'd worked in the department. Military contractors, freelance and available to the highest bidder. They weren't licensed to work within the U.S. Didn't mean they weren't based here.

"Do you ever feel like one minute she's paying attention and the next we're utterly superfluous?" Locke didn't sound insulted.

"Yes," Remington's crisp reply also didn't invite further conversation. "Then, she is doing her job and we should let her do it."

I shuttered the conversation fully. They could talk, I didn't need to focus on that. I needed to pay attention to what was happening on the screen.

The decryption programs were going to work. The keyword program flagged page after page for me to review and cross-reference. I continued to rock the pen as I read, only putting it down to type in new commands. Some files had to be destroyed.

A new security system, kind of like watermarking, had infected the files that had been skimmed. Not a virus, but also not a worm. It simply wanted to report back the IP address for the latest read.

Subtle, delicate work. Respect to the coder,

because it was ingenious. It wouldn't register on most virus scanners. Technically, it wasn't even a trojan program. It was just a little executable that sent out a ping. One, tiny little ping so that it could log where the file had been opened.

Quarantined as the files were the secondary partition, the ping had nowhere it could go, but it kept trying to send it. I set the pen aside as I checked the auto logger to see *where* it was sending the ping to...

Sophisticated. It tried a series of addresses. When it failed to reach any of them, it started over. Sophisticated *and* persistent. I'd have to nuke all of it before I could open the drive again.

I created a dummy file and masked it as a server to receive the ping the file sent out and then logged the information it provided. Oh, that was clever. Now that it had logged the IP, or thought it had, it tried to add a couple of lines to the primary OS that would send another ping with updates the next time the system booted.

Insidious little program. Big brother was watching you, always watching.

It took me a few hours to find the thread of the logger, and pull it apart. The code was—elegant. It was only a handful of lines, but it took every advantage of the fact that whoever "stole" the file would have to encrypt then decrypt. So the decryption was precisely what activated those handful of lines.

Without the quarantine, there was every chance it would succeed in sending the ping without a trace. Well, the trace would have been there but only if you were looking for it. I was going to have to add another layer to the programs I ran specifically for code like this.

Instead of a poison pill it was a tainted cookie. That made me like it even less, even if it was clever.

I'd like to stab the coder in their clever little eye with my pen.

Piece by piece, I pulled out the useful data and began to build a timeline of sorts. The events I added were not defined beyond mission names unless they were target oriented. Combing through the other packets netted some details I could use to flesh out the framework.

The task took every ounce of my focus. Because of the little tags on the data, I had to go through each piece of it individually, extracting the core of what I needed before sending the actual file to be destroyed.

Tedious work. Absolutely tedious, but this was exactly why I'd built these programs, so I could locate and retrieve any file that might be related to my capture and subsequent incarceration. It also let me drill down on them to determine if the link was genuine or not.

McQuade appeared in my line of sight and I dragged my attention from the screen to look up. Since the day I confessed I had trouble sleeping, he made a point of staying in my room until I was asleep.

I hoped he did sleep, but so far I'd always woken alone. I could ask, I supposed, but—a part of me wasn't sure I wasn't already pushing it with these three men. Did they know they'd each kissed me? Did Locke and Remington realize Mc-Quade stayed in my room most evenings until I passed out?

Did I even understand why his presence made sleep not only possible but something I didn't dread? The nightmares were still there, I snapped awake from them. Maybe I should ask him to stay, it seemed even more difficult to go back to sleep after one when he was already out of the room.

Don't go crazy. They are going back to their own lives and business soon enough. You're going to have to do this on your own again.

As bleak a thought as that was, I knew I could do it. As soon as we dealt with the department and my kidnappers, I'd rebuild my life some-where else, somewhere new, and disconnect from what came before—even this.

"Time to eat," McQuade said and I had to blink rapidly as past, present, and potential fu-ture kind of collided. "You're zoning out—that means you need a break."

"No, it means I need to focus more."

Then before he could argue because the nar-rowing of his eyes promised me the argument was coming, I raised a hand to hopefully forestall him long enough to get my point across.

"I'm close. Closer than I've been. I finally got past some of their external firewalls with this skim attempt. I'm finding files on me and on the open bid they are making for my ac-quisition."

"If you don't decrypt it right now, it'll still be there," McQuade said. "Right?"

"Well… yes." That wasn't the point. I frowned at him. "We need everything on these people so we can—well, so you three can plan, though I want to be in on that planning as well."

"No one is keeping you out of it," he answered with an easy shrug as if to say and *no one* would. "However, the work you're doing requires you to refuel. You are putting that beautiful brain to work and you're still healing, that means you need to eat and you need to rest. If the information isn't going anywhere if you take an hour, then we're taking that hour."

I opened my mouth to argue then snapped it shut again as I glanced at the screen. The files were all quarantined. Because of the tracer program, I had to go through them individually. If I took a break, no they weren't going to expire or disappear, but they were also not going to be decoded.

"An hour now might cost us more later." As arguments went, it was a weak one and the bland look he gave me said as much.

"Then it costs us more later," Remington stated from somewhere behind me. "I can't imagine it will cost us much except for time. Time we'll have because you will have healed."

"If we're voting, then we're three for three on you taking a break." Locke wasn't going to be left out. One on one, these men were powerful enough. As a team though, they could overwhelm everything about me. Even my good intentions…

"I don't want to vote." That came out so surly that I wrinkled my nose.

"You don't care about the vote." Trust McQuade to call me on it. "You just don't want to lose."

"Does anyone *ever* want to lose?" Since they weren't going to let it go, I pushed back from the computer and stood. Having learned my lesson the other day, I took my time and stretched. My normal routines used to involve walking or running in addition to daily stretching.

I'd not resumed either here because I was healing and while they may not be feeling the crush of time *I* was. If I wanted to reclaim any semblance of the life I'd made for myself, then I needed to cut all the ties to the past. That included these new ones.

I rolled my head from side to side, then turned away from McQuade's too watchful gaze only to collide with the assessing looks from both Locke *and* Remington.

"Yes, I'm sore." Might as well address it head-on. "I expect I will be sore for some time. My ribs feel better. I can take deeper breaths. The bruises are still pretty stiff along my back, but my legs are fine for the most part."

When I trusted myself to walk without too much of a limp, I left my desk and headed for the dining table where they'd put out food. It was even set right down to the plates, glasses, and cutlery. The roast was on the table...

Remington pulled a chair out for me. "Problem?"

"I thought the roast was for dinner."

"It is for dinner," he said as I sat slowly and he pushed the chair in. "That's why we're all taking a break."

It was dinner time. That meant... "I worked through lunch."

"Hmm-hmm," Locke said as he opened a sparkling water and poured it into my glass. Like me, they'd also refrained from alcohol, though I wasn't sure it had been discussed.

"You guys let me." I was still turning that over as McQuade took the seat across from me. He couldn't take the ones to my left or right at the four seater table because Locke and Remington had already claimed them.

"You're welcome," McQuade said before he filled his glass from a pitcher. At my frown, he motioned to it. "Lemonade?"

That sounded amazing. The smell of the roast and the potatoes were all hitting me at once. They'd prepared a huge meal. It was divine and my mouth watered.

"Thank you," I murmured as Remington served out slices of the meat then the potatoes were handed to me. I got the first serving of everything. It was a huge meal. Now that I was aware of it, I was starving. "Guys..."

All three of them focused on me and the air backed up in my lungs. There was no mistaking their attention, no matter how much I tried to ignore the meaning behind each of their kisses or the depth of feeling they aroused in me.

In their own ways, they were all predators.

Apex predators in their particular fields. While they were extremely dangerous, they were also incredibly gentle with me. Even when I didn't pay as close attention as I should, I could see that they were.

They also capped their own impatience with the process and me, instead, they looked after me in their own ways.

"Thank you," I murmured, taking a moment to meet each of their gazes. "I don't know that I actually said that in all of this. Thank you for coming for me and for getting me out. Thank you for—" I motioned to the cabin. "All of this."

"You're welcome," Locke said easily, a sentiment echoed by Remington.

"Just remember that the next time you get pissy that we're making you take a break," McQuade said and Locke groaned.

"You really don't have a sense of when not to push it," he muttered.

"I don't need to," McQuade retorted. "She has you and the Brit here to hold hands with and skip merrily to her doom." All at once his gaze locked onto mine. "That's not what you want or need from me, is it, Sugar Bear?"

No, it absolutely wasn't. I swallowed, unable to look away from the ferociousness in his eyes. The feeling unfolding in my chest sent waves of heat and cold to every extremity.

"Of course not," I murmured, fighting for normalcy. "I would never ask you for something outside your wheelhouse."

The corners of his lips twitched. Yeah, it wasn't a denial...

"Nor skillset," I continued and his eyes narrowed at the tweak. "It wouldn't be kind."

Some of the tension bubbling there eased and I could take a breath. It wasn't like I didn't know how to talk to them. I always had.

"I'll remember that," McQuade reminded me.

"Of course you will." I managed to look at Locke who seemed to be shaking his head at McQuade and Remington both. The latter lifted his chin as though encouraging me to continue. But I just smiled and saluted him with my first cut of the meat. "This smells wonderful, Remy. Thank you."

"My pleasure," he said and a fresh shiver raced over my skin, leaving tingles in its wake. These guys were—a lot.

But I could handle it, I reminded myself. I knew them. I'd handled them for years. Maybe if I told myself that enough times the pragmatist in me would stop reminding me that for years there'd been miles between us with only the internet and a phone for contact.

Yep, the pragmatist in me was a real bitch because she highlighted the fact the only thing between us now were clothes and based on those kisses—that didn't have to be a thing either.

Heat flushed me and I fixed my gaze on the plate as I ate. The food was wonderful, but all the air in the room seemed to escape as it filled up with their presence.

I really needed to get us the information we needed so we could get out of here in one piece. All four of us.

CHAPTER
THIRTY-TWO

LOCKE

The clock ticking down had grown more audible over the past few days. Initially, the only time constraints had been to find her as soon as possible. Then it was to get her out. After—the drive was to get her to safety and keep her there.

Once we reached Michigan and dug in, the clock had all but stopped. For me anyway. Then it was a series of tasks that needed to be completed —side quests as it were. McQuade and I handled the bulk of it.

He took care of weapons while I handled everything else. I didn't even mind it. Granted, I'd spent more time in jeans and flannel shirts than I thought remotely reasonable. The fact I'd not worn a tux or anything involving silk ties or shirts was almost amusing.

I didn't hate it though. The fact I'd more or less gone totally off the grid wasn't that unusual in my life. My accountant would make sure all my bills were paid—including his own. I had a housekeeper who looked after my home and she handled the bills there.

In fact, the only person likely missing me at all was my tailor. Food for thought, I supposed. The sound of a bedroom door closing quietly had me pivoting. I'd gotten up early, done my stretches and pushups in my room and come out to see about food.

While our rooms were located near the back of the house, we'd given Patch the largest room that was literally on the other side of the wall from the living room. The ensuite gave her privacy and it wasn't that many steps from her work area to her bedroom.

Was she up this early? If she was, I'd make her espresso. I didn't touch the machine before she woke up cause the grinder was noisy.

Instead of Patch coming down the short hall from her room it was McQuade, carrying his boots in one hand and his shirt in the other. His jeans weren't even done up. He looked like he'd just rolled out of bed based on the disheveled hair alone.

He paused mid-step when his gaze hit mine. It was just after six in the morning and he'd just let himself out of her bedroom. *Her* bedroom. My teeth clicked as I snapped my mouth closed before the first comment escaped.

"You're up," McQuade said and I raised my eyebrows.

"Obviously." The uneasy feeling in my gut expanded. His interest in our operator hadn't been lost on me. Remington was equally taken with her. I thought, however, we'd all been on the same page about bedding her. She needed time to *heal* and to recover.

McQuade tilted his head from one side to the other, the pop of sound seemed to offer him some relief. It only served to amp up my own tension. He took another couple of steps toward me.

I tracked his every move. There were any number of items around us that could be turned into weapons. Not the least of which was the metal carafe we brewed coffee in. Apply enough force and it might even dent his stubborn skull.

If I did strike, I'd need to do it swiftly and with minimal awareness on his part. Largely because I wouldn't lie to myself. He was an extremely dangerous man. Reprisal would hurt.

Didn't mean I wouldn't do it, I just needed to weigh how badly I needed to strike him and whether I could wait to extract my pound of flesh later.

"Spit it out," McQuade said as he finally reached the border between kitchen and living room. We were on opposite sides of the breakfast bar. Arguably, we were on many other opposite sides than I'd earlier believed.

I eyed him as he set his boots down and then tugged his shirt on over his head. Saying anything wouldn't be prudent. We needed a certain amount of peace for this alliance to continue. Patch needed our alliance.

At the rate she was going with her research, we would all be splitting up sooner rather than later. Then McQuade and Remington would be gone and I could find a way to insert myself back into her life.

She would need additional security for a while. Who better than a thief to make sure hers was impregnable?

The standoff stretched into the most uncomfortable of silences. He wasn't going to give an inch, in fact, he seemed to be practically *daring* me to say something.

"She needs her rest." Not my best material, yet wholly accurate.

"She does. That's why I made sure she got it," he countered. There was just the faintest of smirks on his face.

Cocky asshole. "She also needs patience and to not have anyone making demands on her. We don't know she wasn't raped."

"We can probably guess she was, we know she took enormous physical abuse." McQuade shrugged that off as if we were discussing the changing of a tire on a vehicle. "What's your point?"

"Why the hell are you in her bed instead of out here, keeping watch, like you're supposed to be?" The icy tone Remington spoke in came far closer to matching my thoughts than his words did. I wouldn't have put it that way and at the same time, I wanted an answer.

"It's none of your business," McQuade said, then he tugged a phone out of his pocket. "I also have all the exterior cameras on here. The motion sensors would alert me—and they did. We had a very curious bunch of deer come through last night."

The screen had been divided into four and flickered from one location to another. All places we'd put up cameras to give us the widest possible angles and the best views if anyone came at us from the road *or* the woods.

"So you put her safety into the hands of motion sensors." Contempt licked every single syllable the British assassin spoke. Frankly, I couldn't manufacture that level of disappointment or disdain. I wonder if it came with Remington's pedigree. I hadn't heard him come up the hall, but good to know we were on the same page.

His increasing anger seemed to let the air out of my own. The motion sensors were out there for a reason. They were tied into *all* of our phones. We also had extraction plans in place. The one *with* or closest to Patch got her out while the other two dealt with whatever incursion there was.

Chances were good, I'd be the one running with her since these two were a lot deadlier. Still, if it came down to firing a gun or letting her get hurt—I'd happily take on my share of the bloodshed.

"Second guessing your own idea, *mate?*" McQuade was just baiting the bear now. "That was the point of the motion sensors. Another layer of security. Don't worry, I had an exit plan ready to go if we were compromised. She would have been fine."

The smugness was a bit much. "You don't have to be a dick about it."

"Why not?" McQuade swung his gaze toward me before he motioned to the coffeemaker. "Also are you planning on making that or just having your judgment for breakfast?"

"Look, asshat," I said, flattening my hands against the counter. "Fuck off with that attitude. You're acting like you're the only one involved."

"No, I'm acting like I need coffee and you jackasses are too busy wondering if I'm dipping my dick to worry about whether you have a right to ask that question. What I do and who—"

"The only who in the equation is Patch," Remington said, cutting him off. "Don't use her that way."

"What makes you think I'm using her at all?" Every single part of that question was an insult. Did he think we were blind *or* stupid?

Remington held McQuade's stare. The air around them crackled with danger and the oxygen began to leak out of the room. There was no way I wanted to be between them if a fight started...

The creak of her door opening might as well have been a gunshot, the pair backed up at the same time. They each gave ground and like me, they looked toward the bedroom. Patch emerged. She wore sweatpants and an oversized sweatshirt. She loved the warmer, thicker clothes. Layers offered comfort.

Her disheveled hair was a lot like McQuade's

had been, but she was already pulling it back into a ponytail with a huge scrunchy. I rather liked the black tips on the golden silk hair. It was like she'd been the light, dipped into the darkness, but she survived.

If that wasn't a metaphor for everything she'd gone through, I didn't know what was. The effect with her hair all pulled back added another dimension to her. It registered that whenever she'd initially disappeared from her life, she'd changed her hair color.

I wasn't entirely sure why that hadn't occurred to me before. Of course she'd changed her hair color. Hair, eyes, and use a little cosmetics to change the dimensions or the contours on her face.

If she had any gift with stage makeup, she could also use putty to alter her nose and jaw. With the right glasses, the whole effect would change her entirely. I wasn't sure they could reduce the magnetic look of hers, but she could look like someone else entirely.

"Guys?" Her voice came out a little raspy and hoarse. She had just woken up. "Is there a problem?"

"No," McQuade and Remington answered in the same breath.

"Yes," I told her, unwilling to lie and I ignored the dark looks the other two shot in my direction. "To be perfectly honest, it's been a small miracle we've had few issues this long. We'll work it out."

Because I wasn't dumping this in her lap,

even if I'd been thinking about the kiss I gave her a hell of lot more than she had been.

Squashing that thought, I shook off the negativity. I had no idea what she'd been thinking about beyond obsessing over the information she'd been trying to coax out of her research.

"I'll get your coffee started. What's your plan for the day?"

She stared at me for a long moment, then glanced at the other two before coming back to me. "Are you sure?"

"That we'll work it out?" I asked. At her nod, I pursed my lips. "For the most part, yes. Because currently, our goals remain aligned. We might not have met until we literally ran into each other at your house, but—we have proven we can work together to protect you. I'm confident enough in our skills and relative intelligence that we can maintain that."

Doubt crept into her eyes and she chewed her lower lip as she studied us. The assassin and the mercenary were both unusually quiet. If I were to have picked which one would break first, I would have been right.

"Locke is correct," Remington said. "We do have issues. We will, however, manage them and they won't impact our work. You don't need to worry about us."

"Alright," she said slowly, but despite my best effort, she clearly didn't believe us. "If that changes, please read me in. I get that I am taking up a lot of oxygen in the conversation right now and I appreciate all of you for everything you have done. But if we're a team, then we all have a voice."

"No one here is arguing that," McQuade told her. "You want coffee *and* food, right?"

"Coffee yes. Food can wait..." Then she sighed. "Or not because otherwise all three of you will hover, so something small and just make me whatever you are having. I should probably start volunteering to cook."

"When you're done with your part of the job," Remington told her. "Right now, we need your brain on those tasks. We can handle the domestic chores for now. Locke, coffee. I'll take care of food."

"I guess I'll just starve," McQuade muttered.

"I have a faster way to kill you," Remington offered in a low voice and I shot a look to where Patch had moved to her computer. The bruises were looking better but she didn't seem to have caught that last.

"Bring it on, *mate*," McQuade jabbed at him verbally.

"Stop calling me mate," Remington ordered him in those same chilly tones.

"Stop it entirely," I told them, with my back to Patch. These words really did not need to carry, at all. "I bought us time to resolve this without her being in the middle. At least respect it..."

They both gave me baleful looks.

"Or don't, but if you keep it up, I will steal her away so she doesn't have to deal with your shit."

With that said, I got the coffee grinder going. They didn't say a word to me, but eventually, McQuade headed back to his own room and Remington got the food going.

I focused on the task at hand. Make her coffee, and keep things even so she could heal. That meant not fighting in front of her. These two could always beat the shit out of each other later...

I'd just finished her coffee when Patch said, "Holy shit...I found them."

"Found—"

I didn't get to finish because Remington was at her side, one hand on her chair as he stared at the computer.

"Section Five," he said and I swore the floor fell out from under me.

"Section Five is a myth," I argued. "A boogeyman to scare terrorists." That was the rumor. They'd gotten very powerful in the years after 9-11. Homeland Security was supposed to facilitate communication between all the alphabet agencies, but Section Five had been composed of those who just didn't play nicely with others.

A government-sanctioned operation that was utterly unscrupulous and buried so deeply, no one held them accountable.

"They aren't a myth," McQuade said as he rejoined us, still tucking his clean shirt into his fresh jeans. "They are the boogeymen, but they are no myth."

"Let me guess," I said. "You worked for them."

"No," he answered. "My father was one of the people who pushed for it to form in the first place."

Fuck.

THIRTY-THREE

PATCH

The discovery of Section Five was like manifesting all of the worst possible outcomes into one horror story. The department I'd worked for was Section Five. A division that seemed to exist only in the tabloids and debunked online rumors and legends. Every once in a while, a meme got started, sharing some bullshit story that was quickly discredited.

Or even if it wasn't discredited fully, it was dismissed by the general populace leaving only the most paranoid of conspiracy theorists. Hell, at one point, I'd even thought it would make fun material for a book or Netflix movie. Conspiracies were all the rage, but this...

If the department had actually been a part of Section Five, it made so many of the things I'd done while working for them worse. Government funding coupled with no oversight for an operation that shouldn't exist made this worse.

And McQuade's father was involved with it? I

wasn't even sure what to do with that. After the initial shock wore off, I spent the next few days truly digging down on all of it. I need confirmation.

Just turning up Section Five in a deep dive could have been a distraction. Something to stir up the conspiracy nuts so they would cloud the issue for the next several weeks to months.

Internet chatter was a great way to farm information. It was an even better way to spread disinformation. Recent studies indicated that more than fifty percent of the populace got their news from social media. More than half of all social media users out there sharing the latest breaking news or posts about politics did so *without* verifying the facts.

They said they did. Everyone *claimed* to be an informed source who had *done* their *research*. I wasn't really sure if the lies they were telling were to themselves or to the people that followed them. The numbers of people who believed broadcast news, no matter what actual bias it might have, was scarier still.

Just because the name Section Five came up, and my heart fell all the way to my toes, didn't make the information accurate *or* actionable. The fact that all three men knew exactly who I was talking about didn't make me feel better. Far from it.

We need confirmation. Confirmation had to come from at least two unrelated sources without awareness of what I was looking for. Otherwise

—what? I just triggered a trap they set into play for all the conspiracy theorists out there.

Worse, I sent us chasing after the wrong people. The biggest question was *how* did we verify a super secret organization? It started with a trip to the dark web, and arranging a meeting in Detroit.

Locke was against me going at all, particularly because it involved leaving the house. McQuade, surprisingly, seemed to be on my side and stressed that I would never be alone.

Remington was Switzerland.

"The person you're meeting has no idea what you look like, right?" Locke confirmed. We'd formed a circle around the island in the kitchen where I'd briefed them. It was—a strange way to do a briefing. Usually I used files and had a headset on.

"She already told us they don't have physical confirmation. That's why they are using objects to identify themselves." McQuade leaned against the other counter, his arms folded and his expression neutral. Despite saying he backed my plan, he didn't give off the strongest vibe of support.

Locke had his hands flat against the counter, his expression far more grim. "Then it doesn't *have* to be you," he said, pinning me with a look. "I can play your part. They don't know you at all. You could be male, female, non-binary, it doesn't matter—"

Technically correct, however, I shook my head. "It has to be me, because the conversation is not something I can just talk you through. If they ask specific questions that I need to answer then I have to be the one there—and before you keep arguing..."

It was my turn to cut him off before he could launch into his lists of reasons. I got it, I really did. But it was important that they all understood I wasn't making this call lightly. His teeth clicked together and he straightened. I held Locke's gaze until he finally blew out a breath and motioned for me to continue.

"If I were setting this meeting, which I am, I would make sure the meeting took place in a very public area where it's hard to knife someone but also where signals are scrambled to avoid anyone listening. That means, even if we have comms in, there's a very strong chance you would have to wing it on questions that I should be able to answer easily. The same is said for them."

"I don't like it," Locke grumbled and I smiled. The worry in his voice and his eyes weren't manufactured. He really didn't like the idea of me being out there.

"Not sure I like it either," I admitted. "I'm going to be out in a public place with a lot of people. After the last several years of being on my own, you guys are almost too much sometimes."

My nerves jangled with the very idea and my pulse raced.

"I have two choices, I can keep being scared of everything or I can put myself out there again. We need confirmation. I can't—make any kind of action or work out an infill and exfil without being dead certain of who we are dealing with. You thought it was a mercenary outfit. You found information on where I was being held because you broke in and stole hard drives."

"All that matters is it worked." He waved off their choices which led to my rescue. "We were getting it one way or another. That opens up another question, if it is Section Five, would they have hired mercenaries?"

"Yes," McQuade answered before I could. "It gives them credible deniability. It also means any trail that's picked up leads to them and not Section Five. Hard to be a secret organization if you're trackable."

He wasn't wrong. I shifted so I could straighten. I was still sore. Most of my bruises had faded. The scars on my arms weren't going anywhere. I just had to keep them covered. My feet were healing the slowest of all, but they *were* healing. One problem at a time, that was all I could do.

"Do I want to take the risk of meeting my contact? Not really. A part of me just says, dig in and dig deep. Wait, play the long game." That part of me gestured to every move I'd made more than five years ago to get out. The plan worked. I'd been safe.

The rest of me, though, wholeheartedly rejected it. How much deeper could I bury myself? I'd have to cut all ties to the world, including these guys. Of all the options, I found that one to be the most abhorrent.

"You don't want to play the long game any-more." The one statement was the first time Remington contributed to the conversation since I presented the plan. It wasn't a question. He dropped his chin as he studied me.

"No," I said. "I don't. If they had never come after me, I'd still be in my house in Estes Park. I'd locked myself in that cell and threw away the key. I stayed there, a very comfortable prisoner. My work was all I really had and I didn't even allow myself to get a cat because what if something happened?"

I shook my head.

"Five years. I spent five years of my life staying off the radar and out of sight. They still sent people after me. They want the files. They want all of it. Whether the *they* in this equation call themselves Section Five or the department or the division or the damn greenhouse, I'm tired of running. That plan failed."

"It kept you alive," Locke reminded me.

"We still don't know *how* they found you," McQuade said. "That's a door that still needs to be closed."

"If we can close it, great. If not—that means I'm still hiding with no guarantee they won't find me again. It also means I never come out of hiding." Head back, I stared up at the ceiling. "I mean, I suppose we could do that. It might take time to set me up so I can still be your operator. Though to be truthful... If I cut everything again, I should cut my work as your operator too. That connection could have been the thing that compromised me."

Whether through a contact, a job search, something. I was careful, painfully so, but maybe I'd missed something. Something so innocuous that I wouldn't identify it now.

"I don't want a different operator," Remington said finally. "You don't deserve to go back into a cell no matter how comfortable."

"You're voting with them," Locke said abruptly and there was no mistaking his disappointment. He scratched at his jaw.

"So are you," Remington countered and I jerked in surprise. "None of us want a different operator."

The three men stared at each other. All the crackling tension of that morning when I'd made the discovery seemed to boil up to the surface.

"Then let's plan," McQuade said. "Every angle covered."

"Agreed," Remington stated and then they both looked at Locke who stared at me.

Did he want me to let him off the hook...?

"Promise me if one of us calls it, for whatever reason, even if we don't have time to explain, that you will drop everything and walk away. We'll cover your exit, and get you out."

That was a huge ask.

"Agreed," McQuade said. "If you told me to drop everything and go, I would."

That wasn't fair.

"Same." With Remington's agreement, all three were firmly on the same side again.

"Usually when I do that, it's because I can see what you can't," I said and that was when I saw their point. They might see or notice something I didn't. Surrendering operational control was not my favorite thing, but I wasn't going to be behind my computer for this one. I would be out there, in the field, taking a risk.

I really had lost my damn mind.

"Fine, done. If any one of us calls it. I'll walk away."

Their relief sent a dagger of guilt plunging through me. They were doing a lot for me, this was the least I could do.

"Okay, coffee and planning." McQuade pointed at me. "Possible locations, I want us to control the where, so whatever deal you strike, make sure that's on our side. Let's start with where you were thinking?"

The tension ballooned again but this wasn't with the same violence as before. No, it bubbled with anticipation and anxiety. I was really going to do this, which meant, we needed to go over *everything*.

~

"Go over the plan again," McQuade said from the front seat as Locke drove. We'd left well before sunrise, the drive to Detroit was going to take several hours. I'd set the meeting for a little after two. Well past the lunch hour and before the evening crowds would fill the area.

Open, and public, but not so dense with

people we risked anyone getting hurt. An icy heat kept sweeping over me each time I thought about the fact I would be meeting face to face with someone I had only ever spoken to online.

That apprehension would probably have been present when I met these three, had circumstances been wildly different. The only objection Remy had made initially had been related to the fact the mobile unit wasn't quite ready for this operation.

Still, it should be a simple meet and greet.

Should be.

"Meeting location is the coffee shop near the clocktower. We will make contact *at* the clocktower and enter the coffee shop together. Tiffin—my contact—will be wearing a navy, orange, and white hat with a sports logo on it."

"Detroit Tigers," Locke said over his shoulder. "Stylized D."

"Does it matter?" I countered. "It's a sports logo, I know the one to look for."

"Aren't you the one who usually reminds us that preciseness is important?" McQuade's teasing tone stroked over me.

"Yes, fine. Navy, orange, and white cap with the stylized D for the Detroit Tigers. In addition to the cap, he will be wearing a black hoodie and carrying a denim backpack. If he has taken off the hoodie or is dangling the backpack rather than has it on his back, the meeting may have been compromised. Back off."

Tiffin and I had spent an hour working out the details. It was complicated and as much as it might seem unnecessary, it was far from it. Tiffin and I had contact for years via the dark web. He'd always been a reliable resource. For this—for this I needed face to face before I read him into what was happening.

No way I'd drag a relative innocent into the possible crosshairs of some shady, disavowed government conspiracy. It was insane if I tried to think about it too closely. How was this my life?

"I'm wearing this dark purple 'Get a Life' sweatshirt. My hair will be pulled back into a braid and I have a pair of sparkly sunglasses." They were the most ridiculous things. Locke had found them at a service station about seven miles away from the house. They were shaped like stars and sparkled in the sunlight.

Gaudy as hell.

I loved them.

"If something is worrying me, I'm to push them up onto my head. If something feels off or is wrong, take them off entirely. If I want immediate extraction, pull my braid free." It was a lot simpler than Tiffin's outfit.

"Locke and McQuade will be in the crowd," Remington said. "I'll have overwatch. Whoever is closest is the one who gets you out when extraction is called."

"And if comms don't work or it's too noisy?" Because that was the biggest reason *I* would be taking the meeting instead of letting Locke play the part of Patch.

"In the event of communication failure, I'll move to your line of sight," Remington said. "I'm better at a distance, but I'll be where you can see me and I can get to you. They won't be far."

"For the record," Locke said. "I don't like this plan."

"Neither do I," McQuade agreed. "But it's the best of a shit situation. You're wearing the body vest, right?"

He'd strapped it on me before I'd pulled the loose sweatshirt over my head. So the question wasn't for him, it was for Locke and Remy.

"Yes," I said. "Still not sure it will protect me from a headshot."

"Me neither," McQuade said, exhaling. "This is a risk. We can still call this off and do it another way."

"I thought you agreed with me that they wanted me alive, so they wouldn't go for the headshot?"

Sweat slid down between my shoulder blades and it took serious concentration to not start panting. I curled my fingers into my palms. The anxiety was there when they were the ones on the ground and I was at the keyboard.

This was a whole new level.

"I said it wasn't in their interests to shoot you," McQuade muttered. "I don't want them to get stupid abruptly."

"You're going to be fine," Remy said, the steadiness in his gaze stabilizing me. "You have us. We have a plan. We have three separate extraction routes planned. If necessary, we can come up with more on the fly."

"We got this," Locke added. This was my plan, but they were comforting me.

"Should we go over it one more time?"

McQuade grinned at me over his shoulder and Remy covered my hand with his and I clasped his gratefully. I wasn't the only one who needed comfort.

"Okay, we're meeting..."

THIRTY-FOUR

REMINGTON

Every plan, no matter how precise and well-researched, had an inherent flaw. They could go wrong. Plans, most often, relied on people. Though we'd gone over the plan repeatedly both before and on the way to Detroit, I couldn't shake the niggling feeling of something going wrong.

Patch was an invaluable resource behind the computer. There was no other operator I wanted backing me. Putting her out in the field, even at her own insistence, set off every internal alarm I possessed. Yes, we'd covered nearly all angles except for every other person who would be present.

Tiffin and Patch were not "linked" online anywhere, but what exactly did that offer us? The faux promise of security and anonymity? The minute he identified her, her anonymity would be gone.

Truth be told, her anonymity had been stripped the moment her captors had taken her.

They dropped me off first so I could check for the best perch. I had a couple of ideas based on the maps.

Online mapping and satellite coverage was great, but they could also be out of date. It was always better to case the physical location with time to adjust. We didn't have time, at least not the time I wanted.

"No good sight lines," I commented into the phone. The line was open to the vehicle. "I'll have to be on the ground with her."

Not one hundred percent true. There was *one* sight line. The clock tower itself. The problem with it, though, was she would be out of sight while at the base and if they deviated from course by even a meter, there was a solid chance I'd lose them.

This was not an acceptable margin of error.

"Understood," McQuade said. "We're coming around to drop her off. South side."

"Copy."

The sun played peekaboo with the clouds. The weather had called for partly cloudy, but I didn't think anyone had actually informed the weather itself. The clouds were thicker and darker. They carried the promise of rain and something chillier.

So far, the only thing going according to our intel was the moderate size of the crowd coming and going from the outdoor mall. Wind swept through, bringing a slash of icier temps with it.

I caught sight of Patch the moment she slipped out of the car. McQuade didn't exit with her. He wouldn't. They'd pull forward to another set of cameras and let him get out there before Locke went to park.

Maybe one of us should stay with the car.

"I have her," I said. There was a distinct crackle on the line that had me adding, "umbrella and I was going to pick up lunch. Thoughts on dining out?"

As codes went, it wasn't sophisticated.

"Not really hungry," Locke said. "But she might have picked up something already. So check with her *first*."

He didn't have to tell me twice. I cut across the quad on a direct path toward her even as I scanned the crowd. Locke had already seen two people trailing her? That was fast.

Unless the entire meeting had been a set up to reacquire her. It was the biggest risk we'd taken. Another reason to have me on the ground with her. Locke and McQuade had gone into the facility, they might have their faces.

They didn't have mine.

Music filtered through the outdoor speakers muddying the ambient sounds. Conversations flowed around me, some strident, others more relaxed. One couple was arguing about expenses. Another man snapped out something to his office on the phone. A couple of teenagers playing truant from school and walking hand in hand.

A disparate crowd filled the outdoor area with hundreds of intersecting points. So many places it could go wrong. I caught sight of the man right behind Patch, but he diverted before I even got there. His whole expression lightened as he hugged a woman hurrying to meet him.

False alarm?

Patch's expression was taut and I could feel her gaze even through the sparkly star shaped sunglasses. They looked ridiculously cheerful in light of the deep gray twilight out here.

Thunder rippled in the distance. The itch between my shoulder blades intensified.

"Call it," I said. "Extract now." I held out my hand to her and it helped that she took my hand without question. My instincts said get the hell out of here and I was going to listen to them.

A corner of a concrete planter poofed up in a spray of dust and dirt.

Sniper.

I dragged her to me.

"Heading out the southwest side," I said into the comms and tucked her under my arm as I didn't pretend to ignore the gunfire. A second later, the sniper stopped playing it safe.

Shots rang out, the sound echoing off the buildings, as a spray of bullets shattered glass and ripped through people. Two fell ahead of us and I switched directions abruptly.

A good sniper led their target.

"Zig zag," I told Patch. "Keep changing where you're going." Most people in a panic would just run. They didn't look at where they were going. It made leading the target easier.

I had to keep my head.

"Where are you?" I demanded but the crackle over the line said the one of the things we'd been worried about had come to fruition. Our comms weren't working. The mobile lines and towers were probably overloading.

Patch tripped, stumbling forward and something hot sliced across my shoulder. I ignored the latter while keeping her on her feet and then we were in between buildings. It wasn't much cover but it was cover.

"Come on," I said. "We need to keep moving."

"I am," she answered in a slur, and I slowed to get an assessment. Then I saw the blood. A lot of it. All from a crease along her temple that vanished along her hairline. Her eyes glazed and she stumbled again.

I pushed up her hair. It was a strike. The bullet had sliced over her head, like the one had my shoulder. Another explosion of concrete dust erupted next to us. A piece splintered out and cut my cheek.

"Patch?" She blinked slowly then stared up at me. Her pupils were expanding. Not good.

The sound of wheels screaming as the brakes were applied jerked my attention around. There was a man in a car, an SUV. Not Locke. Not our car. But it was a car.

I pulled my gun. "Hold onto me," I ordered her, and thankfully she listened, as I strode forward, gun pointed at the man behind the wheel. His eyes widened. He picked up his hands. "Get out of the car."

"I—"

"Get out of the car or die in the seat, I don't really care which." The man was probably a civilian. A noncombatant most likely. Didn't matter.

I couldn't let it matter. Right now, anyone could be the enemy. Patch sagged next to me as the guy finally jumped out of the car, I pulled open the back door and got her inside after scanning that no one else was in the car. The blood soaked the side of her face and the sweatshirt she was wearing.

Head wounds bled a lot. I just kept reminding myself of that. I stripped off my jacket and pressed it to the wound, then put her hand on it.

"Keep up the pressure."

The driver had already taken off running. More people were fleeing the outdoor mall. It was utter chaos. The comm line was nothing but static.

"Stay awake," I ordered Patch and she stared up at me.

"What?"

"Stay awake," I said before I was behind the wheel. Movement had me claiming the gun again and I hit the button to lower the window and sighted the man pointing a gun at us—no not at us—at her.

I shot him twice in the chest. The third shot went into his head. All the screaming around us seemed to climb and I hit the button to roll the window up as I slammed my foot down on the accelerator.

"Stay awake, Patch."

"Not so loud," she said. "Head hurts."

A flick of a look in the rearview showed her expression going more lax. Nope. Not okay.

"Stay awake, luv," I ordered her. "Need you to stay awake, so we can take care of you."

"Where are we going?"

"Somewhere secure."

Back to the cabin if necessary, though we'd need a different car and I'd have to burn the interior on this one. Distance didn't seem to matter to the comms.

Locke and McQuade were both painfully silent. The plan if it went tits up was to scatter. Well, this had definitely gone tits fucking up.

"I'm tired..."

"Stay awake," I said, turning on a side street to avoid the oncoming stream of police vehicles and ambulances. "Talk to me..."

There was no answer and I twisted to find her slumped, chin down and eyes closed.

Bloody hell.

"Goddammit, Fallon. *Talk to me...*"

The adventure continues in the stunning
conclusion of the Switchboard Duet:
Don't Let Go.

Afterword

Whew.

When I write, I sometimes become utterly absorbed by the story and it plays out like a movie in my head. More often than not, my brain will begin to go much faster than my fingers. In those moments, I'm in the zone and I can feel the pulse of the story.

That happened so many times while writing this book, I dreamt about it. Now, I know I left you on a cliffhanger, don't worry, *Don't Let Go* is already tearing up the track.

xoxo

Heather

P.S. Yes, I'm in my corner with coffee, snacks, and my laptop.

About Heather Long

I *love* books. Not just a little bit, but a lot. Books were my best friends when I was growing up. Books didn't care if I was new to a town or to a class. They were always there, my trustiest of companions. Until they turned on me and said I had to write them.

I can tell you that my own personal happily ever after included writing books. I've always said that an HEA is a work in progress. It's true in my marriage, my friendships, and in my career. I am constantly nurturing my muse as we dive into new tales, new tropes, new characters and more.

After seventeen years in Texas, we relocated to the Pacific Northwest in search of seasons, new experiences, and new geography. I can't wait to discover what life (and my muse) have in store for me.

Maybe writing was always my destiny and romance my fate. After all, my grandmother wasn't a fan of picture books and used to read me her Harlequin Romance novels.

ALSO BY HEATHER LONG

82nd Street Vandals

Savage Vandal

Vicious Rebel

Ruthless Traitor

Dirty Devil

Shamelessly Loyal (Novella)

Brutal Fighter

Dangerous Renegade

Merciless Spy

Reckless Thief

Fierce Dancer

Bay Ridge Royals

Shamelessly Loyal (Novella)

Battle Lines

Deceptive Truce

Wicked Surrender

Violent Chaos

Desperate Victory

Blue Ivy Prep

Problem Child

Mad Boys

Party Crashers

Money Shot

Bravo Team Wolf

When Danger Bites

Bitten Under Fire

Cardinal Sins

Kill Song

First Chorus

High Note

Last Word

Chance Monroe

Earth Witches Aren't Easy

Plan Witch from Out of Town

Bad Witch Rising

Fevered Hearts

Marshal of Hel Dorado

Brave are the Lonely

Micah & Mrs. Miller

A Fistful of Dreams

Raising Kane

Wanted: Fevered or Alive

Wild and Fevered

The Quick & The Fevered

A Man Called Wyatt

Heart of the Nebula

Queenmaker

Deal Breaker

Throne Taker

Lone Star Leathernecks

Semper Fi Cowboy

As You Were, Cowboy

Shackled Souls

Succubus Chained

Succubus Unchained

Succubus Blessed

Shackled Souls (Omnibus)

STANDALONES

Kiss of Fate (w/Blake Blessing)

Taste of Karma (w/Blake Blessing)

I'll Be Home... (w/Tate James)

Untouchable

Rules and Roses

Changes and Chocolates

Keys and Kisses

Whispers and Wishes

Hangovers and Holidays

Brazen and Breathless

Trials and Tiaras

Graduation and Gifts

Defiance and Dedication

Songs and Sweethearts

Legacy and Lovers

Farewells and Forever

Hellos and Happily Ever Afters

Wolves of Willow Bend

Wolf at Law

Wolf Bite

Caged Wolf

Wolf Claim

Wolf Next Door

Rogue Wolf

Bayou Wolf

Untamed Wolf

Wolf with Benefits

River Wolf

Single Wicked Wolf

Desert Wolf

Snow Wolf

Wolf on Board

Holly Jolly Wolf

Shadow Wolf

His Moonstruck Wolf

Thunder Wolf

Ghost Wolf

Outlaw Wolves

Wolf Unleashed